FORBIDDEN

KARLA SORENSEN

To the person who holds onto their heart tightly.
It's precious, dear reader, give to it someone who will cherish it.

FORBIDDEN

PROLOGUE

Aiden

Two and a half years earlier

"**D**OES THIS MEAN I'LL GET A NEW MOMMY?"

Amazing how kids could say the most innocent things and make you feel like you'd just taken a knife to the gut.

Shielding my eyes from the California sun, I glanced up at Anya, sitting at the perch of her slide. When I could breathe enough to form words, I tried to keep my face even. "Why would you get a new mom?"

She kicked her legs, staring at the bank of windows where Beth's hospital bed was set up—at her request—so she could watch Anya play. "If Mommy is going to heaven soon, does that mean I'll get a new one?"

I'd learned how to explain a lot to a five-year-old in the past few months.

Cancer.

Why Beth had decided against chemo.

Hospice.

Heaven.

But this … this was new. And I had to pinch my eyes shut to fight the brutal wave of fresh grief as it hit me.

Every day was a new one, despite the reality that we'd been living in for ninety-two days since her diagnosis. And I was convinced every wave was the worst, and the next one might not knock me to my knees until moments like this.

Beth's cancer had forced me to discover a side of myself I'd never known. A wellspring of patience, of acceptance, of realizing that everything I'd dedicated my life to didn't really matter very much in the grand scheme of things. Being good at something didn't automatically make it vital.

Fighting used to be everything. And now, it was simply something I used to do, and in no way did it prepare me to bury my wife before we both turned thirty-five.

Nor did it help me when my daughter asked about a new mommy.

"Maybe we can talk about this later, okay?" I said wearily. Sleep was scarce for me even though Beth was doing more and more of it. Her nurse couldn't give me an exact timeline, but as her appetite waned and her energy decreased, we knew we were down to weeks. Maybe days.

"Okay, Daddy." She swooshed down the slide, running back around to the ladder. Instead of stopping on the platform, she hopped nimbly up to the beam stretching across the top of the swing set. "Look!"

I shook my head. "Anya, you know you can't be up that high."

My fearless girl, she giggled, moving to stand on the beam. I was on my feet in the next breath, holding my arms out. "Come on, big jump and I'll catch you."

If I freaked out, she'd do something even crazier, like trying to land on her feet, and yes, I'd learned that the hard way too. This was the same child who, at the age of three, was found swinging from the dining room light fixture after climbing up on the table.

Anya stood carefully, arms out, tongue trapped between her teeth. "I hope Mommy can see this. I know it'll make her feel better," she said.

I smiled. Another knife. Another knock to my lungs. "I'm sure it will, gingersnap."

"Ready?"

I nodded.

She jumped, and I caught her, swinging her down toward the ground, then back up into the air as she squealed happily.

"You're so good at that, daddysnap." She was a little unsteady on her feet when I set her down, and her tipsy expression had me smiling.

"Glad I'm good at something."

Anya crouched by the grass and plucked a small weed that resembled a white flower. "I'm gonna go bring this to Mommy!" she yelled, hair flying out behind her as she ran into the house.

I sighed heavily, swiping a hand over my mouth as I tried to get my bearings. The nurse aide was still at the house, so I stayed outside doing yard work, letting my muscles heat, my blood flow into something productive. Something I could control. By the time Anya ran back outside, clutching a paper in her hand, I wasn't even sure how much time had passed.

"Look! I got a list!" She held the paper out to me, beaming excitedly.

"What's the list for?" My hands were sweaty and dirty, and I showed her. "I don't think I should mess up your pretty drawing."

She dropped to the grass and laid the paper out carefully. I tilted my head and tried to make sense of what she'd written. Kindergartners were not known for their spelling skills.

But I could see a cookie.

Flowers.

A woman with long yellow hair and a big red mouth. She was either screaming or laughing, I wasn't entirely sure. I scratched my head.

"Why don't you explain it to me, gingersnap?"

Please, dear Lord, explain it.

"I asked Mommy about my new mommy someday." She grinned up at me. My heart stopped. Just stopped. No beating. So did my lungs. Anya started pointing at the paper while I simply tried to breathe. "She told me that she'd be sweet and funny and make you laugh." She tapped the paper. "See? She's laughing."

Her finger moved to the cookie.

"And she'd make really good cookies, just like Mommy, because Mommy said you suck at measuring and will need someone to do it."

My eyes blurred, and I crouched carefully next to my daughter, laying my hand on her back as I stared at the horrifying picture that she worked so hard on. I wanted to rip it up. I wanted to burn it.

Anya pointed at the stick figure. "And Mommy said she'd be soft where you're hard, and I didn't know how to draw that, but anyone who'd be a good mommy might already have kids and know how to hold me when I'm scared and sing me to sleep. And I just added the flower because I like drawing them."

I rubbed the back of my hand over my cheek so Anya didn't see. "You did really good on your picture, gingersnap," I said in a choked voice.

She ran her fingers over the jumbled letters that must've made sense to her. "I didn't want to forget. This way you don't have to talk about it if you don't want to." Then Anya carefully folded the paper and handed it to me. "You can keep it, Daddy. So you'll know who to look for."

I licked my lips, taking the piece of paper like it was a bomb set to explode. But I smiled at my daughter. "Thank you."

She flung herself at me in a tight hug, and I stared up at the sky.

When Anya ran back into the house, I stood slowly, paper in hand, and made my way to Beth's bed.

Her eyes were closed, her chest moving with shallow breaths. I took the chair next to her, and as I slid her bony fingers into mine, her eyes opened.

"Why'd you do that?" I whispered.

She smiled faintly. "I knew you'd be mad at me."

"I'm not mad," I told her. "I'm …" My voice trailed off when I didn't have any words. This time, I let a tear fall unchecked, and Beth watched it with a sad expression on her face. "I just hate that she asked you."

My wife—my funny, outgoing, loud, passionate wife who could no longer muster the energy to get out of bed—tightened her fingers around mine. "She's worried, Aiden. I just wanted her to …" She made a small shrugging motion. "I wanted to make her feel better."

"I know." I sniffed.

"Promise me something, though," Beth whispered.

Immediately, I was shaking my head.

"Promise me that, if you find someone like that, you won't ignore it." Her voice wavered, and I wanted to rage. Scream. Break something.

I sighed, finally meeting her eyes. "All I got out of that picture was that she has a mouth the size of my face and likes cookies."

Beth breathed out a laugh. "That's a gross oversimplification of what I said."

"What did you say?" I asked quietly. "Who'd you conjure up for me, Beth? Because they won't be you." I shook my head again. "I don't care what list you just gave her. They won't be you."

My wife ignored my attitude. She'd known me too long, knew it was easier to brush past it. She'd learned that lesson when we were eighteen, and she kissed me for the first time when she got sick of waiting for me to do it.

"I told Anya that hopefully someday you'd find someone kind

and funny, someone who smiles and laughs easily because we both know you don't." I held her eyes, unable to argue. "Someone soft where you're hard, someone who will know how to handle all the things that Anya will need help with. Someone who can bake cookies for her, and sing her to sleep, and teach you how to handle all her big emotions because I know they scare the shit out of you, Aiden."

I closed my eyes. I didn't want to hear any of this, but like any conversation I had with Beth these days, I forced myself to soak up every word. Every nuance. Every second.

"And for fuck's sake, don't fall for the first tight-bodied fangirl who fawns over you," she teased. "I'd haunt you for the rest of your life."

Somehow, I managed a smile. "Would you?"

"I'd make a bitch of a ghost." Her frame was wracked with a rib-rattling cough.

Lifting her featherlight hand up to my mouth, I kissed her knuckles. She smelled like medicine. Her fingers were cold against my mouth, and all I wanted to do was warm her. Fix her.

And I couldn't.

The helplessness had me wanting to wreck everything. Especially when she kept talking. Her words were so much worse than the knife; it was like a hundred of them. The girl next door, who I'd known for more than half my life, who'd had my heart for almost a decade was going to leave a gaping hole, and I didn't want to think about the fact that I couldn't fill it.

"You have excellent taste, Aiden Hennessy," she said quietly. "You must if you chose me."

I gave her a look. "I think it was you who did the choosing. The way I remember it, at least."

She hummed, eyes falling closed. "That's right. I had excellent taste." She slid her hand over my cheek and down the line of my jaw. "That's why you should trust me."

"I do," I whispered.

"Good." Gently, she exerted pressure on my chin until I couldn't look away. "That's why I answered Anya's question. Because you two will be okay, and she needed to know that. You will be happy again, even if I'm not there."

"Beth." My voice cracked on her name, eyes burning dangerously. "Please."

"You will be okay without me," she repeated, her own gaze clear and strong.

It was like she pulled the knife out—every single one—and everything they'd held in came pouring out in a messy rush. I dropped my head onto the side of the hospital bed, and while my wife stroked the back of my head, I wept.

CHAPTER 1

Aiden

"IT'S A *LITTLE* CROOKED."

A slow sigh escaped my lips, not that my daughter could hear with the unicorn-covered blankets pulled up past her nose.

Hand on my hips, I stared at the offending item. "I don't know, gingersnap. It looks like it did last night, right?"

That stumped her for a solid thirty seconds. Her blue eyes stared straight up, unblinking and unwavering, and I could practically *see* her trying to dig up reasons the hot pink tulle canopy was off center and thereby unacceptable. If it was unacceptable, she wouldn't be able to sleep.

Her eyes darted toward me, then back up to the pink cloud. "Did Uncle Clark measure it?"

"Uncle Clark measures *everything*."

The sound of her giggle was muffled by the mound of blankets. But nonetheless, I heard it, and something eased in my chest. Bedtime had been our biggest struggle in the two years since Beth died. It began about six months after we buried her and with just little things at first.

Daddy, can you move that lamp a little closer to my bed? It's too far away, and I can't see it.

Can I have one more blanket over my feet? They're cold, and I won't be able to sleep if they're cold.

Can I get one more stuffed animal from the playroom? Four isn't enough, and I think I need five to sleep.

Over the next year, the things that bothered her got a little bit bigger and a little bit harder to accommodate. But it faded as we rounded the eighteen-month mark. Her bedroom stayed untouched, and I was able to slip out after reading her a story, saying a prayer, and wishing a good night to each and every plush character that filled the queen-sized bed with her.

Then we moved from California to Washington to be closer to my family so I didn't have to raise my daughter completely solo. So Anya could have grandparents and her uncles and aunt around. And the first night in our new home—where we'd been for the last two weeks—it began again.

"How about this," I said slowly. "I'll go downstairs and see if Uncle Beckham brought his tape measure over, and he can check Uncle Clark's measuring skills. Sound good?"

She nodded, tufts of white-blond hair sticking up around her head.

Carefully, I bent over and dropped a kiss on her forehead. "Love you, gingersnap."

"Love you more, daddysnap."

My lips curled into a smile.

"You're coming back after you talk to Uncle Beckham, right?"

"Yes."

Anya sighed, slipping the covers down a couple of inches, enough that I could see the gap where her two front teeth used to be when she smiled at me. "Okay."

9

The bedtime routine was a dance the two of us had performed countless times on our own, and I could do it half-asleep.

Turn on the small lamp on her nightstand.

Adjust the framed picture of her and Beth so that Anya could see it easily.

Adjust the canopy so it enclosed as much of her bed as possible.

Stop just before I left her room, blow her a kiss, which she caught and smacked over her mouth.

But my smile dropped as I descended the stairs down to the main floor, where my brothers Beckham and Deacon waited for me.

They were on the floor of the sprawling family room, assembling something pink and white and covered in glitter.

"What *is* that?" I asked.

Deacon brought a glittery crown up to his forehead. "I think it's supposed to be one of those vanity things."

My eyebrows rose slowly. "Who bought her that?"

"Eloise," they said in unison.

"Ahh." Our youngest sibling had taken to purchasing anything Anya could possibly want since we moved here. My parents weren't much different, given she was the only grandchild—which meant the only niece for my four unmarried siblings. If Anya wasn't a complete monster by the time she turned ten, it would be a miracle.

With a weariness I felt in every bone and muscle, I sank down onto the couch while they continued to work.

"What was it tonight?" Beckham asked.

I sighed. "The canopy. She wasn't sure it was centered over her bed."

His face cracked into a smile as he screwed a leg onto the small white vanity bench. "Clark hung it," he said by way of answer.

Which meant yes, it was centered. Our middle brother, aka genius boy, was never wrong when it came to things like that.

"I should go up with a measuring tape just in case she's still awake."

Beckham and Deacon shared a look.

"What?" I asked.

"You sure you should still be indulging her?" Beckham asked. His eyes stayed firmly planted on the furniture, though.

My fingers found the bridge of my nose and pinched tight. "No, I don't know that. But if either of you have any helpful advice in how to help a seven-year-old girl who lost her mom, then I'm open to suggestions."

"Maybe you should take her to talk to someone if she's still doing stuff like this."

"It was getting better back in LA." I dropped my hand and studied the crisscrossing scars along my knuckles. "Once she gets used to this house and her new school, it'll get better here too."

"It's been two years, Aiden," Deacon added.

Like I didn't know when my wife died. I could've counted the days with ease. Without looking at a calendar, I knew how many hours it had been. Maybe even down to the minute, if I had Clark's skill with numbers. A pervasive emptiness came from losing the person you loved, and maybe that emptiness eased with each passing minute and hour and day, turning into something manageable, but it was always there.

But instead of telling him that, of trying to explain to someone who didn't have a family of his own and had never loved someone whose loss would carve a hole into his being, I simply nodded. "I know."

One of the strangest things about being back was moments like this, when my younger brothers helped me. With anything, honestly. Not just that they'd been here every day doing things like hanging hot pink tulle canopies and assembling princess vanities, but they were giving me parenting advice.

The stool assembled, Beckham set it on the floor and gave the

11

cushioned seat a pat. "Not bad. Maybe I have a future in furniture assembly."

Without looking up from the vanity, Deacon pointed at the front leg. "That's on backward."

"The hell it is." Beckham turned it over, then cursed under his breath.

It was easier to smile than it had been leaving Anya's room. My brother's worry only underscored my own. My daughter, seven going on seventeen, was smart and sweet and a complete daredevil. But come bedtime, when the dark took over the skies, she let every fear in her head take the wheel.

"Beer in the fridge?" I asked.

Deacon looked up, then nodded. "Might not be cold yet."

"Fine by me."

The house was unpacked, even if it was light on the furnishings. Our bungalow in LA was half the size—and twice the cost—as the home I'd found for Anya and me overlooking Lake Sammamish in Bellevue. And the fridge was no different than the rest of the house. Just shy of empty. Inside was a case of beer, leftover pizza, deli meat, and whatever my mom had bought for Anya's meals. I moved aside a bright pink water bottle and snagged a bottle of beer.

I didn't drink often, which my brothers knew, but today was a day I could justify it.

The bottle opened with a twist of my hand, and as the metal top clattered onto the tile floor of the kitchen, I took a deep swallow.

Since the day I retired from fighting, I hadn't second-guessed any decision I'd made. But today, as I scrawled my signature on a hundred papers in front of a stone-faced notary, effectively making the biggest purchase of my entire life—a gym about to be renamed Hennessy's—gave me my first moment of pause.

My instincts were always, always spot-on. If I didn't trust my instincts, I'd never have survived a single fight. Sometimes your body reacted before your mind had a moment to wonder if it was the right move. That was what training was for. Because a shift of your leg in the wrong direction meant you were pinned with your arm above your head. If you didn't block an uppercut to your jaw or your kidneys, it was a hundred times harder to win.

When I visited the gym for the first time, about a year after Beth died, I felt a shift when I walked in the door. It was the only way I could explain it. Something in my gut screamed at me that it was the right gym, the right place, the right time for Anya and me.

"What's with your face?"

I blinked because Beckham walked into the kitchen without me realizing it. "Thinking."

"Get your paperwork squared away?"

Nodding, I took another sip of beer.

He pointed at me. "You're doing it again."

Sure enough, my forehead was wrinkled, and my mouth turned in a frown. I took a deep breath, trying to smooth out my expression.

"I'm fine."

Because my little brother knew me, he didn't push on that comment. Grabbing a beer of his own, he cracked it open and took a long drag while he stared out of the kitchen window overlooking the lake. "Remember your last fight?"

I gave him a dry look.

Beckham smiled. "The details, I mean. How well do you remember?"

Over a career that spanned almost a decade, I had a few fights that I remembered every move, every pivot, every fall to the mat, every strike as it hit my body, and that was one of them. I knew it was my last, not that I'd announced it yet.

It was my quickest win, over and done in less than three minutes.

Pure rage, anger that was being funneled through my fists and feet and legs, fueled those three minutes. Inside that ring, I was in control. As I thought about it now, until I decided to move and buy Wilson's Gym, it was the last time I really felt that way.

But instead of explaining that to Beckham, I simply said, "I remember enough."

"Do you miss it?"

"Yes." I took a drink of beer and sighed. "And no."

Before he answered, Beckham stared through the window by the kitchen sink overlooking the lake. "You sure you want to be stuck at a desk all day?"

I shrugged. "I don't think I will be, once I get the lay of the land. Amy said I could call her if I needed help, and there's a manager that's been running the place for her for the past seven or so years."

"He any good?"

"Don't be sexist, Beckham."

He grinned. "*She* any good?"

"*She* is not aware she has a new boss, so I don't know anything other than what Amy told me," I admitted.

"That'll be fun."

I rubbed a hand over my eyes. "Appreciate you pointing that out."

"It wouldn't be so bad if you weren't so … you."

My hand dropped. "What's that supposed to mean?"

He tipped his beer in my direction. "Aiden, you have the charm of a rabid porcupine."

"Don't you have somewhere else to be?"

"Nope. Just quality time with my brothers while we assemble bright pink princess furniture."

I rolled my eyes.

Deacon poked his head into the kitchen. "Anya just called for you." He held out a measuring tape, which I took with a sigh.

I took the steps two at a time and schooled my face when I pushed open her door.

"Was the tape measure lost?" she asked.

I shook my head. "Sorry, gingersnap, I was talking to Uncle Beckham about my new job."

She snuggled back underneath her blanket, and in the dim light of her room, I could see the curiosity light her eyes. The canopy was effectively forgotten, which wasn't a bad thing. Surreptitiously, I tucked the measuring tape into the pocket of my gym shorts.

"Is it your first day tomorrow?"

With a nod, I sat on the edge of her bed. "I signed all the papers today, but I'm going to go just for a little bit in the morning so Miss Amy can show me a few things on the computer. Grandma will be here when I leave, so she'll probably make you breakfast when you wake up."

Her lips pursed in thought. "Can I have blueberry pancakes?"

"I don't see why not."

Anya smiled, turning on her side with her arm gripping a small plush dog. "Are you scared for your first day? Do you think they'll be nice to you?"

In the innocently spoken question, I heard her own fears about starting a new school, even if it was still a couple of weeks off.

"Yeah," I told her. "I think they'll be nice to me. The important thing about meeting new people is making sure you treat them the way you want to be treated, right?"

She nodded. "Mommy always said that too. The Gold Rule."

"Close," I murmured, ruffling a hand over her head.

"You're really quiet when you meet new people, though, Daddy."

"I suppose I am."

"Does that mean you want people to be quiet with you too?"

she asked, completely innocent, and like she did just about every day, she broke my heart just a little further.

But I decided to answer her honestly. "Depends on the person. I like hearing you talk, gingersnap."

She giggled. "You have to say that."

"Nah. I only say it because I mean it."

"I think you should figure out what your new people like, Daddy. They may not be like you."

"You're pretty smart, you know that?"

Anya sighed, snuggling her face into the stuffed animal. "Maybe you should take The Mommy List with you," she said quietly. "Just in case."

The Mommy List, as she'd started referring to it, was tucked in the frame behind Beth's picture, at Anya's request. Over the past two years, anytime I went somewhere new, she asked me if I needed it. Just in case.

I always said the same thing. And she never pushed it.

Like I could forget that damn list anyway.

"Maybe I should." I smiled. "You ready to go to sleep now?"

She nodded. "I think so."

I stood, leaning over to drop a kiss on her forehead. By the time I walked into the hallway and pulled her door closed behind me, her eyes were already closed.

Anya's words rang in my head, and I pulled out my phone and decided to send Amy a text.

Me: I know I'll be there in the morning, but so I don't forget to bring it up, I'll take any tips on the best way to introduce myself to the staff.

She responded almost immediately.

Amy: Most of them were aware this was a possibility, so I don't think anyone will be too shocked, but we'll set up a time for you to meet Isabel before we do a meeting with everyone.

Me: How do you think she'll take it?

Amy: She'll be your biggest ally in this. She's smart and dedicated, and completely unflappable. I swear, I've never seen anything knock her off-balance.

Me: Unflappable sounds pretty good right now.

Amy: Tomorrow is her day off, but she'll probably show up at some point. Not many surprises when it comes to Isabel.

I tucked my phone away and sighed. "No surprises sounds pretty good to me."

CHAPTER 2

Isabel

N O ONE IN MY LIFE KNEW ABOUT IT, BUT MY FAVORITE POS-
session in the entire world was a metal box. My Nan—my
half-brother Logan's mom—gave it to me when I turned ten,
and she told me it was the best way to keep important things safe.
Things I wasn't ready to share with anyone else or wanted to make
sure were taken care of. It came right after a screaming match with
Molly because she'd found my diary and made fun of me for something I'd written about a boy in my class. A place to lock things
up from my sister's prying eyes sounded like the best possible gift.

It was sleek and black, a little beat up around the edges, and
had a thick lock that had grown dull with age. Along the heavy
metal top was a red stripe, and I always liked that surprising pop
of bright color. The rest of the box was so forbidding, but that little
bit of color gave it personality.

She told me it was vintage, that they didn't make lockboxes
like it anymore. Stamped into the metal along the bottom was 43
Bond, not that I even really knew what that meant.

Over the years, I was very selective of what I put into that box. There were a few keepsakes, some that brought happy memories, and some that served as an important reminder, good or bad.

A silver locket Molly bought me for my eleventh birthday after saving her money for months because she knew I wanted it. I used to look at it when I wanted to remember why my older sister was, in fact, not the bane of my existence.

A ribbon from my senior prom corsage. The date had been forgettable, but his sweaty man-child hands trying to figure out what to do with me were ... not. That guy—just like the few others who'd made the sad attempts to date me as I stretched my long legs into adulthood—couldn't carry a conversation if it was strapped to his back. That one came out of the box if I ever needed to remember why it was easier to say no.

A bracelet our mom gave me just a few weeks before she left us on our brother's front porch. I'd never worn it. Usually, that one stayed tucked way the hell back because even the smallest glimpse of that delicate silver pattern had my heart racing. People knew when they're going to leave you. The bracelet didn't need to come out of the box in order to remind me of that.

Some of the items weren't that maudlin, don't worry.

The first pair of hand wraps from the kickboxing gym that had been my second home, my life, since I started working there at eighteen. I was fourteen the first time I wore them.

Some were silly, or made me feel silly, which was a little different. I didn't usually pull those out to study them. But I was getting there. All of the storytelling had a point, I promise.

As I got older, I realized the box—strong and secure and protective—was a fitting symbol for me.

How sexy, right?

Isabel Ward, the human lockbox.

I was tough and strong. Everything important stayed safe where no one could touch or ruin it. There was space inside me for a lot more, but the older I got, the less opportunity there was for the lid to be opened.

To be honest, I didn't even really try, which was fine. Nothing that required pity or embarrassment. I *liked* keeping my lid locked, if you know what I mean. No man had pried that baby open yet, and I was perfectly, one-hundred-percent okay with that.

Not that I judged people who ... let someone open their box with frequency; this was just a better choice for me. Safer. Letting it stay closed was better than having it be mishandled.

The box, stored safely in the spare unused room at Logan and his wife Paige's house, was something I hadn't touched in a long time. Hadn't added anything to it since I was eighteen.

But for some reason, I thought about the box and the silly items I didn't usually look at, before going to bed.

I wasn't claiming to be psychic or anything. But a few times in my life, I'd fought sleep for hours, consumed with the overwhelming urge to look at something in that box. Urge wasn't even the right word. It was so strong, my legs jittered and my fingers twitched restlessly.

The night before my mom left us, I swear to you on my Nan's grave (which I only did when I really, really meant something), I felt that box calling to me like it was *alive*. At that time, it was in the back of my closet where my nosy-ass sisters couldn't find it, and I pulled it out while the sky was dark. There wasn't as much in it back then, so it didn't take me long to rifle through the contents. Checking that the bracelet was still there, it helped, and I'd been able to sleep.

What an omen *that* turned out to be.

A couple of years later, it happened again. A different home housed me and the box—the one Logan had bought for our new makeshift family. Something made me open it again, and I studied a picture that I'd tucked inside. It was the five of us. My sisters, Molly, Lia, and Claire, and then Logan. Our protector, the parent who wasn't a parent, the one who stepped in and righted our world when my mom had turned it upside down.

The next day, he brought Paige home and introduced her as his future wife. This time, the change was good. The red-haired tornado, someone I'd take a bullet for, became the mother I always wanted.

That was the last time it happened.

Until now.

I laid in bed and stared at the ceiling, trying to visualize the box that I hadn't opened in probably seven years. I cataloged everything inside it, trying to decipher what it meant. What change might be on the horizon?

Lemme tell you. Women who likened themselves to metal lock-boxes did not like change. We hated change.

It was terrifying, like standing outside knowing that a storm was bearing down on you, but you hadn't yet felt the first fat raindrop.

Even though it was my day off, I showered and dressed to go to work, donning the emotional armor of my favorite dark purple quarter zip shirt with the gym's logo over my heart. Before I left the apartment, I ate strawberry Pop-Tarts, my version of the breakfast of champions. I sipped coffee on my drive with no music on the radio because all I could think about was what proverbial bomb was about to go off in my life.

For months, I knew my boss, Amy, was going to sell the gym, but she'd never actually said anything to me about who might replace her. But still, as I took the familiar route to work, where I'd invested every ounce of my heart since the day she hired me to manage the place, I had a sinking suspicion that my premonition was about this place that was so dear to me.

My headlights cut a swath through the empty parking lot in front of the low, square building that housed the gym. Instead of pulling around to the back where I normally parked, I decided to come through the front.

I locked the door behind me and punched the security code as it beeped on the wall. The gym was dark when I walked in, which suited me just fine. I'd memorized every inch of the place years earlier, so the weak light of the sunrise was more than enough for me to navigate back to my office.

If I could stay busy enough, with the boxes of merchandise I needed to unpack and display, the training schedule I needed to finalize, and the timecards I needed to finish, maybe I could ignore the bad juju feeling.

I took a sip of my coffee and stretched my free arm over my head with a wince. Went a little too hard in class the day before, and I groaned loudly when my muscles screamed in protest at the movement.

The groan is what had the door to Amy's office opening, the light of her small corner lamp illuminating the space. The shades were drawn over the glass that looked out over the gym, which I hadn't noticed earlier. Amy's head popped out. "Iz. You're here like, really early."

I stopped, my heart beginning to tumble over each thudding beat. "Why do you look nervous about the fact that I am?"

I'd worked for her and known her for too long to tiptoe around anything.

Amy sighed, her face falling in a look that had my stomach falling too. She'd been my boss and known me too long to tiptoe around *me*. This was it. As soon as she looked over her shoulder and spoke to someone in her office, I knew this was the thing I'd been dreading.

A new owner.

A new boss.

But that dread was nothing on how I felt when Amy turned back to me and gave me an apologetic smile. It was the apology I saw that set my heart hammering.

My skin felt too tight and my bones too big because I knew whoever was in that office was the thing … the feeling I'd had.

Suddenly, I wanted to run. I didn't want to face whatever—whoever—it was.

Amy's dark eyes searched my face. "I was going to do this tomorrow a bit more formally, but I had a feeling your ass would show up on your day off."

"I needed to unpack those boxes," I said, but my voice trailed off when she moved aside, and *he* filled the doorway.

Holy. Fucking. Hell. It was even worse than I thought. Like all the things that terrified me were rolled into one big, muscular, better-looking-in-person package sent to make me feel wildly out of control.

I hated that I was right, that my sleepless night had indeed warned me that something like this was going to happen. I knew what item in the box had called to me, and oh, my hell, now I wanted to shred it to bits just so I could pretend it didn't exist.

It would be fine, I told myself.

This was no place for the teenage version of Isabel, the one who'd been a little uncertain and a lot terrified of what people thought of me. I was not her anymore. No matter what was in that fucking box with his name on it.

It was the only reason I didn't watch where I was walking, and my foot caught on the edge of the ropes.

With a gasp, I pitched forward, my coffee falling with a wet slap onto the ground, my hand dripping from the mess that was left of my cup after I squashed it to death in my hands.

"I am so sorry," I said.

Amy laughed. "This is the unflappable Isabel Ward I was telling you about."

My face burned, but she leaned over to toss me a towel, which I used to wipe off my hand, and toss it over the spot of coffee that I'd undoubtedly be mopping up in a few minutes. As I pushed the towel around the mess with my foot, I felt his gaze on me. Carefully, I lifted my head to meet it head-on. See if I was capable of it.

This could.

Not.

Be.

Happening.

Honestly, I knew so much about him that it was ridiculous. From my years of study, of keeping tabs on his career, keeping tabs on *him*. I knew he was six-foot-three, and in his prime fighting days, he weighed in around two forty-five, tiptoeing him into the heavyweight class that he dominated for years. He'd lost weight since he retired, not that it lessened his impact.

I knew what it was like to watch him fight because I'd watched every one.

Every one.

I knew that his name was scrawled into the pages of fifteen-year-old Isabel's diary because when he had his first fight, I was utterly convinced I'd meet and marry him someday. For years, every fumbling boy who tried to flirt with me, ask me out, anything with me, was held up to the standard of him in my mind. With the stench of my spilled coffee hanging around us, I swear, I could've died from the mortification.

I knew his eyes were dark green, and his mouth rarely ever curved up into a smile.

I knew he'd retired a couple of years ago, after the death of his wife, in order to care for his daughter.

Having him stand in front of me was like having someone hand you the single thing you used to want, used to crave, and now you just had to pray that it was as good in real life as you'd imagined it would be.

If he was anything like what I'd built up in my mind, I was absolutely fucked.

Amy cleared her throat, and it broke the connection between his gaze and mine.

"Iz, you might as well be the first to know," Amy said.

He took a step toward me, mouth flat but not mean, eyes dark and curious, and when he held out his massive hand, I took a step of my own. Unfortunately, I inhaled shakily before slipping my palm against his. The reason this was unfortunate was because it was loud and impossible for him not to hear.

When our hands touched, his brow lowered, and his gaze held on that single connection point. Slowly, I pulled my hand back, hoping he didn't feel the tremor in my fingers.

"Aiden Hennessy," he said.

Like I didn't know his name.

When he opened his mouth again, I almost slapped my hand over those lips because I didn't want him to say it. But my hand stayed at my side, and he spoke the words anyway, all low and dark, and I felt a shiver of foreboding at how my life was about to change.

"I'm the new owner."

It took a few seconds to find my voice, and when I did, it was softer than I would've liked.

"N-nice to meet you." Gawd, I could've slapped myself for that one single hiccup on the first word. But, honestly, it was hard to speak over the roaring in my ears. Quite easily, I could count on one hand the times I'd met an athlete that gave me butterflies—butterflies!

Aiden Hennessy, my new boss, who I'd see *every single day* unless he fired me for being completely incompetent, didn't just set them off in my belly. From my head to my toes and every inch between was coated in flittering, fluttering, vividly colored, beating wings.

I wanted to douse them in gasoline and light all those little fuckers on fire.

Amy was giving me a weird look because soft-spoken and me did not go together. Ever.

He studied my face for a second, then nodded. "Amy tells me you've worked here a while?"

Amy laughed, laying a hand on my arm before I could formulate an answer. "Isabel walked through these doors when she was, what, thirteen? Fourteen? I may not have hired her until she was eighteen, but since the day I laid eyes on that scrappy little girl with a killer right hook, I haven't been able to shake her."

My cheeks felt hot again as he appraised me. I gave Amy a slight smile. "She tried, too."

"Please. I would've been crazy to get rid of you," she said. "She's the reason we're doing as well as we are, and don't let her tell you a word differently. The clients love her, and so do the employees. We all do."

"Yet you're leaving," I heard myself say. My mouth snapped shut because it wasn't exactly the kind of thing one should say in front of the new owner.

Amy's eyes watered, and to my abject horror, I felt mine do the same. "You knew this was coming, Iz."

Slowly, I nodded. "I know."

When she dropped her chin to her chest, her long, black braids fell over her shoulder, and I heard the quietest of sniffs. The big hulking man watched us carefully, without a lick of judgment in his expression at the display of emotion.

"I'll give you two a minute," he said, voice a low grumble that I felt in my bones.

The sound of it, holy hell, I almost shivered. This was so, so much worse than I could've imagined.

Amy lifted her head, teeth white and straight as she smiled gratefully. "Thank you, Aiden."

He dipped his chin, eyes flickering in my direction once more, then disappeared into the office.

As soon as it was just Amy and me, I gestured to the edge of the boxing ring that dominated the center of the main room. She sat first, and I followed.

"I didn't …" She paused, shaking her head. "I didn't mean for it to happen this way. To take you by surprise like this."

I didn't trust myself to answer just yet, and even worse, I felt my eyes burn at the thought of not working for her.

And Amy, because she'd known me for so long and knew me so well, just kept talking.

"Aiden came in last year. I don't know if you noticed."

I snorted, which made Amy laugh quietly under her breath.

"Of course you did." She shook her head again. "He genuinely wanted a training session, but he was doing some research, too. And when he approached me a few months ago to start negotiating, Iz, it was an offer I couldn't refuse."

The air hissed slowly from between my pursed lips. "How did he know you wanted to sell?"

"I mentioned it to a neighbor because he knows a lot of former athletes. Thought he might have insight as to how I could go about finding someone who would be a good fit."

My hands tightened into fists. "You could've asked me."

Amy glanced at me in surprise. "For your input?"

I swallowed. "To buy it."

She nudged me with her shoulder. "You got that much cash laying around, Isabel Ward? I know I haven't paid you enough to be able to afford something like that."

Lifting my eyes to her, I nodded. "I have a trust fund from Paige that I've never touched. Maybe I'm underestimating how much this place is worth," I admitted quietly, "but I could've probably made you an offer."

Amy sank back against the ropes, mouth slack. "The hell, Ward? You're loaded, and I didn't know? I should've been letting you pay for the coffee all these years."

I smiled. "Maybe. She put the money aside for us, but none of us could do anything with it until we were eighteen, and even then, we needed Logan and Paige's signature to release anything until we turned twenty-five."

She hummed. "Well, maybe you could've made an offer, and maybe not. But his offer was more than what it's worth."

"Why do you think he did that?" My eyes wandered back to the office where he sat quietly, waiting for us to finish talking.

"He's got a huge family, like four or five siblings or something. They all live in this area, and it's close to his daughter's school. It allows him to take what we've already built and just ... make it even better." She glanced sideways. "And I think he will. He's passionate about this, and he doesn't want to come in and redo everything, I promise."

I nodded.

The sleepless night was perfectly clear now.

Change had come knocking again, and yet again, it was digging a foothold in the one place I felt the safest. The one place, outside of my family, where I felt the most comfortable.

This was the one thing I worried would test any of the metal-strong barriers I'd put up.

He was.

But because I respected Amy, and I wanted her to be able to get an offer so good she couldn't refuse and be able to travel the world with her wife, Renata, like they'd always dreamed, I nudged her shoulder back.

"I trust you," I told her.

"Thank you." She sighed. "I dreaded telling you the most."

That had me smiling. "Why's that?" I asked.

"Because you're stubborn as hell and don't think I don't know you probably had his matches memorized because you watched every single one, and you'll *hate* that now that he's your boss and you feel like you did something wrong."

Cue me choking on the bubble of hysterical laughter trying to push up my throat.

She had no freaking idea.

My stupid cheeks burned stupid hot for the eightieth time since

I walked in the door, and I refused to look at her. "I don't know what you're talking about."

Amy snorted. "Like you'd share if you did. Promise me you'll give him a chance, all right? He'll need you more than anyone else here if he's going to pull this off. I already told him you'd be his biggest ally."

His shadow, tall and broad, moved in the office, visible behind the closed shades, and the sight of it—the sight of him—had the knots pulling tighter and tighter in my stomach.

Give him a chance.

To what, exactly? My options were slim. Either he was nothing like I imagined, or he was better. I'd already tripped over myself in front of him, so this whole boss/employee dynamic was off to a fantastic start.

"Iz?" she prompted when I didn't answer.

"I promise."

And I'd keep it. But it was the scariest promise I'd ever made because the feeling it gave me made it perfectly clear that my sleepless night was just the beginning. Change was here, and his name was Aiden Hennessy.

CHAPTER 3

Isabel

"**Y**OU'RE ACTING WEIRD, AND YOU'RE HIDING, AND I DON'T know which of those two freaks me out more." Kelly's voice came from over the large stack of boxes I was sitting—i.e. hiding—behind.

Ladies and gentlemen, the unfortunate side effect of knowing my co-workers incredibly well was that they had no problem calling me on my shit—even if I was their manager.

Without sparing her a glance, I pushed aside a stack of sweat towels and marked them on my inventory sheet. "I'm working, Kell."

"You've been back here since the minute he walked in the door."

The top of her blond ponytail poked up over the tallest box in the stack, but I couldn't see her entire face.

What Kelly McKendrick lacked in height, she made up for in boundless energy and enthusiasm. So much so that I wanted to dislike her for it, but I quite literally could not because she was one of the nicest people I'd ever met. "Normally, you work in your office on Wednesday mornings. But since your office is empty …

I figured you were avoiding him, and I wanted to make sure you were okay in case you needed to talk about it." She sighed. "Not that you ever want to talk about what's bothering you, but there's a first time for everything."

When I rolled my eyes, she climbed behind the boxes with me, bracing her back against the wall and stretching her pink legging-clad legs in front of her as she started folding the towels. The gym had a handful of part-time employees, and Kelly was the one who'd hung around the longest of that group. "I'm quite sure I don't know what you're talking about," I murmured. Before I reached for the next box, I handed her the inventory sheet.

"I couldn't believe how sad I was after the meeting yesterday." She sighed. "Amy is such a good boss, and he's so …"

In her pause, I found myself holding my breath. I could certainly think of a few words to fill in the blank, but I wasn't entirely certain how I wanted Kelly to answer.

"So what?" I asked. I took the clipboard back as she began unpacking the box of new gloves.

"Serious," she whispered. "I don't think he smiled once yesterday while she introduced him."

Kelly's comment, which was totally accurate, had me serving myself a stern mental pep talk.

Yes, she and I were the same age.

Yes, I considered her a friend because we'd worked together for five years.

And yes, I desperately wanted to talk to her about this entire thing. I wanted to tell her how I was hiding from the hot man who now signed my paychecks and covered my body in butterflies, and at one point in my life, I practiced signing my name as if we were married. The embarrassment was so real.

It was so bad that I hardly spared him a single glance during Amy's meeting the day before.

Not one.

But I couldn't tell her any of that because I was not in friend-mode for this particular conversation. I was the manager. I also didn't tell anyone anything if I could help it.

I chose my words carefully. "Seems like he's always been a pretty serious guy." When she gave me a curious look, I shrugged. "I watched his fights, so that's my guess, as much as you can judge someone you've never met."

"I'll have to take your word on that. I can't stomach watching professional fights, so I didn't even really know who he was when she introduced him." Ohhhhh, to have that problem. "Isn't he supposed to like, win us over?"

"Actually, I think it's the other way around," I told her. "He's the new owner, Kell, and it's up to us to show him we know what we're doing."

"Even if he's physically incapable of smiling?" she asked in a glum voice.

I tossed her some gloves. "Even if."

"These are some badass motherfuckers right here," she said, pulling the plastic sleeve off so she could admire the matte and glossy black design. "Can I try a pair?"

"If you're paying for them."

She laughed. "You don't think Mr. Smiley would let me have them for free?"

As the words hung in the air between us, his giant, non-smiling shadow appeared. My face fell, and Kelly started coughing—a horrible, hacking sound that did nothing to erase the fact that she'd just called our new boss *Mr. Smiley*.

My stomach pitched sideways as I saw the muscle in his jaw—which looked carved straight from a mountain—clench dangerously.

"Morning, Mr. Hennessy," Kelly said.

His eyes flipped from my face back to hers. "McKendrick, right?"

She nodded.

Because half of his body was covered by the boxes, I didn't know what he was looking at when he glanced down at his hands. But when he came around the side, he was holding a disposable coffee cup, capped in a white lid, with her name scrawled on the side. He handed it to Kelly, who, after taking it carefully, sniffed at the opening.

In my peripheral vision, I saw her jaw fall open.

He produced another cup, this time handing it down to me. My whole body locked down like someone had poured me into concrete.

His eyebrow, dark and slightly foreboding, rose slowly.

Kelly cleared her throat loudly, and I blinked.

Coffee.

The cup.

Right.

On the side of the cup was my last name in black Sharpie, and I swear, my hand didn't shake in the slightest when I reached forward to take it from him. Our fingers didn't touch because I damn well made sure of that.

His eyes, steady and, *yup*, unsmiling, watched me as I took a wary sip.

My eyes widened when it hit my tongue because it was exactly what I normally ordered.

With a slight dip of his chin, he murmured a short, growly, "Ward," in greeting and was gone. As he walked away, long legs striding easily over the black rubberized floor, I caught sight of another full drink carrier in his massive hands.

"What the fuck," I whispered.

Kelly burst out laughing.

I gave her the side-eye. "You never heard me say that."

She notched two fingers to her forehead in a salute. "Aye aye, boss."

Like I was handling a pin-less grenade, I set the coffee cup onto the floor next to me and kept unpacking boxes with Kelly's help. Only a few regulars were in, using the bags and the weights, so the gym was quiet.

After how long I'd worked there, the noises hardly even registered to me anymore. The clang of weights hitting a rack, the laughter of people talking, the music playing over the speakers, and the rhythmic tapping of someone on a speedbag in the corner should have all been comforting and made me feel better.

But everything was just ... off. I couldn't find my bearings in the place that was my touchstone.

"How many for your class today?" I asked Kelly.

Her face scrunched up as she thought. "Twenty-five, I think? I checked about an hour ago when I got here."

"Yeah, why *are* you here this early?"

"I wanted to get in a workout."

I glanced at her taking a leisurely sip of her coffee. "How's that going for you?"

"Quite well, as I am helping my beautiful manager unpack these beautiful gloves from her hiding spot," she said with a magnanimous gesture. Picking one up, she studied the design. "Now I get why Amy didn't want the logo on the wrist strap. She knew what was coming."

The pair I was holding lowered slowly into my lap because I hadn't even realized it.

A change had been on the horizon for longer than I realized, peeking over the edge of my days unnoticed. It was me who hadn't been paying attention.

Kelly chattered happily in my silence, but very little of what she said registered. Beyond the boxes, Aiden was familiarizing himself with the computer programs we used and reviewing the policies, schedules, and day-to-day information I knew like the back of my hand.

And I was hiding behind boxes because my reaction to him made me feel like I was bungee jumping naked from the Space

Needle. A teenage crush was nothing to be embarrassed about, but there I was. Hiding.

"Iz," Kelly said. By her tone, she must have been trying to get my attention.

"Huh?"

She grinned. "You didn't hear a word I said, did you?"

"I …" My shoulders fell. "Not really. I'm sorry."

Kelly waved that away. "I said that you should go in there and thank him for the coffee." An innocent enough statement, but then she fluttered her long eyelashes.

My head tilted. "Are you high?"

"Never on Wednesdays," she answered gravely. Her wide smile broke across her face, and I found myself laughing under my breath. "I'm only half kidding. You should thank him, but honestly, that man is gorgeous, and he's single, and you two have a million things in common."

I wanted to shove a towel in her mouth to shut her up because hearing her talk about us together had my palms going a little sweaty.

"Kelly," I said quietly.

She beamed.

"Stop talking about it."

Kelly sighed.

An alarm went off on my phone, and I cursed under my breath.

"What?" Kelly asked.

"I forgot I have a bridesmaid dress thing with my sisters." I blew out a hard breath.

"Am I invited to Molly's wedding?"

I gave her a look.

Kelly sighed. "I *know*. But she's marrying *Noah Griffin*. He's Keith's favorite player on the Wolves, and your brother is his favorite coach, which means half the team will be there, and then my boyfriend could die a happy man."

I smiled. This was the byproduct of being in a family that was practically NFL royalty. I was constantly surrounded by world-class athletes, but look how it did me absolutely no good when it really counted. The mental image of spilling my coffee at his feet would haunt the hell out of me.

"As fun as that sounds, I don't think siblings' co-workers are invited," I said. "Can you take my session with Glenn after your class? That's the only thing I had on the schedule."

She nodded. "No problem."

I stood, stretching my arms over my head.

Kelly pointed at the untouched cup on the floor. "Don't forget that."

I swear, I looked at that cup like it was a snake coiled up around my legs, ready to sink its fangs into my skin.

She laughed, shaking her head as she left to get set up for her class. "You're so suspicious, Iz," she said over her shoulder.

Maybe to her, it was that simple. A thoughtful gesture from a serious guy. To me, though, it felt like something else entirely. If I drank that coffee, I'd start thinking about how—in his first week owning a new business—he took the time to figure out what every single employee on the schedule liked to drink. I didn't want to think about Aiden Hennessy, with his excellent eyes, wide-as-a-house shoulders, and long-legged stride, doing quietly thoughtful things because it would shred my already embarrassed heart into a heap.

What it did was make me feel like that fifteen-year-old girl again, and I hated that.

Not because fifteen had been a bad year. On the contrary. Our family finally felt settled and right when I was that age. Paige was pregnant with Emmett, and I felt safe. Loved. It was why doodling in my purple diary about marrying MMA fighters who were ten years older than me felt completely acceptable.

The reality of my adulthood might look different than the one I'd dreamed up, but everything about it was great.

And what I didn't need was Aiden making me feel like a starry-eyed young girl whose heart was soft enough to be crushed into bits. Been there, done that, and had a T-shirt and abandonment and control issues to go with it. I did not need to put myself in that position ever again.

And sure, it was great if he didn't turn out to be an asshole, but holding that coffee, it felt far, far more dangerous that he might be more than what I'd built up in my head so many years ago.

That was why I walked that coffee over to the drinking fountain, took off the top, and slowly poured it down the drain. It was a small way to assert control over all the flutteries.

The brown liquid swirled quickly through the holes, and I breathed deeply once it disappeared. Decisively, I capped the travel top back onto the empty cup and tossed them both into the trash can next to the fountain.

"Guess I got your order wrong."

I froze. His voice came from right behind me, all low and growly. My eyes fell shut because holy shit, I was destined to get off on the wrong foot with this man, wasn't I?

Blowing out a slow breath, I turned to face him. His eyes betrayed the slightest hint of amusement that he caught me, but everything else about his face was even and steady. In fact, every physical feature that made up Aiden Hennessy seemed carved straight from stone.

Not just his face, which was handsome enough, but his shoulders and arms, the veins running down toward his massive hands.

I'd seen the gracefully inflicted violence his body was capable of, the speed and strength.

And as he towered over me, I hated that I had to lift my chin in order to meet his gaze.

"The order was fine," I told him. "Drank too much already this morning."

The sound he made in the back of his throat was so ambiguous that I had to physically chomp down on my tongue to stop from defending myself. When the front door opened and a group of members walked in for Kelly's class, his attention moved from me to the sound of their bright laughter. Immediately, the pressure on my lungs eased. There was some magic voodoo he had going on, and I did not like it one tiny bit.

"Seems like the classes are always well-attended," he said. His gaze left the group of women and came back to rest on my face.

I nodded. "Especially on the weekends." I sucked in a deep breath and held his eyes. "I hope you don't intend on getting rid of those."

He shook his head. Nothing else. Just a shake of his head.

"Good."

His lips twitched just a fraction before they settled back in a firm line. "Glad I have your approval, Ward."

My cheeks were flaming, and I hated it. My hand lifted in a small gesture toward the door. "I have to ... I'll be back in a little bit."

Aiden nodded, and as I turned to go, I knew he was watching me.

꩜

"So let me get this straight ..."

"Yes."

Molly paused. "You don't know what I was going to say. How can you say yes?"

Even though I was behind a dressing room curtain and she couldn't see, I rolled my eyes. "I already know what you're going to say."

"You just left?"

"Yes."

"Isabel!"

Angling to the side, I slid the zipper of the sky blue dress up and huffed when I couldn't get the eye hook closed. "What? It's not like I expected him to be standing over my shoulder like a giant hulking shadow, and yes, I just … left."

"Guess I know who's not going to win employee of the month …" Her voice trailed off. I stuck my hand out from behind the curtain with my middle finger raised. She swatted it back inside. "I never knew you to be a chicken."

Instead of arguing with her over something so stupid, I simply rolled my lips between my teeth and tugged one last time at the zipper. As I studied my reflection in the mirror, I couldn't decide if the dress just wasn't right for me, or if my body was so used to workout gear that it now actively rejected any finer materials.

"Are you dressed yet?"

My hands fell by my sides. "Yes. I don't think this color works on me, though."

"One, I find that highly unlikely, and two, show me." Molly tugged the curtain aside, and when she caught sight of me, her smile was massive. "Iz, I love it. You look so pretty!"

With a skeptical glance at the mirror, I tugged at the drapey things over my shoulders. "There are frills. On my body."

She laughed. "You don't have to choose that style. I'm just trying to decide on the colors. I like the blush pink, but it might be too summery for a fall wedding."

"The blue," I insisted. "I will feel naked in that pink one."

"Definitely blue," Lia called from across the space.

Our two youngest sisters, Lia and Claire, separated by all of two minutes at birth, were sharing a dressing room. "Come on, you two," Molly called. "Iz is already dressed."

"Hang on. Lia's new mom boobs are huge, and she can't get her dress zipped."

Molly and I grinned at each other because really, they were. She'd given birth about eight weeks earlier, and honestly, she had the rack of a centerfold if I'd ever seen one.

While we waited, Molly pulled out her giant wedding binder and made some notes after flipping to a bright pink tab. It was no surprise that Molly was the most organized bride-to-be on the planet, and also no surprise that she had zero Bridezilla tendencies so far, something that was making this whole "watch my big sister get married" thing a lot easier.

"Where's Paige?" I asked.

"She had to stay home with Emmett. He wasn't feeling well, and Logan is at training camp." Molly held up her phone and snapped a picture of me. "But I promised I'd send her pictures."

As her fingers tapped out a text to our sister-in-law, I took a seat on the large ivory ottoman in the middle of the room. No one else was in the dress shop with us, so I leaned back on my hands and listened to the laughter of Lia and Claire as they struggled to close up Lia's dress.

Out of nowhere, I felt very, very lonely sitting in that room with my sisters.

Molly was getting married.

Lia was living with her boyfriend, Jude. With the addition of their son, and Jude's new gig playing soccer for Seattle, I knew it was only a matter of time before they made it official too.

Even Claire, the shyest of the four of us, found her person in bad-boy snowboarder Bauer Davis.

And none of this was new; none of their relationships were new. Was I allowed to blame Aiden for this? I tried to imagine his face if I came back to work in a rage.

Yo, bossman, seeing you has me all twisty inside, and I don't like it. And when you're nice and thoughtful, it makes it worse, and I start feeling like a lonely petulant teenager around my very wonderful, happily-in-love sisters because I'd rather gouge my eyes out than explain it to them. Please stop. Thanks.

"What are you smiling about?" Lia asked.

Belatedly, I noticed all three of them staring at me.

"Nothing." I cleared my throat.

Molly nudged Claire. "She's terrified of her hot new boss. Did I mention that yet?"

Lia's eyes widened. "Oooh, are you?"

"How hot is he?" Claire asked.

Molly held up both hands, all ten fingers wiggling. Claire laughed.

I gave her a steady look. "Are we deciding on dress colors or not?"

Lia held her hand out to help me off the ottoman. "Sorry, Iz. We've never been able to tease you about a man before."

Molly snickered. "Yeah, because normally, she eats them alive once she's done with them."

The words I muttered under my breath would've set a nun's ears on fire. Lia was the only one who heard and started laughing. The idea of me as a man-eater, casually licking my fingers after I'd had my way with them was so laughable. But immediately on the heels of that was a startlingly clear mental image of Aiden lying on a bed, spent and wrecked with me equally spent and wrecked next to him. My heart rate jumped at the vivid picture in my head. But that kind of inner-vixen reaction would be welcome after how I'd started off with him.

The tripping, coffee-spilling me was nothing like they imagined me.

It was so much easier to let them think it. Let them believe it.

"Fine." Molly sighed. "Let's get this done so she can go back and hide from him for the rest of the day."

With a deep breath, I shoved down everything they'd just brought up. Way, way down. "You're going to be missing your maid of honor if you keep this shit up."

Molly held up her hands. "Fine, fine. I'm done. Ladies, show me what you've got."

CHAPTER 4

Isabel

UNTIL I STARTED WORKING AT THE GYM, LEADING CLASSES, and working with clients, I never understood exactly how deep my sadistic streak went. But when one of my favorite clients limped up to me after class, shirt soaked with sweat, it was the only time in my life I was all hearts and rainbows and smiles.

Sally's eyes narrowed in a glare. "I don't know who hurt you, Isabel, but I can't tell whether I should set you up with my therapist or give you a hug."

I laughed, running my sweat towel along the back of my neck. "Is that your way of saying you liked my class today?"

As she dumped her gloves and tangled hand wraps back into her bag, she snorted. "Something like that."

"I added those extra burpees just for you."

Straightening slowly, she rolled her eyes and slung her bag over her shoulder. "Next time? Don't."

"Bye, Sally."

She waved.

My mood felt light, probably because I'd yet to see any glimpse of Aiden. For the day, at least, my office was my own. And it wasn't like his presence weighed me down; it was simply that added awareness and the way my skin vibrated at a different frequency when he was in the building. It was something I was going to have to get over because Aiden Hennessy was here to stay.

A college-aged girl approached as I started wiping down the bag I'd used during class. She slipped in just before I started, so I didn't get a chance to speak with her like I liked to do with new members.

"What'd you think?" I asked her.

She exhaled a small laugh. "That was … intense. But one of the best workouts I've ever had."

"Excellent." I held out my hand. "I'm Isabel, the manager."

"Brenleigh." She pointed at the ring in the center of the gym. "I was just glad you didn't make us hop up in there for some ass-kicking."

"Nah, we wait until at least your second class for that. You bought the ten-class punch card, right?"

Brenleigh nodded. "I came in yesterday after I saw one of your Insta posts about the special you're running." Her cheeks were already flushed from class, but when she glanced around, the red deepened even further. "Is it true that Aiden Hennessy is the new owner?"

"That is true. We're very excited to work with him."

Excited. Terrified. Hiding from him. Whatever.

She licked her lips and lowered her voice to a conspiratorial whisper. "Is he, like, taking one-on-one clients or anything? You know, like, *private* training sessions."

Ahh. The fangirls were starting to descend. Now this was something I hadn't anticipated. I knew he had plans to do some training sessions, but no formal coaching like some speculated he might after he retired. So a co-ed coming in and asking for private sessions … that was not in my managerial wheelhouse. It wasn't in my personal wheelhouse either. My ability to fake it with people was about as stellar as my cooking skills.

I sucked at both.

Now that I looked at her more carefully, she was wearing one of those sports bras that wasn't really a sports bra, the kind that flashed more cleavage than a Victoria's Secret ad.

Gawd, I sounded like such a judgy bitch. So I softened my smile. "Not that I know of, but he's still getting settled. I'm sure in the next few weeks we'll know a lot more. If he decides to take on clients, we'll definitely post about it on our social, so keep an eye out."

There. I sounded polite. Professional. Go me.

Brenleigh and her cleavage leaned in toward me. "What's he like?" she asked, big brown eyes wide.

I paused. What did she want me to say?

"He seems very nice," I answered diplomatically.

"I hope he's not like, too nice." She grinned. "What a disappointment, right? He can be hard on me *any* day."

Then she bit down on her lip and giggled.

And it was the giggle, along with the criminal overuse of the word *like*, that had me imagining what it would be like for Brenleigh if I like, elbowed her in the face.

It wasn't her fault, not really, because what Miss Brenleigh and her strappy bra and her burning curiosity did was nothing more than hold a mirror up in front of my face. Something about him turned me a little crazy and made me feel like I was Brenleigh. A caricature of the worst side of me.

The silly, unsubstantial side.

Even though it killed me to do so, I kept my smile firmly in place. "Are there any other questions about the workout today? I'd be happy to review anything since I didn't get a chance to talk to you before class started. Normally, I'd go over the basic moves if this was your first time."

She waved a hand in the air. "Nah, I'm good. Will he like, be here tomorrow if I come back for your four o'clock class?"

"I couldn't say. He doesn't have a set schedule." I shrugged. "Perks of being the owner."

Brenleigh sighed. "I guess. Well, I'll see you tomorrow. Thanks!"

And she bounced off. Actually, physically bounced. I pinched the bridge of my nose.

As she walked toward the front, where she sat on a bench to change her shoes, I did a lap around the bags, snagging two water bottles that had been left behind and a few wipes dumped just outside the garbage container. Only a few people were using the weight machines, with one person on the treadmills facing the TV Amy had installed a couple of years earlier.

My office was quiet when I walked in, and when I took a deep breath, I caught the slightest whiff of something masculine.

I sank into the chair and dropped my head in my hands. He wasn't even here, and I could smell him. That was when I noticed the sweatshirt folded on the edge of my desk. He was wearing it at the meeting and must've left it. My fingers reached for the edge, tugging it toward me before I thought too hard about what I was doing.

The shirt was well-loved. A faded logo of a California gym on the front, the seams of the front pocket were ripped at the edges.

When I lifted it toward my face and took a deep inhale to see if that was the source of the smell, I shoved it back into place with a groan before I could go any further down this crazy-ass rabbit hole.

I know you don't know me, but I'm sixteen, and I think you're amazing, and even though I'm younger than you, I know we're meant to meet.

My eyes pinched shut, and my heart raced uncomfortably when I thought about that silly, silly letter, folded carefully and locked inside the metal box.

I was no better than the bouncing co-ed fangirl and her substandard bra and her giggles and her *like*. Sitting up straight, I took a deep breath and stared hard at my own reflection in the glass overlooking the gym.

No more, I thought. No more sniffing. No more butterflies. No more wondering when he was going to come in or obsessing about whether we'd share space or he'd buy coffee. No more tripping at his feet or childish displays to make me feel better about my embarrassment.

"Isabel Ward," I said, "get your shit together. This is fucking ridiculous."

Sweatshirt back in place, I made the chair spin from standing too quickly and marched out of my office. With only one more class on the schedule for the rest of the day and no training sessions of my own, the gym would most likely be quiet for the next couple of hours.

It was easy to keep myself busy, and I popped in one earbud so I could listen to some music without missing anything that might need my attention.

Exiting the now cleaned women's bathroom, I did a quick scan of the gym, something I did constantly when I was the only person working, and noticed that the gym was empty. A glance at the digital clock on the wall told me it would probably stay that way until we got our usual post-work day group.

Which was why I stopped short as a young girl sprinted across the room, white-blond hair flying, and then shimmied straight up one of the heavy bags until she'd hooked her tiny arms over the top and hoisted herself up onto the iron beam that held the entire rack in place.

In no more time than it took me to blink, she'd climbed to the top of the beam, where she now sat perched, legs swinging like she didn't have a care in the world.

It took a concerted effort to close my gaping mouth, but I set down the cleaning supplies and looked around the gym. Not a parent in sight. It was completely normal for a few kids to tag along with their parents if they came to class, but this was not normal.

Nor was it safe.

The last thing we needed was someone's kid falling from an iron beam and breaking her leg. I approached carefully, channeling all my big sister vibes. Her eyes were wide and clear and bright blue, and they tracked every step that I took.

I set my hands on my hips and glanced up at the beam. "Impressive," I told her.

She didn't answer, but her lips quirked in a smile.

"What's your name?"

"You're a stranger, so I shouldn't tell you."

I nodded slowly. "That's very smart."

"What's *your* name?"

"Isabel. Where'd you learn how to climb like that?"

She shrugged. "Dunno. I've always known how."

"And you're not afraid of heights?"

Her hair swooshed when she shook her head.

"Do you think you could hop down to me?" Again, the hair swooshing and the head shaking. Okay then. "It would get pretty uncomfortable sitting up there all day."

Her legs swung. Yeah, she was in no freaking hurry. How nice for her.

"I don't know if I could climb up onto the beam," I said, "but I do have one other trick I could do."

Interest sparked behind those eyes. "What is it?"

I clucked my tongue. "Can't tell you unless you hop down, kiddo."

Her lips screwed sideways as she pondered that.

"Who'd you come here with?"

"My daddy's in the bathroom. I heard him on the phone and got bored waiting."

"Okay, well … maybe if you hop down now, I can show you my trick, and he won't even see you up there."

"He's already mad at me because I pretended I had to puke so I didn't have to go to day camp, but that place is dumb, and I don't want to go, but my grandparents were busy and couldn't watch me."

I blew out a slow breath, imagining all the ways this could go sideways. "Can't blame you, kid. I'd probably fake sick too."

Her smile was bigger this time, and I caught a glimpse of an adorable gap where her front teeth would eventually grow in. My nephew Emmett lost his when he was almost eight, so I took that little nugget and ran with it.

"Especially because you're, what, nine?"

She giggled. "Nope. I'm only seven, but I'm *almost* eight."

"Yeah? When's your birthday?"

"In ten months."

I smothered my smile. "So close."

"How old are you?" She shifted on the beam, and I fought the impulse to stick my hands out in case she fell, but apparently, only one of us was nervous about her perch, and it was not her.

"Twenty-five," I whispered. "Super old."

She giggled again. "You're only old once you turn fifty."

"Ahh. Very good to know."

Her eyes darted to the side and then back to me. "Do you like to sing?"

My head tilted at the change of subject. "I'm not a very good singer, so no… I can't say that I do."

The line of her eyebrows lowered.

"Okay, I'll come down, but only if you show me your trick first."

I narrowed my eyes. "Bargaining, huh?"

"My aunt told me I should always stand up for what I want, so that's what I'm doing."

Well, her fricken aunt wasn't here trying to get her down from the fricken metal beam, now was she? I kept my smile even, though.

"Okay, but you've got to promise you'll come down, right?" I held up two fingers. "Girl Scouts honor?"

She nodded vehemently.

"Okay." I pointed at the beam. "Turn your one leg so you're straddling it like you're sitting on a horse, okay? Then hold on with both hands."

I breathed a bit easier when she obeyed immediately.

"What're you gonna do?" she asked.

"I'm going to hang on the bag," I whispered. "With no hands."

Her eyes widened. "No way."

"Way."

With a quick glance back by the bathroom, there was still no sign of her dad, so I shook my head and jumped, grabbing the chain along the top of the bag and pulling my body weight as high as I could go. Hoisted up like that, I tugged my legs up, wrapping them around the upper middle of the heavy bag, and crossed my feet at the ankles.

With a glance in her direction, I let go of the chains and let my upper body slowly fall back.

"Whoa," she whispered.

My braid was swinging toward the ground when I lifted my upper body and did a couple of sit-ups from that hanging position. She clapped excitedly.

"How many more should I do?" I asked her.

"Twenty!"

"Oof. Okay. Then you'll hop down to me?"

"Uh-huh."

"Count for me then, boss lady," I told her.

"One, two, threeeeeeee," she stretched out. I groaned as I did number four, and she giggled.

"You should be a trainer here," I told her. "I pull that slow counting crap in my classes too."

We made it as far as seven when I noticed someone approach

from the corner of my eye, a tall shadow blocking the overhead lights of the gym.

Aiden.

Today, he was wearing a white T-shirt, snug across his boulder-like chest. His arms were folded over that chest, and even though I was hanging upside down, I could see the tightness in his mouth as he surveyed our little scene.

The girl stopped her counting. "Hi, Daddy! Look at the lady's cool trick!"

That was when my ankle lost its grip, and I fell off the bag, landing at my boss's feet in a tangled, graceless heap.

CHAPTER 5

Isabel

MAYBE, JUST MAYBE, I THOUGHT, IF I PRETEND THAT DIDN'T *happen, he'll be gone when I open my eyes.* My legs flopped to the ground, and I winced when I rolled to my side, eyes still pinched shut.

"Whoa," the little girl's voice said. *Aiden's* little girl's voice. "You fell super hard, Miss Isabel."

Fuuuuuck me, honestly.

"You okay?" he asked. His voice was close—low and rough—and it raised the hair on my arms.

Was I okay? Such an interesting question. Because no … I wasn't.

I wanted to erase every freaking interaction I'd had with him, scrub it from my brain with bleach because somehow, they just kept getting worse.

But was I actually, physically fine? Uh-huh, sure, let's go with that.

I let out a slow breath and took stock of my body, because if I'd hurt anything, hopping up was a terrible idea. "Yeah, I am."

When I pried open my eyes, Aiden was crouched down, hands hanging in between his bent knees. His face was lined with concern, but he made no move to touch me, thank the Lord in heaven above.

If I was this much of a klutz when he breathed the same air as me, I'd probably spontaneously orgasm if we made skin-to-skin contact.

He nodded, rising slowly as I stood off the mats. Bracing his hands on his hips, his eyes turned toward his daughter, still swinging her legs up on that steel beam like she was at the freaking playground.

"Anya," he said, all steady and calm, but I saw the tension in his jaw. "Time to get down."

Her chin stuck out. "I'm not getting down for you." She pointed at me. "I'm getting down because of her trick."

"Fine," Aiden said evenly.

"Can I jump off the top?"

"Absolutely not."

She sighed dramatically, but reached her arms out. He moved underneath the beam and as I watched those arms extend toward her, I felt this dangerous swelling in my heart. Something I didn't want to touch or poke at, but she hopped off the beam with such ease, such trust, that I almost had to look away.

Before he set her down, Aiden hugged Anya to his chest, her skinny arms wrapped around his neck, and I saw him release a quiet breath of relief.

Instead of watching the scene in front of me, I moved my gaze to the floor and smoothed a hand over my now-wrecked braid—a fitting symbol for my bruised pride.

"Sure you're okay?" he asked.

I nodded.

"She's not a good singer," Anya chimed in. "She told me that."

Aiden closed his eyes, while I ... I tried not to stare awkwardly at his daughter because honestly, could this get worse?

"Anya," he chided.

"I asked her." She fiddled with the collar of Aiden's shirt. "But I didn't ask anything else."

He gave me an apologetic look. "I'm sorry." Aiden let out another breath. He glanced around the gym. "There's a class at six, right?"

Again, I nodded, because this was the signature move in the Isabel Ward library of reactions to this particular man.

"You teaching?"

Don't nod, don't nod. My tongue unstuck from the roof of my mouth. "Not usually, but I'm covering for Kelly."

Anya's eyes widened. "Do you show people how to punch like my dad?"

Aiden's mouth softened, but still ... it wasn't quite a smile.

Maybe this little girl with her strange questions and horrible love of climbing could help me ease my way into 'normal Isabel' around him.

I tilted my head. "Show me your strongest fist," I told her.

She curled up her little fingers so tightly that the skin over her knuckles went white.

"Very good." I showed her mine, then tapped my pointer and middle finger knuckles. "Always aim to hit right here, okay? And don't tuck your thumb inside your other fingers."

Anya rolled her eyes. "Everyone knows that. You'll break your finger."

I set my hands on my hips. "Maybe I should have you teach class."

She giggled, glancing up at her dad with an expression so adoring, I could feel every ounce of my body melt like a stick of butter.

"Okay, gingersnap, you can play on your iPad while I get a little work done," he said, and oh holy hell, *he called her gingersnap.* His eyes came back to rest on me, and I prayed to all the deities in all the religions in all the world that he couldn't see what that did to me.

Honestly, it was like he was trying to be the most attractive man alive. And the fact that he didn't realize he was made it even more attractive, which was an entirely separate issue. She motioned him down to her own height, and whispered something in his ear. If his face had been angled in my direction, I might have seen his lips curve in a smile, but instead, I simply saw the edge of his cheek move. But he nodded to whatever she said.

Anya gave me a shy smile. "You're really pretty, Miss Isabel. I think you look like Wonder Woman."

Instead of laughing her off, or dismissing it because Aiden was watching, I held my arms up in an X over my chest, and winked. When her face transformed into a wide smile, for the first time, I felt okay about an interaction with my new boss. Sort of.

Each embarrassing moment could get tucked away, in the corner of the box, held in place by each time I managed to take baby steps into something normal with him. I didn't want to fawn over him, I didn't want to study each nuance of each moment, because it felt wretched.

Anya ran off to his office, and to my surprise, Aiden didn't follow.

"I owe you, Ward," he said.

I blinked. "For what?"

Aiden jerked his chin toward the top of the steel beam.

My cheeks flushed hot. Honestly, with the flushing and the falling and the nodding. "No, it's okay. You don't owe me anything."

"Yes," he said evenly, "I do."

There was nothing for me to say, because 1—I was afraid I'd keep arguing because no, he didn't owe me anything for getting the small child off the very high beam, and 2—it seemed safer not to initiate a conversation with him.

Problematic, that.

"Anya," he said, lifting his chin toward where his daughter had disappeared, "she's done that her whole life." At the lift in my eyebrows, he clarified. "The climbing. Doesn't give me a heart attack like it used to, but every once in a while she goes a little too far."

The way his voice softened when he spoke of his daughter had all sorts of melty, gooey things happening in my body. At first, all I could do was nod. But when I said nothing in response, I felt his curious regard.

Promise me you'll try, I heard Amy say in my head. At the time, she'd had no clue what she was asking of me, but I'd given her my word all the same.

Before I could form words though, Aiden spoke again.

"You don't like that I'm here, do you?"

My eyes zipped to his. "What?"

Aiden's gaze was steady, searching. He didn't repeat the question. Not to be rude or intimidating, but because we both knew that I'd understood him perfectly.

"I," my voice faltered, and I shook my head. *Try, Isabel.* "Change is hard for me," I forced out. Pushing aside all butterflies, all off-kilter feelings with a sweep of my hand, I dug past the embarrassment and found a kernel of truth. "I still don't know what your presence here means," I told him.

Handing him that piece of truth, even if I had no clue exactly what it meant, was like tugging out a part of my body. But his reaction … I'd be lying if I said it didn't make it just a little less painful.

The way he watched me talk without ever rushing or pushing me helped loosen something tight and uncomfortable behind my ribs.

Aiden tucked his hands into the front pockets of his dark jeans. "How about this," he said slowly. "I promise I won't make any big changes without discussing it with you first. New name aside," he added.

My heart hammered. He wasn't required to do that. And his approach—the calm, the steady—wasn't something I expected.

"You don't have to do that," I told him. "This is your place, not mine."

A few people walked in—lawyers from a local firm—and effusively loud greetings came my way as they entered. I waved.

"You sure about that?" he asked dryly.

I hid a pleased smile. Just barely. It'd felt like my place since the first day I walked in.

"All the same." I kept my reply even, professional. "It's your name on the building, or it will be soon enough. You can make your mark on it without my say-so."

After I said the words, I wanted to take them back. Or for a moment, I did. Because I'd known so many athletes, ego-driven, prideful, who preened obnoxiously under any spotlight they were given. And still, I wasn't entirely sure how this particular former athlete would respond.

"All the same," he responded. "I want you to trust me, Ward."

My eyes could hardly meet his, not with the way he said my last name. If he looked hard enough, he'd see goosebumps rise along my bare arms. The impulse to smooth them down with the palm of my hand was almost impossible to ignore. Before I could react, Anya popped her head out of his office.

"Daddy, my iPad froze. Can you help me?"

With a slight lift of his chin, he walked toward his office, and I breathed out slowly, my cheeks puffing with the loaded exhale.

Back to work. It was the only way I'd survive it.

Soon enough, as I'd told him, the building would bear his name, and the thought had me wandering to the front area.

As I faced the shelves of merchandise by the desk, I thought about what the hell we were supposed to do with all the stuff labeled Wilson's Gym when I knew Aiden had already ordered the new signage to make the switch to Hennessy's. Fortunately, he wasn't champing at the bit to slap his name over everything. He wanted to handle the transition publicly in a way that was smooth. Staring at the racks of T-shirts, sweatshirts, wraps, gloves, all of it, I started thinking through ways to clear the inventory as quickly as possible.

I took a seat at the front desk and yanked open the bottom right drawer.

"There you are," I murmured, tugging on a clear container that held bright-colored round stickers. I eyed the racks of shirts and wondered if Aiden would have an opinion on starting with half off everything or maybe a BOGO sale to see how much we could move.

There it was again, the pause in my entire body when I thought about going to his office to ask him.

This was ridiculous.

I set my elbows on the desk and covered my face with a groan. While I sat in that dejected position, the gym phone rang. I picked it up, but before I could say anything, I heard Aiden's voice coming through the handset in his office.

"Wilson's Gym, this is Aiden."

Gawd, his voice. I rolled my lips between my teeth and allowed, just for one moment, my eyes to fall closed so I could just … listen to him speak.

"Mr. Hennessy, this is Chandra at the Seattle Youth Sports Foundation. Thank you so much for your call. We were thrilled to receive it."

Slowly, I started setting down the phone even though there was a nagging, naughty whisper in the back of my mind that wanted me to keep listening. Because the way he formed words, the way something simple and innocent came out of his mouth, had me picturing him behind me, whispering in my ear. Things I'd never imagined someone telling me to do.

If I were to text Amy where she was currently exploring Greece, I didn't think this was the kind of trying she'd had in mind.

The front door opened just as I had the phone set back down on the receiver, revealing the smiling face of our newest college hire.

"Emily, how's it going?"

When she sucked in a deep breath, I knew the answer was going to be very, very dramatic. The word vomit started immediately about her boyfriend and another girl, and I'm sure my eyes were so wide in my face that it looked like I'd just been smacked over the back of the head.

"So, you're stressed then," I said when she finally took a breath.

Emily plopped into the chair that I'd vacated behind the front desk. "I just know he's cheating on me."

Early arrivals for my six o'clock class started filtering through the front door, and I greeted them with a smile.

"But you can't be sure," I told her. "You just suspect based on a couple of ... vibes, right?"

My sisters always came to me for no-nonsense relationship advice, and honestly, sometimes I thought my ability to be no-nonsense was because I'd never gotten myself tangled up in any of the dramatics. Or any body parts, really.

Vibes had never been my forte, or at least ... not until Aiden walked through the door. As much as I didn't want to admit it, I was creating all *sorts* of those in my own imagination.

Emily paused to swipe a member's card as he struggled to check in with the scanner on the desk. He thanked her with a smile, nodding to me as he passed. I pulled my favorite black and pink wraps from the top drawer and unraveled the tightly wrapped ball.

"They were strong, though," she said, leaning against the desk. "*Heavy* eye contact."

Yeah. Heavy eye contact. I shifted uncomfortably. "What else?"

Emily hummed. "Really loaded subtext in the things they said." Her face got serious. "They were saying one thing, but you knew they meant something else."

"And that's a sign of ...?" My voice trailed off.

"Sex, *for sure.*"

Sweat popped along the back of my neck because *check, check,* and *check.* One-sided vibe, courtesy of me.

Someone else walked in, and I stifled a groan at the sight of him. I know, customer service and all, but this guy was the bane of every female trainer's existence. He stood too close, talked too much, stayed after class too late, and had a seriously annoying tendency to stare at either our tits or ass through the entire class.

Talk about getting a vibe from someone. This guy was the absolute king of inspiring douchebag feelings.

"Mike," I said politely. "Haven't seen you in a while."

He slicked his tongue over his teeth. "Where's Kelly? I didn't know you were teaching tonight."

Not surprising. Mike did not seem to stay too late or talk too close with me. He favored Kelly, probably because she was petite, and he could stare down at her chest from his lofty five-foot-six.

Also, Kelly was friendlier than me.

In her absence, he did a thorough examination of the bubbly blond behind the desk. The way he looked Emily up and down had me clearing my throat. I held his gaze steadily when his attention was back on me.

"She hurt her ankle." I continued wrapping my knuckles, angling the wraps around my wrist, and then back around my palm. Flexing my fingers, I gave him a tiny smile. "You're stuck with me tonight."

"You're new," he told Emily.

She gave him a friendly smile, but not quite as friendly as the one she'd given everyone else. Emily, apparently, *was* a very good reader of vibes and heavy eye contact. "Started a couple of weeks ago."

He nodded. "Sweet. Another reason to love Tuesday nights."

Because he wasn't looking, I rolled my eyes. "You better go

stretch, Mike. I have my angry rock playlist, which means you need to be all warmed up and ready to get your ass kicked."

He snorted as he walked past, and I had to grit my teeth.

Someone was going to get a lot of extra burpees tonight, and it wasn't me. As the manager, I might not be able to be outright rude to him, but I could make him curse the day he was born.

Emily shook her head. "So creepy."

I finished wrapping my other hand and sighed. "He is. Unfortunately, he's never done anything blatant that would get him kicked out. Next week, if you're here with Kelly, and he's the only one left, don't leave until she does. That's one of our unspoken rules. No female trainer here alone with someone new, or someone like jackass over there who's just kinda slimy. Got it?"

She nodded. "Got it. Thanks, Iz."

I picked up my bottle of water and tipped it back to take a drink. That was when I saw her eyes widen again and her back straighten. Mid-swallow of cold water was when he decided to speak from right behind me.

"I hope that rule applies to you, too," Aiden grumbled.

The choke came first, and I slapped a hand over my mouth, but in the process, I tried to exhale.

Which brought water right up my fucking nose.

The cringe on Emily's face was more than enough for me to know just how mortifying I must have looked, but when she carefully handed me a towel to wipe my face, I knew it was bad.

"Sorry," he said. "I seem to have a bad habit of taking you by surprise."

No shit, Sherlock.

I finished wiping my face and glanced at Aiden. "It's f-fine."

He watched me set the bottle and the towel down, and when his gaze returned to my face, I saw the slightest hint of amusement.

And that did nothing to lessen my abject humiliation at how stupid and silly I felt around this man.

I took a deep breath and faced him. "Does what rule apply to me?"

He tilted his head to where Mike was stretching out his arms in front of his bag. "What you just told Emily."

"Most of the time," I answered honestly. "But Mike doesn't bother me."

"Yet."

I nodded in concession. "Yet."

"I can revoke his membership if the trainers are uncomfortable around him."

My eyebrows lifted slowly. "Even if he hasn't done anything other than being a creep?"

"Even if."

His brusquely spoken words did nothing to soothe my feathers that seemed to naturally ruffle in his presence. If anything, they made it so much worse. Something about our exchange earlier, the bag, the daughter, the way he came at me head-on. Aiden made me feel like I was all raw, exposed edges, and there was nothing that I hated more. I turned away briefly to grab the microphone battery pack, hook it onto the back of my leggings, and then attach the earpiece around my ear so the mic was in front of my mouth. I made sure it was switched off before I spoke.

"I'll let you know if it gets to that point."

Aiden clenched his jaw. "Okay."

Oh, look at that. I managed one whole conversation with him, and the worst thing that happened was spitting water out of my nose. Things were looking up.

"Did you need something?" I asked.

He glanced over at the racks of merchandise. "New merch should be here in about two weeks."

"I can have Emily mark this stuff down to half off if you want to move it fast."

But Aiden shook his head. "Just box it all up."

"Don't you want to try to sell it?"

He handed me a slip of paper, and along the top, I saw the logo for the Seattle Youth Sports Foundation. "I'd rather just donate it. They'll disperse it to various foundations across the state for underprivileged kids. They need the equipment more than I need the money."

For a moment, I stared at him. The hard line of his profile and the slight bunching of smile lines that fanned along his eyes. Honestly, screw Aiden Hennessy and his big heart and protective gestures and cute daughter and biceps that were the size of my head. This was about to get ridiculous.

"If that's okay with you," he said lightly.

Holding his eyes to gauge his sincerity, I found nothing to make me doubt what he was saying. Finally, I nodded.

As I took the paper from his outstretched hand and he walked away after a murmured thanks, I knew if I stayed in this headspace for another week, I'd be head over heels in love with my boss.

I couldn't predict what he was going to do, what he was going to say, and I found myself waiting with bated breath for whatever came next.

He was locked away in a box of his own, and for the first time, I was the one wanting to dig my fingers in and pry off the top.

CHAPTER 6

Aiden

"**W**HAT'S YOUR PROBLEM?"

I blinked, glancing over at Clark. He was sitting at my desk, sketching out an idea for adding an open loft space over the main workout area.

"I don't have a problem."

Which wasn't a lie because it wasn't the right word.

"You look like you have a problem," he said, pencil flying steadily over his graph paper.

"Why do my little brothers always ask me that when I'm trying to think?"

Clark didn't hesitate. "Maybe because you look perpetually pissed off when you're thinking too hard."

Crossing my arms over my chest, I turned my attention back toward the middle of the gym where Isabel was leading a class.

She moved in and out of the bags, shouting encouragement and occasionally stopping to help someone. Her hair, as always, was slicked off her face, and when she dropped to the floor to demonstrate something she wanted, it was long enough over her shoulder that it almost brushed the floor.

Wonder Woman, Anya had called her. And she'd asked her if she liked to sing. I knew she was thinking about that fucking list the moment she said that.

"You're doing it again."

This time, I didn't look at Clark. "Can't figure out my manager."

In my peripheral vision, I saw his pencil slow, stop, and then start again. He always thought best when he was either drawing or building. "Why not?"

"I can't get a read on her," I said slowly. "But I feel like she's … uncomfortable around me."

Clark stopped drawing, spinning in my desk chair until he faced me. "She do a good job?"

"Yeah."

As it always seemed to, without my permission and without any approval or forethought, my attention strayed to her. She was an irritation under my skin, not because of anything particularly vexing but simply because I felt like she was hiding something. Hiding herself.

And I didn't like how that felt.

Because it lit the fuse on an urge that I'd long since buried.

Interest.

Everyone else at the gym had made a concerted effort to seek me out and get to know me. And it was the exact opposite with her. Maybe that was why I found my gaze drawn to her.

The softness she'd shown my daughter was the most disconcerting of all. Before that, all I'd seen of Isabel were shifting pieces that I couldn't pinpoint, like she was standing in front of a funhouse mirror.

Clumsy one moment, graceful the next.

Impenetrable with a client, blushing in the next interaction.

Kind with the employees, refusing my kindness in turn.

Warm with those who knew her, candidly wary with me.

She was beautiful, as my daughter had said. Rarely smiled, rarely laughed. Not that I'd seen yet.

And I hated, more than I could've put into words, that I wanted to figure her out.

Hated that I'd checked her employee file, musing uncomfortably over the fact that she was a decade younger than I was yet seemed so much older than her age.

None of those things would I verbalize to my brother, who was already watching me with that analytical brain of his. I'd probably said too much as it was.

Because the second I saw her making Anya laugh, the second I watched them interact, the very first thing in my mind was absolutely terrifying:

Not this one. It can't be her.

For a host of reasons. Too many to count.

Before I knew what Anya had asked her, I'd mentally cataloged each piece of Isabel that I knew. When she came up as the opposite of each thing Beth had listed to our daughter a million hours earlier, I felt the impact of it like a blow.

Disappointment.

"Aiden?" Clark asked.

"Forget I said anything," I murmured. "I'll get over it."

I had to.

CHAPTER 7

Isabel

"**C**OULD YOU POSSIBLY BE MORE OF A BITCH?**"**

Not a single person at the table blinked when Molly glared at me. I smiled because surrounded by the sheer chaos of our family, I was in my happy place.

"Because of this?" I lifted my fork, each tine loaded to the edge with rotini noodles. My gaze stayed right on Molly as I sniffed deeply. "Mmmm, the sauce smells so good, doesn't it?"

Her eyes narrowed. I shoved the entire bite in my mouth and groaned. Molly picked up her own fork and stabbed her salad like it was a teeny tiny Isabel voodoo doll.

My sister's fiancé, Noah, rubbed her back and set a small piece of bread onto her plate. "You can have some carbs, Molly."

"Yeah, Molly," I said, "you can have carbs."

She threw the bread at me, and I caught it with a laugh.

Paige sighed. "Isabel, don't poke the carb-deprived bear."

She set her jaw, my happy, kind, friendly sister who was so carb-deprived angry that she looked like she was plotting my death.

"Easy for you to say, you work out for a living." Then she glanced around the table. "Oh my gosh, half the people here work out for a living. This is bullshit," she grumbled, spearing a piece of asparagus.

She wasn't wrong.

Logan held up his hand. "Don't include me in that. Coaches don't have to be in shape."

"You sure expect your players to be, though," Noah grumbled between bites of his own pasta.

Logan exhaled happily. "Great conditioning today, wasn't it, Griffin?"

Noah gave him a long look.

"Speaking of people working out for a living," I said, "where's Bauer?"

Claire sighed. "He's up in Vancouver for some training thing that he couldn't miss."

I held my fist out across the table. "Hey, now I'm not the only single one at the family dinner."

She bumped my fist. Our nephew, Logan and Paige's ten-year-old son Emmett, scoffed. "I'm single too. Thanks a lot."

Claire fist-bumped him, and I reached across to do the same.

Paige grinned over the rim of her wineglass. "This is the closest we've had to the whole zoo at one table in like … a year."

"Is that why it's so loud?" Logan asked.

"Yes," Claire and I answered.

From the kitchen, Lia walked toward the table, balancing two plates in her hands. Behind her was her boyfriend, Jude, carrying a sound asleep Gabriel. He glanced around the table. "Anyone want a sleeping baby?"

Paige, Molly, and I all raised our hands.

Jude cast a skeptical look at all three of us, then lifted his chin at Molly. "You're up, then."

"Rude," Paige muttered.

I frowned. "You're just picking her because she's got that look in her eye like she'll cut you."

Noah choked on his food. Molly sat back down in her chair, Gabriel tucked into the crook of her arm, with a beatific smile on her face. "I can't wait until you get engaged someday, Iz, and we'll see how *you* act when you're a couple of months away from your wedding, and you don't want bread making you puffy because you ordered your dress just a little bit too small on accident."

Isabel Ward Hennessy. Isabel Hennessy. Isabel and Aiden 4-ever.

If I pinched my eyes closed, I could see the purple-inked doodles in my head. That damn diary might not be in the metal box, but it was probably still up in my old bedroom, and oh, my gosh, I wanted to go find it and burn it.

I may never send this letter, but would you come to my junior prom with me? I have a light purple dress that my brother bought I bought for myself. And I love daisies, if you'd want to get me a corsage made of those. Only if you want.

Shutting off my brain would've been lovely because my face immediately went flame hot. After that, Aiden's face was what popped into my head like an asshole. And my older sister noticed immediately. "What's that face?"

"Nothing." I shoved another bite of pasta in my mouth. "Involuntary physical reaction at the idea of giving up carbs."

She rolled her eyes.

I could feel the weight of Paige's gaze on the side of my face, which was why I ignored her.

At some point, I'd always known that the right person would wedge their foot in the proverbial door before I could slam it shut.

But it would have to be a big foot. No pun intended. The thought of big feet and big hands and big ... arms had me shoving food in my mouth again. It was just hard to imagine how everyone else seemed to have such an easy time letting that happen, opening up, and just being normal.

But because it was me, of course it wasn't that easy.

The first guy to flip all the right switches was part fantasy, part forbidden reality, and all fricken perfect from what I could see.

"How's the new boss, Iz?" Logan asked.

That delicious pasta turned to ash in my mouth because there was no way he could've been following my thoughts. It was my turn to glare now.

"What?" he asked. "Are we not talking about that?"

Paige stifled a laugh.

He sighed. "You're supposed to tell me when I'm not allowed to ask things," he said to his wife.

Molly laughed. "Iz is just touchy because she had such a raging crush on him when he first started to fight."

"I did not," I protested, but it was a weak one at best. I wouldn't have believed me either.

Lia laughed. "You used to cut his picture out of *Sports Illustrated* and tape it up on the back of your door. You told us after he was at the gym the first time."

Hands shaking as I gripped my plate, I stood from the table. I'd rather face a firing squad than that topic. "You know, I think I'm done eating."

Paige smacked Lia. "Should we remind you of who *you* used to tape up on your wall?"

Her laughter faded. We *all* remembered the Bieber-with-the-long-hair phase Lia and Claire went through. It lasted a solid two years.

"My eardrums are still recovering from that block of time," Logan muttered.

Jude hummed. "Kate Winslet for me. I met her at a dinner a few years ago, and I about passed out when she shook my hand."

"See?" I gestured to Jude. "It's not just me."

Molly snuck a piece of bread from Noah's plate, pointing a finger at me when she was done chewing. "He's your boss, though.

Your ability to separate your past feelings is vital if you're going to keep professional boundaries."

"Are you *serious?*" I asked.

"What?"

Noah gave her a look. "You're one to talk. Do I need to remind you of how our past caught up with us on the job?"

Molly's cheeks turned pink. "No."

I gave him a smile. "Thank you, Noah. You're my favorite almost-brother-in-law."

"I'm your only almost-brother-in-law."

Jude held up his hand. "Hello, sitting right here."

My brother gave him a level look. "Is there a ring on Lia's finger we don't see?"

Wisely, Jude didn't argue. He just slid his arm around my younger sister, who beamed in his direction.

Setting my plate down on the kitchen island, I tried to ignore the way Paige was looking at me from the table. She wasn't even trying to hide it, and when Logan whispered something in her ear, she smiled, but her eyes stayed trained on me.

She saw too much. From the day she showed up in our lives, she had this uncanny ability to see through me like I was made of plastic wrap. I hated it. And I needed it.

My sisters, for whatever reason, and though they loved me eternally, never had the same talent. They saw the same thing that everyone else did. Isabel, the intimidating sister. Isabel, the one you didn't mess with. Isabel, the one who'd fight the world if someone messed with her family.

But every once in a while, I wondered at how they couldn't see what was underneath all of that.

Sometimes I felt like everything truly good I could offer someone was lined in metal and locked under the surface. Even I wasn't sure how to pry the lid off. Aiden, all of this, it made me realize just how long I'd gone being content with that.

As I cleared my plate, Paige quietly stood and joined me in the kitchen. Nudging me with her shoulder, she leaned in to whisper, "Talk to me."

"About what?"

She sighed. "Are we gonna play that game where you act like there's nothing wrong? Just let me know if we are, and I'll put on my stubborn pants."

I took her plate and rinsed it off, setting it in the dishwasher next to mine. "I just don't know what they want me to say. Yes, teenage Isabel had a ... thing for him. I can't change it, and it doesn't mean anything now."

Liar, liar, pants on fire.

"So why do you look like you want to teleport out of here when they ask you about him?"

I closed the dishwasher and leaned against the counter. With a shrug, I gave her a helpless look. "Because I do. And I just ... ugh. All of this makes me feel so ..." I shuddered.

Paige studied me, nodding slowly as I spoke. "He makes you feel off-balance and out of control, which you *would* hate. Come to think of it, I don't think I've ever seen you get like this over a man."

With a groan, I covered my face with my hands. "Can we stop talking about it?"

She laughed. "Okay, okay. I'm done."

Logan joined us. "Sorry, Iz, I didn't know that was a forbidden topic."

What an interesting choice of words. Aiden was certainly that.

Something I wanted but couldn't have. For all I knew, he still hadn't grieved his wife. Who, by all accounts, had been beautiful and kind. His high school sweetheart, from the article I read one day when I'd felt a little maudlin. He was starting over, taking care of his daughter, and more than likely, he'd remain as he was. An active participant in all my best fantasies until I'd get over it one day. Hopefully.

"It's fine." I sighed.

He glanced at Paige. "Did you ask her about Emmett?"

"What about Emmett?" I asked.

"Paige wants to come to the away game in Tampa," my brother said. Paige gave him a look that had him grinning.

"Can you not, with the eye contact?" I asked.

Paige laughed. "Would you be able to stay with Emmett for a couple of days? He's got a school thing that Friday he can't miss."

"Sure. When's the game?"

As I scrolled through my phone calendar, he named the mid-September date. "Molly going to the game too?"

Paige shook her head. "She doesn't want to use any time off that close to the wedding. I think she'll be gone for work, anyway."

Because we'd already teased her relentlessly about it when she first started her planning, I raised my voice when I replied. "Yeah, what kind of bride plans an October wedding in a family of athletes?"

Molly raised her voice right back. "I knew it was a bye week, *okay?* You try to book the venue of your dreams when half the people in your family play in some sort of professional sport."

Paige laughed.

She wasn't wrong. Juggling the schedules of my sisters and their significant others was a nightmare.

"Lia will be gone at an away game with Jude, and Claire is going to be up in Vancouver with Bauer while he trains."

I waved off Paige's explanations. "It's fine. Plenty of time to request the weekend off."

"New guy won't mind?" she asked.

My gaze stayed locked onto my phone. "I can't see why he would."

Emmett ran into the kitchen and dumped his plate into the sink with a crash. Paige rolled her eyes.

"Am I staying with you when they leave, Iz?"

"I think we'll stay here if that's okay."

He nodded. "Totally. Your apartment is so boring."

"It is not. I just don't require seventy-plus inches of my wall space dedicated to television viewing like some people I know." I gave Logan a look.

"*Yeah*," Emmett said, "that's why it sucks. You've lived there for two years, and you watch on your dinky laptop."

Paige nudged him out of the kitchen. "Go do your homework before she changes her mind, you little punk."

"And quit saying sucks," Logan called after his retreating back.

"If that's the worst he says at the age of ten, he's doing better than we were," I reminded him.

He rubbed his temples. "I listen to cursing athletes all day at work, and sometimes, I think the worst language I've heard came from the four of you as you were growing up."

"That's why you love us."

"And that love is why I am going prematurely gray." He sighed.

Paige patted his stomach. "My sexy silver fox," she purred, leaning up for a kiss.

I could handle PDA from about two percent of the population, but when he grabbed her ass, I shuddered.

"And on that note," I said, walking from the kitchen with a hand covering my eyes. "Bye, everyone," I said, with a wave to the group at the table.

"You're leaving already?" Molly asked with a pout. It did not escape my notice that Noah had slowly ripped off pieces of his bread to the point where she'd eaten his whole slice. No wonder she was nicer now.

"I'm beat," I told her. "And I have to teach three classes tomorrow with Kelly gone."

"I'm going to come work out with you," Molly said after blowing me a kiss.

"'K. Just shoot me a text so it goes in the schedule. I don't want anyone else booking me for a time that works for you."

Lia made a pouting face. "Aw, I was hoping we could go through boxes after dinner and find all your *I heart Aiden* paraphernalia."

The look I gave her had Lia cackling, but honestly, if she wanted a guarantee that I'd hightail it out of there, she'd just done it.

Because somewhere just up the stairs, she could find it if she looked hard enough. The metal box, with that damn letter, was in the spare room, no doubt underneath a pile of books and papers that Paige refused to organize. For a moment, I glanced up the stairs and thought about smuggling it out.

Maybe destroying the letter, seeing the ridiculous level to which I'd obsessed over him, would purge him from my system, and I could get back to normal. It sounded so good.

And so terrible.

I said the rest of my goodbyes and got an extra tight squeeze from Paige. But before I left the house, I paused, and without trying to overthink it, I took the stairs two at a time, striding straight for the spare room. It was a mess, but in the large bookshelf toward the back of the room, surrounded by spare furniture, clothes that needed to be donated, piles of toys, and all the random shit we'd accumulated over the years, I saw the black metal edge of the lockbox.

Holding my breath, I curled my hand around it and slid it out from underneath the pile of books that had hidden most of it. It was heavier than I remembered, and when I clutched it to my chest, I wished I could call Nan and tell her about Aiden. She wasn't related to me since Logan and I didn't share a mom, but in all the ways that mattered, she'd taken us under her wing after my dad—her ex-husband—died.

She'd want to know all about what I'd kept in the box in the years since she gave it to me. And why I wanted to hide this one thing away from everyone else.

With the box in my possession, I breathed out a sigh of relief and skipped lightly down the steps, sneaking out the front door before anyone even realized I'd gone up there.

The night air was warm and fragrant as I walked out to my car. The box went into the passenger seat, and for a moment, I studied it like I wasn't sure what it was or how it got there.

My thumb traced the heavy circle of gold where the key, taped to the bottom of the box in a sandwich bag, would slide into place. With my luck, the thing had rusted shut, and I'd go the rest of my life knowing my teenage self could never fully get rid of the evidence of my crush on Aiden Hennessy.

Maybe I'd burn the whole damn box in that case.

Just as the thought crossed my mind and I realized how freaking crazy it made me sound, my phone started buzzing. When I pulled it out, I didn't recognize the number on the screen, but it looked familiar enough that I answered.

"Hello?"

"I'm looking for Isabel Ward," an unfamiliar male voice said.

"Can I ask who's calling?"

He paused. "Yeah, this is Carl from Punch Fitness. Is this Isabel?"

I pursed my lips for a second. Punch was one of our biggest competitors. We'd never had a bad relationship with them, per se; we just ran a different style of gym. And not once, in all my years of working for Amy, had the owner ever reached out to me.

"It is. How can I help you, Carl?"

"I don't really know how to say this any other way than bluntly, but I heard about your shift in ownership, and I'm wondering if you're looking for a change."

My head reared back. "You want to hire me?"

He laughed at my incredulous tone. "Yeah."

"You don't even know me," I pointed out.

"I don't, but I'm aware of your reputation. You seem like someone who doesn't tolerate bullshit, and I like that. So I won't beat around the bush. We've had enough overlap in members in the past five years that I've heard about you. And everything I've heard is good, even if it's bad."

If I kept up the way I was acting, all he'd know about me was that I tripped over air, fell off bags, and fantasized about my boss.

"Thanks," I said dryly.

"I mean, if people have a problem with how you run things, it's probably because they pissed you off, and you held them accountable. That's how I do things too."

I ran a hand down my face and could not ignore the way my heart was racing in my chest. This was not something I expected.

Surprises, much like change, did not sit well with me.

The thought of leaving my job, that building, and my co-workers caused actual pain. I'd bleed out immediately if I even tried to dislodge it. The metal box creaked and groaned in protest at the idea of uprooting all the things that made me me, how much of it was rooted in the building where I worked. Change took on a different form, something I couldn't have imagined when Aiden showed his face. So I answered as honestly as I could without leading this guy on.

"I wasn't looking to leave Wilson's."

"But it's not Wilson's anymore, is it?"

Exhaling slowly, I tapped my fingers on the steering wheel. "It's not. But it's still the place that I love. And right now, I have no intention of leaving."

He hummed. "Well, if you change your mind, you've got my number."

With the call disconnected and my brain spinning at an uncomfortable speed about what it all meant, I set my phone back into my purse and started up my car.

CHAPTER 8

Isabel

THE NEXT DAY, EVERYTHING AT WORK LOOKED DIFFERENT.
Or maybe work was the same, but I was observing it through a different lens. The surprise call from the night before kept me awake for hours as I stared at the ceiling and tried to imagine a reality that didn't include the four walls of the gym that was my second home.

The filter I'd applied started cataloging things that I'd change, if I could.

I didn't like the way that the weight and cardio machines had been set up, but Amy felt it was important to keep a separation from the bags. There was too much dead space around the center ring, and the front desk should be oriented differently. We'd repeatedly had requests for full showers, but the investment was never worth the payoff at the time.

More than once that day, I found myself staring at that side of the gym, mentally rearranging things.

We needed more employees, woefully apparently on days like

the ones I was in the middle of, as I wrapped my hands for my third one-hour class of the day. My throat was paying the price as much as my body was because even though we had mics, it was still a solid hour of yelling over the music. And my body, well … suffice it to say, I was trying to go easy so that I could move the next day.

As I was chatting with clients, I stretched my arm over my chest and caught movement in Aiden's office.

He'd made himself scarce all day, and for that, I was thankful.

If I'd started off with water coming out of my nose, falling on my face, tripping over ropes or something, I might have thought on Carl's offer for too long.

His tall frame filled the doorway, and when his gaze locked onto mine, I felt my cheeks grow warm.

My reaction begged the question, one I didn't want to think about. Could I leave simply because of my reaction to him?

I'd never run from a challenge in my entire life. Not any that mattered.

And if I took this other job, that was what I'd be doing. Even when I didn't see him, I imagined his eyes on me.

I dropped my arms and my gaze because he was still far enough away from me that I should've been immune to his presence.

Should didn't mean shit, though, not when he had me hooked up to some invisible power grid. Even with the few interactions we'd had so far, that man had all sorts of hidden parts of me lighting up.

Hooking the battery pack onto my leggings, I flipped on the microphone.

"Two minutes until we get rolling, everyone. Make sure you're all stretched out, grab a drink, whatever you need to do. I don't give water breaks in my class, so it's up to you to stay hydrated, okay?"

I walked to the wall where the stereo system was mounted on large brackets and tapped the iPad in the holder on the wall, pulling up the playlist I wanted to use.

Along the edge of the gym, Aiden walked slowly, chatting with one of our longtime members. But I felt his eyes on me as I walked the class through the warmup. My blood hummed warm and fast underneath my skin, and I found myself more energized than I had been in my previous classes of the day.

As I walked around the bags, shouting combinations and directions to the thirty people present, it was the first time I felt a different type of energy coursing through my body while Aiden was around. It was something powerful, something that prowled and purred.

What I allowed myself next was stupid. So stupid. But as I taught, I let my mind race. A different scenario played out in my head to the heavy, pulsing beat of the music. While everyone kept working, while people filled the building, he motioned for me to come into his office. Without a word, he shut the door behind us, approaching me silently, sliding his hand against my hip to turn off the mic, and then I was against the door, his hands hard, his mouth demanding, and to the thumping bass, he took me that way. Hand over my mouth so no one heard.

But it wasn't real.

By the time I finished class, walking everyone through a cool down and stretch, I was sweaty and disheveled, hair sticking to the back of my neck as my braid had started unraveling with my effort and my imagination. Clients thanked me for the class, and after wiping down their bags and picking up their stuff, the gym slowly emptied, save for a few people on the machines.

By then, my heart rate had slowed, and my mind had calmed.

One class member, a fresh-faced young woman, approached me with a tentative smile.

"Casey, right?" I asked.

She nodded. "I really like your classes. You always push me harder than the other instructors. I think it's because you're scarier."

I laughed. "Thanks, I think."

"Do you ever do self-defense training?"

I nodded. "Yeah, the setup of these classes is for cardio, but if you wanted something specific, I can get you hooked up with me or one of the other trainers."

"I-I think I'd prefer a female trainer," she said quietly.

"Absolutely." I gentled my tone. "Feels good to know a few moves, doesn't it?"

Casey's eyes were wide in her face, and when she nodded slowly, I wanted to rip apart anyone or anything that made her feel like she needed to know how to defend herself.

"How much are the training sessions?" She winced. "College student budget, you know? I grabbed your punch card promo last month, but I don't know if I can afford anything else."

I looked over my shoulder and didn't see Aiden. "Tell you what, do you have a few minutes now? I'd be happy to go over some basics."

"Really?" she breathed.

"Yeah. Let me get rid of this mic and grab some water."

As I hooked the battery pack up to the charger, I let out a slow breath. It wasn't the first time we'd had a young woman ask for self-defense classes, but nevertheless, something about her big brown eyes and tentative nature had my wheels spinning.

Maybe a once-a-month class taught by me or Kelly with a few other trainers helping out with demonstrations. I'd have to ask Aiden if he'd be okay with something like that. Ideas of how we could connect with the University of Washington and other local colleges had ideas tumbling faster and faster in my head.

I walked back to where she was waiting, her arms folded over her stomach. "Ready?" I asked.

She nodded.

"Okay, drop your arms by your side and take a deep breath for me." I nodded when she complied. "I'll show you a couple right now, and they're nothing that requires you to be stronger than an attacker, okay? The most basic self-defense moves won't require you to stay and fight. The goal is to get away safely."

Her chest rose and fell rapidly, but she was listening.

I pointed at the bags. "So everything we just did in class, that's great for exercise. It's great to know the basics of how to throw an effective punch and use your lower body to your advantage, but you're not going to hit them with a jab, cross, and a roundhouse, right?"

Casey breathed out a laugh. "I hope not. I've always had really weak upper body strength anyway."

"That's okay," I assured her. "If you feel comfortable with it, I'd like you to act as the aggressor right now, and I'll show you a couple of things."

"What should I do?"

From the corner of my eye, but out of Casey's sightline, I saw Aiden lean his large frame up against one of the steel beams that held up all the bags. His face was curious, but he made no move to interrupt.

I swallowed, shifting her so that we were facing each other. "Let's start as if someone walks up to you and tries to pull your arm toward them, so why don't you grab my wrist."

Her hands were still wrapped from class, and tentatively, she curled her fingers around my wrist.

"Good." I held her eyes. "Now feel how I'm going to put my hand over yours. It's not about yanking my arm out of your grip. It's about taking back the control."

I wrapped my hand over the top of hers and pushed down slightly, her body moved toward me, and I swung the arm she was holding down and around, so I could use that hand to grab her forearm. Once I'd done that, her upper body was forced to turn away from me, and I pushed down gently. Almost immediately, she was down on one knee.

"Whoa." She laughed.

"Now try to stand up," I told her, hand still holding her arm in position.

She couldn't.

"See? I'm not trying to overpower anyone. I just want to put myself in a position where I can disengage and escape. So now that you're down like that, I'm going to let go and run."

Casey stood, her eyes lit with excitement. "Can you show me again?"

A bit more slowly, I went through it two more times until she felt like she could try it on me.

We reversed spots, and after one correction of how she was gripping my hand, she had me down on one knee, body turned away from her.

"Excellent," I told her. "Let's do that one more time, and we'll move on to another move."

Casey did great, pushing me down and away from her with more ease, and her smile was broad when I stood back up.

"Okay, how do you feel about grabbing me by my braid? I can show you a really easy way to escape if someone grabs your hair."

Immediately, her face went pale. "I … I don't know."

I held my hands up. "We won't do anything that will make you feel uncomfortable, I promise."

She crossed her arms over her stomach again. "I could grab yours fine, I think, I just … I can't have that …" Her voice trailed off and she gestured vaguely to her own ponytail. Casey squeezed her eyes shut. "I wasn't like … attacked or anything. It was just a drunk guy at a party, and he got a little handsy."

My heart broke as she fumbled for words, and all that fiery rage I'd felt earlier came roaring back. "You don't have to tell me if you don't want to."

Behind her, I saw Aiden drop his chin to his chest, which expanded on a deep inhale.

I took my own steadying breath. "Would you mind if I brought in someone who can show you how this works?"

Casey blinked, looking uncertain.

"He'll only grab my hair," I promised. "He won't touch you at all, okay? Or we could do another move too."

"No," she said. "I can watch. Thank you, Isabel."

I laid a hand on her arm and squeezed. My gaze found Aiden's, and I lifted my chin. "Could you help me a second, please?"

He pushed from the beam and walked over, and I had to curl up my fingers into a fist when I felt the slightest tremor of nerves.

Casey gave him a quick, tight smile, and he answered with a small nod.

"Casey, this is Aiden. He's our owner."

She waved. "Hi. Sorry for being a chicken about this."

He dipped his head down because she was so much shorter than him. "Don't ever apologize, okay? It's hard to let someone put their hands on you, even if it's just to practice."

I had to fight the urge not to think something unfair like, oh, screw him for saying something perfect. I didn't want Aiden to say and do perfect things. I wanted him to screw up. Do something that made me mad. Do something that made me want to call Carl back and tell him I'd take his job offer.

And that was the thing. I didn't want to take Carl's job offer. I'd only do it if I had a really, really good reason. As Aiden faced me, green eyes locked onto my face, I had to make peace with the fact that him knocking my emotions off-kilter was not a good reason.

Imagining us together wasn't a good reason.

Wondering if he had any room in his life, his heart, for someone new wasn't enough either.

Acknowledging it was enough to calm something frantic inside me. Trusting that I knew it was right to stay, even if it took me time to move past this, had me breathing easier.

"Aiden is going to grab my hair, okay?" I said to Casey even though my gaze didn't move from his. "And I want you to watch how I move my arm."

He made no quick moves, nothing designed to surprise. As his arm lifted, shifting the muscles underneath the cotton of his shirt, it was just a little bit harder to breathe. Ribs squeezed in when the thick column of his throat moved on a heavy swallow. Because I'd just imagined us so clearly, there was a blurring in my head of what was real and what wasn't.

Just before he touched me, he hesitated. Our gazes held like that, and I wondered what he saw in my face.

When his hand curled around my braid, his fingers brushed against the nape of my neck. It was so light, barely even there, but I shivered all the same.

And he noticed. His eyes narrowed just slightly.

To the side, Casey moved, and I blinked.

I moved my attention to her. "Don't ever try to yank away or try to pull their hand off your hair."

She'd wrapped her lips over her teeth, but she nodded. Two bright pink spots dotted her cheeks.

"Watch where I pull down, just by his elbow."

I took a deep breath and swung the arm that was between us, hooking it around the top of his arm and yanking it forward in a big C shape. Aiden stumbled forward, and I caught sight of Casey's huge smile.

Aiden quirked an eyebrow at me when he straightened to his full height, and at his expression, I exhaled a laugh.

"Again?" he asked. His tone was warm, and my toes curled in my shoes.

I nodded.

He grabbed my hair again, his grip a bit more firm. I motioned for him to wait. "Watch what I do at the end now. This is only if you feel like you need it."

"Do I get a warning of what you're going to do to me?" he asked.

"Nope."

Casey laughed.

His hand tightened, my skin humming as it did, and I swung

my arm around again—harder this time—and when he stumbled forward, I kicked my foot into the back of his already bent knee, and he immediately fell forward.

Casey clapped. "That was awesome."

With a grin, I gave her a high five. "And I'm not bigger or stronger than him, right?"

She shook her head.

Aiden straightened again, pinning me with a look that almost, almost could've looked amused. Something light and bubbling hit my bloodstream, and I desperately wanted to grip his face in my hands and kiss him when he looked like that.

With all the control I was capable of, I pulled my focus away from him.

"It's not about fighting them off, Casey. Disengage and escape. That's all you ever need to worry about."

"Thanks," I told him.

"I think we're even now," he murmured, pointing at the steel beam where Anya had been perched.

I nodded jerkily.

He gave a quick nod to Casey. "Call tomorrow if you want to set up a free training session with either Isabel or Kelly, okay? It's on me."

"Thank you," she said fervently. "You guys are awesome."

He disappeared off the gym floor and back into his office, and slowly, my heart returned to a normal speed.

Casey set her hand on my arm. "Thank you. Seriously."

"That's my job," I told her.

And it was.

She waved goodbye, and I sat on the edge of the center ring, leaning up against the ropes when I felt him approach.

Neither of us said anything, and I had to close my eyes to fight the urge to escape. The urge to stay. It was a constant battle when it came to him.

"Ward," he said.

Slowly, I opened my eyes. I wanted to hear him whisper that in my ear.

He was staring at the parking lot, where Casey was pulling her car out of her spot. "Whatever you need to get some classes like that on the schedule, you make it happen."

My throat was tight as I nodded.

"If you want," he added quietly.

"I do."

"Good." He exhaled, eyes coming to rest on me for just a moment. But I felt like he'd just wrapped his hands around my hair again, like his fingers tightened in the strands and tugged my head back.

For a moment, we were quiet.

"You taught a lot today," he said.

I glanced up at him. "I don't normally do that much."

"How many more do you need?"

He'd seemingly plucked my earlier thought from my head, and after a deep breath, I said, "Two more would make things more comfortable."

Aiden nodded. "What else?"

"What?"

"What else do you need?" he asked.

I blew out a breath. What a question.

Heavy eye contact. Loaded subtext. Sex vibes, wasn't that what Emily had called it?

There was no way he was feeling what I was feeling, and even if he was, it had to be switched all the way to max in my stupid, never-been-unlocked virgin head. This was a man who'd had an entire marriage with someone good. And I was the silly girl spinning scenes in her mind.

"Nothing right now," I answered.

If Aiden felt the need to push me on it, he didn't. But he did watch me for another moment before nodding.

He walked away, and I had to close my eyes again, allowing the charged feeling to settle and then pass.

Eventually, it had to pass, I told myself. I'd go home that night and think about what had just happened, keep the scenario locked away safely where no one could see it. But before I did, I'd play it back over in my head and imagine it unfolding in another way. One where we were alone, and he was holding me in place to do something very, very different.

In that safe space in my head, I'd pretend he had fingers fisted in my hair and his breath hot on my neck while he came up behind me. My heart raced, sitting there in the middle of the gym, and I had a visceral image of Aiden holding my hip with the other hand. My fingers curled into fists, a helpless gesture I couldn't control as I let it play out for just a few selfish seconds.

What had I thought only a handful of days earlier? Skin-to-skin contact might cause me to spontaneously orgasm. Well, apparently, I had pent-up sexual fantasies that had been lying dormant with Aiden Hennessy as the proverbial fucking key, ready to unlock them.

That small brush of his fingers along the nape of my neck was the most action I'd gotten in a couple of years, and I *should not want* to pretend what those fingers would feel like anywhere else on my body. I really, really shouldn't.

But as I stood and walked back to my office, I think, even then, I knew I was lying to myself.

CHAPTER 9

Isabel

"**Y**OU COMING BACK ANYTIME SOON?" PHONE WEDGED BE-
tween my ear and my shoulder, I waved at the guys leaving as they finished a group training session with Aiden.

Involuntarily, my eyes strayed over to where he was wiping
down the equipment they'd just used. Each flex of his arm had my
body humming some happy little tune. Gawd, I needed a hobby.

Or a better vibrator.

Or a dog.

Or a new brain.

Kelly sighed, yanking my attention back to our conversation.
"Doctor wants me to stay off my ankle for one more week, then I
can try teaching. As long as I'm not going crazy."

"Boo."

"I know."

I pulled up the schedule, squinting at the computer screen. "I
can probably shift around a couple of people so no one takes on too
much to cover you for one more week."

"You don't want to pull another three-class day?" she teased.

"Hell no." I arched my back, which was still sore. "Not when I do two the day before. I'm too old for this shit."

"You're twenty-five, Iz."

"Yes, but my attitude is so, so much older."

Aiden approached the front desk, eyes on a small piece of paper in his hand. His arms were still sweaty from his session, and I wondered—just a teeeeeeny tiny bit—what they'd feel like if I trailed my fingers down the curves of his biceps.

"How many people did you have in class last night?" Kelly's voice pulled me out of my little stare-fest, which was good because so far, I'd done nothing to abjectly embarrass myself. My current streak felt very, very impressive, all things considered.

"Ummm, hang on." I clicked the mouse a few times, leaning in to see the tiny numbers. Maybe I needed glasses. "Thirty."

"Oh, you bitch, my highest is twenty-five for that time slot."

I laughed under my breath. "Anything else, Kell? I need to get some work done before a training session."

"Nope! Love you, bye."

I was shaking my head as I hung up. Aiden's eyes flicked to my face as he set the paper down next to the phone. "Kelly's ankle doing better?" he asked.

I nodded. "She can't teach for another week, but I should be fine with coverage."

Aiden folded his arms over his chest. "How often do trainers get injured like that?"

"Not often," I told him. "I think she aggravated an old injury."

Without realizing what I was doing, I stretched my wrist out and flexed my hands. He noticed.

"What is it?"

My hand stopped. "Oh. Nothing. Still just a little sore from yesterday."

He looked like he was going to say something, opening his

mouth, then closing it with a tiny, almost imperceptible shake of his head. Very slowly, he and I were treading onto more neutral ground.

"My elbow," he said, after another pause. "Hyperextended this more times than I can count. Worst one was my second to last year fighting. Cortez caught me in an armbar, and that asshole would not let go." He unfolded his hand and tapped the side of one thumb. "Comminuted fracture in one of my early fights. I swear, I still feel it sometimes when it gets really cold."

"I remember," I said quietly before I could stop myself.

He studied me carefully. "Do you?"

Turning the chair back to the computer, I started randomly clicking … things. "Kind of. I watched a lot of fights."

My neck went damp with sweat because the injury had ended the fight, and to this day, I remembered worrying about his future fighting after they'd announced the bone had broken in two places.

There was no response from him, but he didn't move away either.

We weren't alone in the building. About half a dozen people were working out on the equipment. But even with those people sharing space, I had to *remind* myself that we weren't alone. Ever since my long-hidden vixen decided to bombard me with all sorts of fantasies involving me and him and dark rooms and whatnot, it was almost impossible to be this close to him.

With the perfectly reasonable amount of space between his shoulders and mine, it felt almost as if he were slowly winding a string. The string, in my mind's eye, was invisible to anyone but me, which meant I couldn't sever it, couldn't apply any boundaries to the way that my body wanted to sway gently in his direction.

"You post about the open positions?" he asked. The clear subject change had me breathing just a little easier.

"Yeah. I've already gotten a few applicants." I brought the schedule back up so he could see. "But unless someone gets sick, we're good with this until Kelly can come back."

As Aiden glanced at the schedule that I'd pulled up on the computer, I closed my eyes and let out a slow breath.

If I could manage one entire day without doing something stupid, I'd feel like it was something I could get control of. If only my imagination would cooperate. For a virgin, my imagination was very, very good.

When I opened my eyes, he was squinting at the screen, and it made me smile. He noticed.

"I can't see these tiny numbers," he muttered, leaning over my shoulder.

"Me neither," I admitted.

"Molly Ward," he said quietly, his finger tapped the screen for the training session I'd popped into the calendar. His arm brushed against mine as it did. "Relation or coincidence?"

"My oldest sister." I gave him a sideways glance. "She paid, if you're wondering."

"I wasn't." He moved away from the desk, and I found myself losing a bit of that closely-held tension. "You make your sister pay, huh?"

I exhaled a laugh. "She can afford it."

Aiden stared out into the parking lot, but I couldn't tell if he was going to say anything else by the way he held himself.

"My brothers think they should be able to work out for free," he said. "I thought about being nice and saying yes."

My attention stayed on the computer screen as I tried to decipher what he was trying to get from me. Small talk was not something we'd mastered. Which made my fantasy life even worse, the more I thought about it. And it wasn't that I didn't want to know about him. I did. But it was so obvious that the more I knew of Aiden, the more I'd want him.

But this tenuous thing we were doing by walking a strange tightrope of tension couldn't continue.

Finally, I glanced at him. "Depends on how many brothers you have."

"Too many."

His dry answer had me smiling. His brows dropped, like my reaction confused him.

"Did Amy ever look into getting a key scan set up on the door?" he asked.

At the change in topic, my eyebrows lifted. "A couple of years ago. At the time, we couldn't swing it."

"Okay." He glanced at a big black watch on his wrist, and I had to fight not to allow my eyes to trace along the veins that mapped his forearm. I wanted to lick them like they were candy. "I have to go pick up Anya from my brother's. Your sister is here after open hours are done, right?"

I nodded.

He gave me a pointed look. "Lock that front door."

"Will do," I answered quietly.

It would have been easy to dismiss him or tell him that I would be fine if I was here with Molly. That I'd be fine even if I was here alone. It would have been easy to take his words for something deeper than face value, like they were meant for me alone, but the hard truth was that he would've said it to Kelly or Emily. He would've told our male trainers that too. My heart wanted to soak up his words and let them bring life to the rest of my body, but my pride slammed the wall shut. Because that would help nothing.

While he gathered his stuff from his office, I kept myself busy. One of our members flagged me down, needing help with his form, so I wasn't even watching when Aiden left for the day. By the time the open gym hours concluded and the last person left, the late summer sun was still bright in the sky. Because the glass front of the gym faced west, it was my favorite time to do work in view of the windows. While I waited for Molly to arrive, I sat on the floor with my back braced against the front desk and started scrawling out ideas for the self-defense class.

Immersed in those ideas, which I'd been thinking about for months before Aiden ever took ownership, I didn't even notice Molly's car pull in. It wasn't until she pulled open the front door and shouted, "I'm so sorry I'm late."

I jumped, hand slapping my chest. "Holy shit, Molly."

She eyed me. "Didn't you see me peel into the parking lot?"

"Apparently not." I tossed my notebook aside and stood.

Her hair was tumbling out of a ponytail, her chest already glistened with sweat, and I tilted my head to the side as I studied her workout tank. "Is your shirt on backward?"

She glanced down. "Ummm …"

"Oh, my word. *That's* why you're late?"

Molly laughed.

"You know what I keep thinking?"

"What?"

"You're not even newlyweds, and you and Noah are already nauseating. What's it going to be like when you're actually married?"

She blew out a hard breath. "Please. We're basically having our honeymoon before the wedding. He was all worked up after training camp today, so … " She shrugged. "Gotta get that tension out somehow, you know?"

Nope, sure didn't.

"Honestly, I don't want to think about you and Noah and the kind of activities you get to have right now."

Molly laughed again, sitting on the bench in front of the window as she tugged on her workout shoes. While she wasn't looking, I studied my older sister. Made me wonder about how it must feel to have someone in your life like that.

And because I was me … I didn't ask.

"Where are we starting first?" she asked.

I blinked. "Umm, I have some bodyweight exercises mapped out. Arm day today."

"Oh, goody," she muttered.

While she made her way over to where the ropes and bands were laid out on the rubberized floor, I cued up some music.

We worked our way through a few things, and like I usually did, I worked out alongside her.

Molly and I were shoulder to shoulder, passing a medicine ball back and forth after twisting to the side, when I asked a question that later, I'd really, really wish I hadn't asked.

"You get all your RSVPs back?"

With a twist, I handed the black ball to her, and she mirrored my movement with a grimace. My quads were burning as I held the squat and waited for her to give it back. But when she turned back toward me, I caught a look ... just a glimpse of discomfort.

"What?" I asked. I took the ball and twisted again.

When it was in Molly's hands, I stood. She did the same, setting the ball down at her feet.

"Nothing."

But she didn't make eye contact when she said it.

"Molly."

"Isabel."

"You had a look, and don't even pretend you didn't. Is Noah still on that *let's invite the entire team* kick?"

She exhaled a laugh. "No. Too many guys travel during the bye week anyway." Molly paused, her eyes finally locking on mine. "But we did end up sending out a last-minute invite this week. And ... and I don't think you're going to understand why."

My head reared back. "What do I have to do with it?"

Before she answered, Molly leaned down to snag her water bottle, and she took a long sip. By the time she set her water down, more than ten seconds could've elapsed, but it felt like an hour.

"I know we have some complicated family dynamics," she said slowly, "but I feel like we can't avoid some of it."

I nodded. "Yeah, I know. And Logan told me that we had to be nice to Nick even though we haven't seen them once since they moved to the East Coast," I said, referencing our other half-brother, who was a total a-hole. Thankfully, we rarely had to see him and his wife. There was about a minute, back when we were younger, when he challenged Logan for custody of the four of us. Gawd, what pricks we'd all be if he'd been the one to raise us.

Molly's eyes searched mine. "I wasn't talking about Nick."

"Okay. Who?"

"Noah and I decided to send an invitation to Brooke's last known address," she said, lifting her chin.

My skin went hot. "What?" I whispered.

She nodded, and my skin went ice, ice cold. The change was shocking, bracing, and my heart went wild in my chest. I felt like Molly had taken a crowbar to my rib cage, prying me open like I was on a hinge.

"It wasn't an easy decision," Molly said calmly. "But Noah agreed that it was the right thing to do."

"Why would you *want* her at your wedding?"

"Because … because this is a big deal! Getting married is a big deal. We're all moving on to these chapters of our lives, and to me, it felt like an appropriate gesture to make, considering how happy I am with Noah." Molly set her hands on her hips and exhaled heavily. "Maybe I'm handling this wrong."

"Maybe you shouldn't have invited the woman who abandoned us."

Even to my own ears, it sounded like a childish reaction, on par with dumping coffee down the drain, but just like I had with Aiden, the thought of facing her also had teenage Isabel roaring back in charge of my brain. But this was not the teenage Isabel who had crushes and cut out pictures. This was the past version of me

95

who lashed out at anyone who might hurt me, and oh, how good I'd been at that.

It was the version of me who felt like she had no control over any part of her life.

Molly inhaled slowly. "I knew it wouldn't be easy to hear this, Isabel, but it's my olive branch to extend."

"She doesn't deserve an olive branch," I said hotly. "*Last known address*, Molly. She can't even be bothered to update us on where in the hell she lives, but you think she should sit in the family pews at the ceremony?"

Molly held up her hands. "If you want to bait me into fighting about this, I won't do it."

I set my hands on my hips. "I'm not trying to fight. I'm trying to understand why the hell you think this is a good idea. You have no clue how she'll act or what she'll do, Molly. Don't you want this day to be perfect?"

Just the thought of it, of Brooke walking into the room, had my hands and fingers and arms racing with pins and needles. I didn't know how she'd aged. I didn't know what she'd say. If she'd pretend everything was fine. And all of those unknowns snapped and snarled in my head like a rabid dog on a rusty chain.

My temper didn't come out often, but this was the one single thing that would make me explode faster than anything else in the entire world. If my reaction to Aiden made me feel off-balance and out of control, then my reaction to Brooke turned me into a walking nuclear bomb.

The combination of them—the first building up for weeks and the second dropping without warning—wasn't pretty.

To my horror, Molly's eyes welled up. "Yes," she whispered. "Of course I want this day to be perfect. I am marrying the love of my life. Don't you think I've thought through every angle of this? I'm inviting Brooke for me, Isabel. Not for her."

I exhaled a laugh, shoving my fingers into my hair. "What could you possibly gain from this?"

Molly shrugged helplessly. "Peace, Isabel. I gain peace from knowing I've forgiven her for leaving, and she realizes it. Maybe Brooke has stayed away all these years because she doesn't know how she'd be greeted."

The look I gave Molly could only be described as incredulous. "We're making excuses for her now?"

"No," she answered simply. "I'm not making excuses, but I won't hide behind some arbitrary wall of anger either. I know therapy was bullshit for you, but it wasn't for me. And sometimes, sister, you figure out a way to forgive someone because it's what *you* need. Not because you're letting them off the hook."

With every word she said, I felt this overwhelming urge to flee. I wanted to slap my hands over my ears and stop listening. It was the same sensation I felt before Aiden said he bought the gym, except much, much worse.

This thing Molly had done was, at the very minimum, like yanking open the worst scar I could think of and watching someone pour saline into the torn flesh. And what that felt like ... well ... it brought out the very worst version of myself. I hated this side of me. This hot-wired, reactionary person who couldn't control what she said or did.

I'd worked really hard not to be her. To let that instinct take me over. And everything in my life seemed to be instinct-driven lately, the wheel spinning wildly in a way that I couldn't stop, couldn't get a hold of.

I swooped down and picked up the bands we'd used, then tucked the medicine ball under my arm. "I think we should end here."

"Isabel, come on, don't be like this."

I stopped, spearing her with a look. "How long have you had to process the idea of this?"

Molly swallowed before she answered. "Three weeks."

"Great." I nodded. "Sounds about right for me too. Now if you'll excuse me, I need to put this stuff away."

When I returned from putting the equipment away, my playlist hit the end, and Molly was in the front area, slowly packing her bag. From where I stood, I couldn't tell if she was crying or not, but I was too upset to stop and ask.

Which was a big deal because anything that made my sisters cry made me want to punch things repeatedly.

And now, it just made me want to run.

Because at the moment, the only thing making my sister cry was me.

Well, me and our mother.

Fucking Brooke and the damage she'd caused with her selfishness.

Molly paused before she left the gym and gave me a long look. Thankfully, her eyes were dry.

"I love you, Isabel. And I hope eventually, you'll understand why I'm doing this."

I rolled my lips between my teeth and nodded. "I love you too."

She exhaled in relief when I said it, but her face was sad as she walked out.

The building pulsed with silence as soon as she walked out, and I inhaled unsteadily. Moving slow, I packed up my bag and turned off the lights in my office. But I couldn't bring myself to leave. I almost looked up at the ceiling because I could've sworn that brick by brick, unimaginable weight was falling on top of me. My hands started shaking, and I curled my fists tight to make them stop.

I needed this tension ... this feeling ... out of my body.

First work.

Now my sister, my family.

Both had me rocked with no place to grab onto. Or that was what it felt like.

And the truth, which I also hated, was that I didn't have anyone who could shoulder it the way I needed them to. To take the brunt of the pressure building and building, no outlet, no valve to release. They all had someone. They all had that person who'd know exactly what they needed at the moment they were most out of control.

My hands shook, and I imagined that metal box splitting angrily at the seams, paint peeling, edges crumpling from what was being held inside.

And what I needed, in the face of all this blistering emotion, was someone to roll with whatever came out of my mouth with no judgment and without trying to soften the blows or tell me I was overreacting, that I was too much for feeling this way.

Striding over to the iPad on the wall, I cued up one of my angry rock playlists and turned the volume up. A moment later, my hands were wrapped and shoved into my favorite black and purple gloves.

If there was no one to be that for me, I'd be that for myself.

I let out a deep breath in front of my favorite bag, stretched my arms out a few times, and started to move.

CHAPTER 10

Aiden

I T WAS A MISTAKE TO GO BACK TO THE GYM WHEN I SAW THE lights on and realized her car was the only one in the parking lot. I'd recognize it later, the ramifications full and clear once all was said and done.

But at the moment, I wasn't thinking about that. Even if I hadn't left my wallet on my desk, the sight of her lone car, the bright lights, and the dark sky around the building probably would've made me stop.

Because it was only a matter of time before I recognized something important when it came to Isabel.

Curiosity and attraction were two entirely different things. Interest was so mundane because so many things held my interest.

Football held my interest, which was how I knew who she was, who her family was.

Working out held my interest because it kept me feeling strong and healthy and sane.

When I had the time, reading held my interest if the story was good.

Those were all easy and peaceful things that kept my attention and reduced my stress.

But if I thought my manager would fall neatly into that category once I figured her out, I was kidding myself.

That became apparent when I approached the front door, and with a grimace and a flare of anger, I found it unlocked. Interest never exploded into a bright ball of fiery emotion, something unnameable, at the realization she was inside with the music blaring while the door was wide-fucking-open for anyone to walk in.

Attraction did that. But I wasn't ready to name it. Not until later.

The music was hard and angry—sort of like the rippling waves of emotion I was trying to keep in check—with guitars and drums and screaming rock, so I knew Isabel wouldn't be able to hear the ding of the bell over the pulsing from the stereo system.

Even then, I could've turned around, locked the door behind me with my key, and left her to work out in peace. Once I knew that my state of mind was hardly polite, hardly civilized.

But I didn't do that either.

"What the hell is she thinking?" I muttered.

When she avoided me, I let her be.

When I caught her dumping out the cup of coffee I bought her, I didn't push.

When she continued, over and over, to do things that seemed completely at odds with what Amy had told me, I didn't engage in the way I wanted to.

When I caught myself watching her, studying her, fighting the urge to pick her apart until I understood all these things that I didn't seem to understand, I'd let her be.

But as I rounded the corner and she came into view, I *knew*

I should have left. Something inside me screamed to turn and go. Leave her be now when it matters.

Because the first thing that came into my head when I noticed the graceful strength in her body, with hair unkempt, limbs and back coated with the sheen of unbelievable effort was, *I could watch her do this all night.*

I'd been lying to myself that I was only curious about her as my employee.

It wasn't polite or professional as I stood and watched her. This had sharp, snapping teeth and a voracious appetite, something I hadn't tapped into before.

Like shaking a limb that had fallen asleep, wincing through the pins and needles as the blood flow returned because for so long, that side of me had been silent.

I stopped to watch Isabel draw her left arm across her body to deliver an explosive back fist to the bag, followed by a right hook and, with a quick snap of her arm, an elbow strike.

Her technique wasn't perfect, but when emotion took over, it was rare that anyone held their body correctly.

Finally, finally, I was seeing the real her. And I knew the truth of that bone-deep.

Crossing my arms over my chest, I tried to fight the warring emotions behind my ribs.

Leave now was the thought battling for dominance, but my curiosity and the completely mesmerizing way she moved held my feet firm on the ground.

No. Not curiosity. Attraction disguised as something far more innocent.

My gaze caught the edge of her high cheekbones and the sculpted line of her jaw. Even from where I stood, I could see how tightly she clenched that jaw, and I wanted to lay my hands on her shoulders and tell her to relax and breathe.

If I tried hard enough, I knew exactly how it would feel if I did. If I drew my thumbs down the line of her neck to unlock the muscles she was holding so tense. She'd go pliant if I did that. If I treated her with softness.

But I didn't want to see her melt. Didn't want to see her go into some sweet, tender place.

The fire in her was palpable, and I knew I was about to walk into it.

It was that instinct that had me leaning down to snatch the focus mitts that laid on the ground next to the ring. The remote for the stereo was on the floor by her bag, and as much as I didn't want to get a roundhouse kick to the face from Isabel Ward, my own seething anger at her leaving the door unlocked had me approaching from her blind spot.

Just to see what she'd do.

Just to see what would happen.

It was stupid. And nothing, not a single thing, had excited me this much in two years.

If this was my chance to see the real, unguarded version of her, I would not waste it. And later, I could curse myself for a moment of weakness.

I shoved my hand into one focus mitt and rolled my neck before sticking the second one on.

When she drew her leg back and kicked the bag with such force that my eyebrows popped up, I held one mitt up to protect my face and touched her shoulder with the other.

With a roar fit for an Amazon, she whirled, glove aimed right at my face. I yanked my hand to catch the right cross on the mitt.

"Not bad!" I shouted over the music. "But next time, go for an uppercut off your back leg."

Her chest was heaving, her blue eyes wide, and she kept her gloved hands at guard.

"What the hell is the matter with you?" she yelled.

I gestured to the door. "Anyone could've walked in here."

Her eyes narrowed in a vicious glare, and for just a moment, I couldn't help but glory in how well she wore anger. Isabel tugged off a glove, then reached down and snatched the remote, turning the volume down to a more manageable level.

Neither one of us spoke, but Isabel was breathing heavily. Since I'd seen her earlier, she'd pulled off her gym T-shirt and stood in front of me in a sweat-soaked purple bra and black leggings. I hated that I noticed, and because I did, I kept my eyes firmly on her face.

This was, without a doubt, the absolute last fucking thing I needed.

And it was the only thing I wanted from her.

No more tiptoeing. No more leaving her be.

Isabel broke the stare first, setting her hands on her hips and letting out a weighty exhale. "This just … figures, doesn't it?"

"What?"

"You!" she yelled, lifting her head, eyes blazing. "Of *course* you'd show up right now."

I stepped around her, and she moved as I did, keeping her front foot centered toward me, just as she should have. "You got a problem with me showing up at my own gym?"

"At the moment? Yeah."

I held up a glove. "Show me."

Without hesitation, Isabel hit me with a jab.

"Why don't you want me here?"

Each strike hit the mitts with a sharp snap. "You want a list?"

What was this? It was so immediate, so unfiltered, and the exact opposite of every interaction we'd ever had. My blood screamed with something hot and pulsing, something new and furious.

"The last thing I need," she said, chin raised and chest heaving, "is you here to see this."

"Again." I held up the gloves.

Snap.

Snap.

"I almost punched you in the face."

"You didn't almost punch me in the face," I said calmly, which made her eyes narrow even further. "More."

She gave me more. Three more in quick succession. But she didn't calm. There were words brewing, and I could see them flaring hot in her eyes. But I knew she wouldn't give them to me. Not easily.

"What happened to your advice to Casey earlier? I thought the goal was to disengage, not attack."

Isabel lifted her chin. "For her, that is the goal."

"And you hold yourself to a different standard?"

She didn't answer. But watching the flash behind her eyes, like someone dropped a match into a vat of gasoline, I knew I was right. This was Isabel Ward. And she was fucking glorious.

I wanted more of it. More of this. No matter how wrong she was for me, how badly this might go, or how much I might regret it. I wanted more.

That was why I leaned in and whispered, "Lock the fucking door next time."

Her mouth fell open.

Satisfied that I'd made my point, I nodded, lifting the mitts. "Let's go. Whatever your problem is, get it out right now."

Isabel eyed me carefully. "Who says I have a problem?"

"Anyone with eyes, based on how you were treating that defenseless bag." I hit the mitts together, the sharp snapping sound echoing around the gym. She didn't so much as flinch. "Come on, Ward."

For a moment, she just stared at me, and I found myself holding my breath at how she would respond.

And because it was the first moment of just the two of us, it was also the first time I saw how carefully she held herself. The sharp edge of wariness in her gaze. What, exactly, did Isabel Ward think I was going to do to her to make her look at me like that?

"No," she said. "Not tonight."

I nodded slowly, waiting until she'd turned away from me.

"What are you afraid of?" I asked.

Her frame, tall and strong and proud, went perfectly still. It was almost like watching her turn into a statue right in front of my eyes. If an artist somewhere had carved her out of marble, those gloves tucked under her arms, hands still wrapped, she would've been called something like, *A Warrior in Repose.*

But when she slowly pivoted back in my direction, the wariness was gone, completely replaced by blade-sharp resolve. Isabel jammed her hands back in her gloves, and I held up my mitts.

"I am not scared," she snapped.

"Prove it." I stepped closer, and she held her ground. "I am the only person in the building you hide from, and that ends now."

"You think you're going to earn it like this?" She raised an eyebrow. "By fighting it out of me."

"Hell yes." I held her gaze, and her eyes went wide at my honesty. "This is probably the only place you feel like you can be yourself, be honest about what you feel. I'd bet the whole fucking gym on that, and if you and I are going to move forward, we work your reservations out here."

Isabel's rib cage expanded, the light from overhead catching on the sheen of sweat coating the curves of her cleavage.

"I'll do this under one condition," she said, bouncing lightly on her toes, arms up to guard her face. "You don't get to ask me what I'm angry about."

Judging by the look in her eyes, like the slightest thing could set her off, it was an easy thing to agree to. I nodded. "Wouldn't dream of it."

We started simple. I kept just far enough away that she had to throw her weight behind each strike, and I called out what I wanted her to do, counting down until she could take a deep breath or a drink of water.

Isabel and I found a rhythm easily, and once we did, her

movements became more precise, less wild. Her chest shone under the lights, sweat dotting her forehead until a few stray strands of her almost-black hair clung to the line of her neck.

After about fifteen minutes, I stepped back, and extended my arm out, tapping by my elbow with the focus mitt. "Watch your form right there, when you go in for the left cross. If I went to block, it would be really easy for you to adjust and hit me with a right elbow off your front leg."

She nodded, breath sawing in and out of her mouth.

I jerked my chin up. "Show me."

We started slow, almost like a dance. She came in with the left. I pushed her arm down, and when I barked the command, she pitched her right elbow up, stopping just shy of hitting me in the cheek.

"Excellent," I told her. "Try again. Let's move a bit faster."

She got that down almost immediately, and I stepped back, swiping my arm over my forehead. I caught a quick flash of a grin on her face.

"I didn't anticipate a workout tonight," I told her.

"Then maybe you shouldn't have interrupted mine."

I exhaled a laugh, gauging her facial expression as she said it. "You sorry I did?"

Instead of answering, Isabel tugged off one of her gloves to pull a long drink of water from her bottle. When she set it back down, she did a heavy exhale of her own.

"No," she said. Then she put her glove back on.

I held up the mitts. "Let's go again. After the elbow, use your right arm to push my blocking arm down, come up with a knee to my midsection while my momentum is in your favor."

She nodded.

We practiced once. Twice. Then faster. And again. Her hair smelled like something citrus when her braid whipped past my face. The fourth time, she had her full strength behind pushing me down, and I grunted when her knee had a bit more oomph behind it than I was expecting.

"Easy," I warned, as I stepped back.

But Isabel didn't smile. She was watching me set up again.

"What?" I asked, dropping my mitts to take a drink of my own. Her gaze was heavy on me while I swallowed.

"I got a job offer from Punch Fitness."

The water stuck in my throat, and I coughed into my hand. She didn't look very sorry about her timing as I tried to compose myself. After another sip, I was able to breathe normally.

"You taking it?" I asked. My voice was so calm and steady, but inside of my body, something roared and snarled. Another dangerous sign. Another impossible reaction to this woman. I wasn't ready for something like this. Like her. Something big, something wild.

"I haven't decided yet."

"That guy's a hack," I heard myself say. Because he was. She'd be wasted at a place like that.

I couldn't read a damn thing on her face, not like earlier, when I'd seen more. This was the guarded Isabel, the collected Isabel. And I found I liked her transparency better. In her anger, no matter how dangerous that was to my well-being, I could see everything she was thinking.

I jammed the mitts back on my hands, even though my forearms were getting a hell of a workout. Holding them up to my face, I barked, "Again."

She set her feet, and we started the dance all over.

But this time, there was an edge.

Each time she struck the mitts and knocked my arms back, I felt more and more coming from her. I blocked her knee when it came up a little too hard and gave her a warning look.

Her lips, full and pink, curled up in a satisfied smile, even as her upper body heaved with exertion.

"You don't want that job," I said quietly.

Isabel's jaw clenched, and she ducked to the side when I was expecting her to throw the left cross. She came in with an upper-cut, and I blocked it easily.

"How the hell do you know?"

I swatted her arm away when she tried to jab. "Because this is not just a job, or a paycheck for you."

Isabel sidestepped and tried to do a low roundhouse, but I knocked her leg down with the mitts. Her eyes flashed hot, because I wasn't holding back as much. But neither was she.

"You don't know me," she said, striking the left mitt hard with a jab.

"Because you don't let me." She hit the mitts three more times in rapid succession, the *pop pop pop* sound echoing around us. "But I see you, even if you don't want me to."

She swore.

"You treat the employees like family," I said. She danced around me, neither one of us making a move. "You do the same to the clients."

I slapped the mitts and she attacked, *jab, cross, cross.*

"Good," I yelled. "And you know every inch of this place like it's your own home. You may think I'm just hiding in my office every day," I leaned in when she backed up, "but I know exactly what this building, these people mean to you."

She didn't say a word, but in only a few sentences, I noticed her movements change again, packed to the brim and overflowing with emotion, whatever my words were triggering in her showing in the ferocity of how she came at me.

"You don't want that job," I repeated, and this time, I felt my own reaction coloring the delivery of the words. I sounded, to my own ears, less steady and calm. "And I don't want you to take it either."

And just like that, whatever we were doing became less chore-ography that we were expecting and more instinctual. The moment

109

she broke out of whatever pattern we'd established, the more I had to anticipate what she might do next. This wasn't about hurting each other because it wasn't a battle. What it felt like was a test.

But I was at a disadvantage wearing the mitts, not my typical gloves, but still ... I blocked and spun, catching each offensive strike before she caught me. I almost smiled when she missed her opening, and when I saw her eyes flash, I knew I was in trouble.

She yanked my arm out with her own and tried to sweep my leg out from underneath me, and I caught it midair. With her shin tucked between my arm and side, she muttered a curse under her breath and lost her footing.

Isabel hit the mat with an oomph, arms splayed out and her rib cage expanding on deep, greedy breaths. I leaned over, mitts braced on my knees, doing some deep breathing of my own.

"You okay?" I asked.

She nodded, but didn't move to get up.

I pulled off the mitt and held my hand out to her. Isabel visibly swallowed, and I had a moment of pause about whether this entire interaction with her was the dumbest thing I could have ever done.

Her eyes, in the overhead light of the gym, were a deep, midnight blue, something I hadn't really registered before tonight.

I didn't want to know the color of her eyes or the smell of her hair, but the feeling coursing through my veins at what had just happened was too potent for me to ignore.

Because it was *life*. When you lose someone you love, a part of your brain and a part of your heart believes you'll never, ever feel again. That forever, you'll walk around with numbness in this one portion of who you are. And for the past two years, it held true.

When Isabel sat up and slowly tugged her gloves off, tossing them to the side, I almost pulled my arm back. But then she took it with hers, and as I curled my fingers around her hand, that numbness was absent.

Pushed aside.

Completely erased.

In its place was ferocious need.

I pulled her to standing, and it was the closest we'd stood all night. She was taller than average, and when she lifted her chin to stare at me, I noticed that her inhale was a little unsteady. And her eyes, they dropped to my lips.

There was no one around us.

No one to see.

And for the first time in two years, I wanted to slide my hands over a woman's body to see what her skin felt like under my fingertips. No, not just any woman. Isabel. She'd be warm and soft. She'd hold the evidence of how hard she just worked, and it made my skin tighten and my heart pound.

This woman, with all that banked fire inside her, had me holding my breath to see what she'd do next.

Because I would not, could not, be the first to move in closer.

Even if I wanted to. Even if I'd think of her like this later, imagine what we'd be like together, no matter how much I shouldn't.

Not just because she was too young, because she was.

Or because she worked for me, which she did.

Because in two years, no one had ever made me want anything, and in a single interaction, she redefined everything, had me imagining her split wide underneath me, sharp nails, soft lips, wet tongue, and the taste of her in my mouth.

That was when Isabel licked her lips, eyelids fluttering. I sucked in a breath.

Then she yanked on my arm, sweeping her leg under mine, and I landed like a giant fucking boulder onto the ground.

She leaned over me with a grin, black braid falling over her shoulder. "You're right," she said breathlessly. "I don't want that job."

I exhaled a laugh as she walked away.

"See you tomorrow, boss," she called over her shoulder.

CHAPTER 11

Isabel

MY CONFIDENT EXIT—WHICH I WAS VERY PROUD OF— lasted as far as the parking lot.

"Holy shit," I whispered, hands shaking as I unlocked my car and slid in the front seat. For all I knew, Aiden was still lying on the gym floor because I'd *put him there*. "Oh, what did I just do, whatdidIdo*whatdidIdo*?"

But for as much as I wanted to dissolve into panicked laughter in that parking lot, a naughty little voice in my head was patting me on the fricken back because I'd had a glorious twenty minutes where he and I existed in this strange little suspended state of sexual tension.

Was it training? Foreplay? I wasn't even fucking sure.

All my awkwardness gone.

He was talking.

I was talking back.

He knew exactly what I needed to settle the snarling angry version of me that I hated so much.

It wasn't the boss and the manager. There was no awkward version of me on display. It was something else entirely. It wasn't something that just played out in my vivid imagination. It had been real.

Because Aiden Hennessy stood over me, staring at my lips, and I swear on the benevolent spirit of Muhammed Ali, I almost died on the spot.

He was so big and tall and strong, his hands so broad and capable-looking, and if he kissed even a fraction as well as he did anything else, I'd never survive it. Forget sex, I'd perish from his tongue in my mouth.

I couldn't even start the car because I wasn't sure I was steady enough to drive home. Adrenaline let down or something. Whatever the comparable version was when you had unrequited lust pumping through your body instead of blood.

My phone was in my hand before I could blink, words crowding my throat before I could even make sense of what I wanted to say.

Paige hardly managed a hello.

"I need your advice," I interrupted.

"Holy shit, finally," she breathed.

Under my breath, I laughed, but really, I was still just … freaking out.

"Have you ever like"—I paused, running a hand through my hair—"wanted something, but you never thought you'd have it?"

Paige didn't miss a beat. "Your brother when we first got married."

I folded my arms on the top of my steering wheel and laid my forehead on them, staring down at my lap. I couldn't do this. I closed my eyes and blurted out the first thing that came to my head. "Cake. There's a cake you imagined eating. You know exactly what it looks like, you had every part of that cake's existence memorized, and you dreamed about it for a really long time, even before you knew what cake tasted like."

"I …" Paige hesitated. "I'm just gonna run with this. Okay, sure. Yes."

Sitting up, I stared at the front of the gym, tried to imagine what he was doing since I'd walked out. "So the cake, suddenly, is right in front of you. You never, *ever* thought it would get taken out of the case. Display only, no touching, pretend the cake … isn't yours because it's not," I said. "And then it's just … there."

Holy hell, I was confusing myself, but I'd committed to the analogy, and I was not dropping it now.

"Cake is there, excellent." She cleared her throat carefully. "And have we taken a bite of the cake yet?"

"No!" I cried.

Paige breathed out a laugh. "Okay. That's okay."

"What if … what if the cake tastes like shit, you know? What if you've thought of it for so long, and never had it before, and your first bite is awful or just, isn't what you expected?"

Silence dropped like a friggin bomb.

"Wait, you've never …?" Paige stopped. "Isabel, I cannot even believe I'm about to ask this, but are you a *virgin?*" she whispered.

My face flamed surface-of-fucking-Mars hot. "That's not what this is about."

"I know we're not talking about dessert, Isabel Ward."

"Yes, we are!" I shouted, the tingling edge of panic coloring my words. "I said we're talking about cake, so *we are talking about fucking cake*, okay?" I covered my face even though she couldn't see me. "It's all I can handle, Paige. Please."

"Okay, okay," she soothed. "So, you're worried he—it," she corrected instantly, "will disappoint you?"

Oh, holy shit, I was going to cry. This was *awful.*

"Or worse," I whispered.

"Oh, Iz," she said gently. "How can it be worse?"

Through the windows, I saw Aiden turning off the lights. With each one, he disappeared from view. For a moment, I thought I saw his silhouette by the front desk looking out at my car, but I closed my eyes so that I'd stop trying to see him.

He'd lost something—someone—incredibly precious to him. And I was the fumbling girl with a vivid crush and a temper, a decade younger than him. There were so many reasons I could think of why he might not be seeing that the same way I was.

That was always my problem, wasn't it? It wasn't even really clear what he wanted from me, but there I was, prying open an impossibly big barrier because that was what he was already doing to me.

Aiden was opening me up, and he had no idea.

"What if ..." I swallowed. "What if it's the most perfect, delicious, amazing thing I've ever experienced, and the ... cake ... doesn't want what I want in return? How would you ever get over that?"

Paige exhaled heavily. "Well, I think that if someone shows interest in you—and why *wouldn't* they because you are a fucking treasure, Isabel—then you should trust that. And trust that you know when it feels right."

Finally, I smiled. "Why does it sound so easy when you say it like that?"

"It's not easy, my dear girl. Relationships are never, ever easy."

"It's not a relationship, Paige." I shook my head. "It's a crush come to life. I feel like a child when he's around, and I hate it. Or I did until tonight," I amended.

"You would," she said, voice full of love. "None of this surprises me about you, Iz."

I sighed.

"Look at it like this, having big feelings for someone doesn't mean you're weak or asking to be hurt. But if you don't want to do any *biting* right now, then don't." Paige's voice took on a soft quality. "You've been hurt, kid. That makes opening yourself hard. But for the right person, you will want to."

"I don't know how anyone measures up to him," I admitted in

a quiet voice. The words hurt coming out. "After getting to know him. I don't see it, Paige."

Paige answered carefully. "I don't think we need to borrow trouble just yet, okay? One day at a time."

"Yeah, I guess."

For a moment, we were both content to stay quiet, even if my reasons were different than hers. Paige, no doubt, was processing all the horrible baked good analogies I'd just tossed in her lap like a grenade. And I was quiet because I could no longer ignore how far down this rabbit hole I'd gone.

Protecting myself from possible pain came at a steep cost.

Besides my sisters and Logan, Paige was the only person in my life who I trusted with anything. The only other person who'd earned that trust. But tonight, Aiden walked in, and without flinching, he knew exactly what I needed from him to smooth the raised hackles along my back.

The more he pushed me, prodded me, the more I'd calmed.

He met me where I was instead of trying to smother the flames.

And not once, despite my growing feelings for him, had I attempted to reach out in the same way.

What he might need in this new season of his life would look completely different than what I'd just needed from him. And all I'd done was avoid. Deflect. Hide.

As the realization came, Paige spoke again, plucking thoughts from my head. "The only thing I'll say—my darling girl, one of the great loves of my life—is that if you want to know what he wants, you may have to ask." She paused, continuing when I didn't raise a protest. "And I'm not just talking about wanting a bite of your own cake, you know? You may know the version of him from behind the glass case, but is that really him?"

What *had* I asked him in the first couple of weeks?

Nothing.

Because the idea of Aiden—and now, the reality of who he

was—had me off-balance and at a disadvantage, even if the disadvantage was in my head.

I tried not to feel ashamed because he'd gone out of his way to make me feel comfortable.

Sometimes you had your guard so far up, you blocked the good stuff too. And I was better than this. I was sure as fuck stronger than I'd been acting. So what if I tripped in front of him and spilled some coffee?

I *liked* who I was, even if it was hard for other people to get a real glimpse.

One of us was a locked box, and the other was on display for the world to see. Neither made it easy to make real connections.

A shadow moved away from the windows, and he walked out of the building. Across the parking lot, even though it was dark, I knew he was watching me.

With a deep breath and pulling from a well of self-control I didn't know I had, I turned the key in the ignition and started my car. As soon as the headlights went on, Aiden dropped his head and walked to his truck.

"One day at a time," I repeated.

CHAPTER 12

Aiden

"**D**ID YOU HURT YOURSELF?" MY MOM ASKED.

Of course, she caught the wince. Anya was sound asleep on their couch, and when I leaned over to make my first attempt to pick her up, I must've made a face.

My sister, Eloise, perched on the kitchen counter with a spoonful of peanut butter in her mouth, nodded slowly in agreement. "He did look very old and slow just now."

I speared her with a look.

She smiled.

Deciding to leave Anya where she was, for the time being, I stood quickly, like I was young. "Just fell hard at work when I wasn't expecting it."

My mom's face wrinkled in concern. Eloise grinned.

"You okay?" Mom asked.

"Yeah. I was … training with my manager and …," I paused, trying to decide if it was wise to even tell them a little bit of this conversation. No part of my interaction with Isabel felt safe for consumption yet. I wasn't even ready to process what it meant, let alone spoon-feed it to my mother and my younger sister, who'd devour it with the same unfettered glee as she was attacking that peanut butter straight from the jar. "I just fell," I finished lamely.

Eloise narrowed her eyes, but I knocked her legs sideways when I passed into the kitchen of our parents' house. She kicked out at me, catching my hip when I cleared the island, and she was lucky I didn't dump her off the counter.

I'd already been kicked at enough by one feisty twentysomething tonight, and I didn't need my little sister added to the ranks.

And dammit, like I needed the reminder that she wasn't that much older than Eloise.

"When did Anya fall asleep?" I asked.

My mom grabbed a spoon of her own and snuck the container from Eloise. "'Bout thirty minutes ago. Colored a picture with El after we had some dinner. Clark was here for a while and played Uno with her. Her forehead was a little warm, and she said she was tired, so I told her to cuddle up on the couch. She fell asleep as soon as I turned the TV on."

I rubbed my forehead wearily. "I wondered if she was getting sick. She was a little off last night too."

Mom's face, as usual, took on that look of concern. "She still getting finicky at bedtime?"

My laugh was dry. "Yeah. Last night we hit a new variant, though. She asked if she could sleep in bed with me, which she hasn't done since Beth died."

Eloise stared down at her lap, and my mom clucked her tongue. The lack of immediate reaction was nothing new to me.

This was my life on a loop.

Sometimes they piped up with suggestions, but for the most part, no one in my family had ever dealt with a loss at this level until my wife died. Their silence was a glaring admission. *This sucks, and we don't know what to tell you.*

It was the largest piece to moving through life-altering grief. Making peace with that unfulfilling truth.

It sucked. And no matter what people said, their words didn't make it better. Better came with getting through each day.

"Did you let her?" Eloise asked. For as much as she gave me shit—that was part and parcel with being the youngest of five and the only girl—my sister always trod carefully in this area.

I shook my head. "I can't move backward now. I'm not really sure what triggered it, but I'll keep an eye on it."

"She climbed up on that armoire in our bedroom," Mom said. "Had to bribe her with cookies to get her down."

"How'd she get up there?"

She shrugged. "I think she used the small end table from your father's side of the bed."

I sank onto a stool at the island and rubbed my forehead. "That's happening more again too."

"Your house?" Eloise asked.

"The gym." I blinked a few times, an unwitting smile pulling at the edges of my lips. "My manager was pretty impressive in trying to bargain her off the steel beams holding up the heavy bags."

Eloise cleared her throat delicately. "The same manager you sparred with tonight?"

I narrowed my eyes at her. "What does that have to do with anything?"

"I don't know, Aiden," she said. "You tell us. You just"—she waved her spoon at my face—"smiled. A little. Sort of."

"I did not."

"You did," Mom chimed in. "Sort of."

I sank my head into my hands.

"Is he crying?" Eloise whispered.

My head lifted just so I could glare at her. My mom laughed.

"I liked it better when you were too young to be involved in these conversations."

"Wellllll, you can thank Mom and Dad for that. Not like I chose to be fourteen years younger than you."

Mom held up a hand. "Don't look at me. It's your father's fault. He couldn't keep his hands out of my pants when we were in high school. Being a teen mom was never in the plan." She leaned over and ruffled Eloise's hair. "But it all worked out. We made all our mistakes parenting Aiden, so by the time the rest of you came along, we knew how not to screw you up too badly."

Pressing the palms of my hands into my eye sockets, I took a few deep breaths.

My mom laid her hand on my back. "What happened, Aiden?"

I paused. "Nothing."

It was the truth. But it wasn't.

I'd made peace with the loss of Beth, and what it might mean for my future. Grieving my wife, grieving the absence of her sweet, funny nature, the knowledge that Anya may not remember her when she grew up. Not once in the past two years had I met a woman who stirred up any sort of reaction.

So, while nothing had happened with Isabel, inside me, it didn't feel like nothing.

It felt an awful lot like someone had flipped a switch whose location had been kept a secret, even from me. It wasn't like I'd been fumbling around in the dark, trying to force attraction to someone. There was no empty gap in my life that I was looking to fill.

But now, all I could think about was how she would've responded if I'd slid my hand behind her neck and took her mouth with mine. How well she'd fit me, how well we'd move together because she already proved she could match me step for step. If I allowed the images to progress with Isabel, I'd never have to worry about breaking her, because the likely truth was that she'd probably have me on my back and at her mercy before we ever got to that point.

"Fuck," I whispered.

Mom tsked. "Language. I raised you better than to curse in front of me."

Eloise cackled with glee. "Ohhhh, this is good. Come on, give us the scoop."

"Is she pretty?" my mom asked.

Eloise sighed. "Mom, we do not reduce a woman's worth to their physical features anymore. She can be pretty *and* a raging bitch monster with the IQ of a salad, and then it's all wasted."

"She's not," I heard myself say. At their stunned silence, I wanted to yank the words back in.

"A bitch monster?" Eloise asked.

"No. I mean, she's not that either." I kept my gaze down at the counter because, at the age of thirty-five, I'd never had a conversation with my mom and my baby sister about women. "Pretty. Or … it's not the right word, at least."

For some reason, the path of my brain caused a tremor of panic down my spine. Trying to define what Isabel was or wasn't, in this context, made my chest feel heavy and tight, and my hands held a slight tingle.

No, Isabel was not someone that I'd ever describe as pretty. It was such a weak word.

Even beautiful felt wrong.

I remember taking Anya to the zoo, maybe a year earlier, and we watched the panther exhibit for a solid hour. Something about that animal—sleek and powerful, as it paced and prowled—mesmerized both of us as we sat on a hard wooden bench. Sometimes it would disappear behind some lush greenery, but when it came back out, a flick of its tail or a stretch of its sleek, extraordinary body, and my breath would catch in my lungs.

That was the closest I could come to what Isabel looked like.

Yes, she was fierce and strong, but she wasn't only those things either. As my heart hammered, I remembered the curve of her lips when she stared up at me. They were full. Perfectly formed. The softest looking thing about her when I tried to separate Isabel into individual attributes.

"What is the right word?" my mom asked gently.

"Just say the first thing that comes to your head," Eloise nudged.

My voice came out as a hushed whisper. "I *can't.*"

No one said anything. Neither of them moved. I wasn't even sure they were breathing. When I lifted my head, they were both gaping at me. The admission still hung there, and I couldn't take it back. I wasn't even sure I wanted to. More than anything I could've admitted to them, it was the most telling.

I'd lost the woman I loved and I still couldn't think about her without feeling that bruise, and I didn't know how to wrap my mind around the idea that anyone else could step into her place already.

"Oh, Aiden," my mom said, her eyes going all watery.

Her reaction set off a small flare of panic, rocking the foundation of this carefully cultivated plan in my head. "All I want is something peaceful, Mom. I came here to make a home for me and Anya, something good and solid that we can settle into. I didn't uproot our life for anything like this. I'm her *boss.*"

Eloise nodded, eyes wide. "Abuse of power is no joke. You gotta know she *wants* it."

"Eloise," my mom chided.

"What? I don't want my brother to be one of those douches who thinks because he looks like he looks he can get away with whatever he wants." She pointed her finger at me. "You can't. Be respectful."

I gave her a look.

"Sorry," she muttered. "I'm done now."

"This is why I don't particularly feel like talking about it." I stood with a sigh. "Nothing happened. Whatever I might have thought or imagined or whatever doesn't matter because nothing happened and nothing will. Moving here was about doing what was best for Anya, not so I can start something with my manager who's a decade younger than me."

"Oooh," Eloise breathed, "Age gap. There are *so* many layers to this."

"Can you muzzle her?" I asked Mom.

She laughed. "I have twenty-one years of unsuccessful attempts that would say no."

Eloise ignored us, sighing happily. "I can't even handle how great of a setup this is. It's like forbidden looks and accidental touches at work, and you're looking for a second chance at love even though you're *way* too old for her, so she's all young and hot—" My mom slapped a hand over Eloise's mouth.

Which I appreciated because my brain went somewhere it hadn't before.

Beth's tired voice teasing me that she'd haunt me if I fell for the first hot, tight body I met.

My gut churned uncomfortably at the realization.

"Thank you," I told my mom. "I'm going to pick up Anya. Can you bring her backpack out to my truck for me?"

Mom nodded. "Yes."

When she went to grab the backpack, Eloise gave me an embarrassed grin. "Sorry, I'm reading some books right now, and I might've gotten a little carried away."

"Might've?"

She sighed dejectedly. My little sister was my opposite in just about every way. She spoke without thinking and felt everything so big and loud, and in moments like this, it was hard to extend grace when the last thing I needed was her talking about abuse of power, and Isabel's young, hot body, and how I was way too old for her.

"It's fine, El." I hooked my arm around her shoulder for a hug, dropping a kiss on the top of her head when she gave me a squeeze. "But trust me, I don't need anyone reminding me of all the reasons nothing can happen between Isabel and me."

"Nothing?"

I gave her a gentle nudge. "Nothing. I'll go back to work with my head on straight because that's the best for everyone."

"So boring," she whispered.

I didn't respond, but it did make me smile. It wasn't until I was walking out of the kitchen that she stopped me in my tracks.

"Beth would want you to be happy, you know."

Slowly, I turned. "I am happy."

She shook her head. "You're settled. There's a difference, big brother. And I hope you don't ignore the possibility for one because you're so fixed on the other."

Her words echoed in my head as I moved a drowsy Anya into the truck and drove us home. I got her into her bed and then sank onto the family room couch with a sigh. The words continued to ring, over and over, like a bell I couldn't shut off.

Even if she was right, it didn't matter.

Whether I imagined kissing Isabel or not, whether my hands itched to slip over her skin, or how at that moment, my mouth watered at the thought of burying myself to the hilt until we both lost our minds, it wasn't the point.

No matter what my sister said, this phase of my life was about finding an even, steady foundation. It wasn't about heat and hormones, about attraction that hid behind the guise of interest.

I'd already married the woman I loved.

Already buried her.

Nothing short of a miracle would make me want to do that again.

CHAPTER 13

Isabel

Aiden: Anya is sick, so I'll be home today, possibly tomorrow. Could you shoot me the numbers of the two clients I had on my schedule today? Thanks, Ward.

The sigh that escaped my mouth as I read his text came without permission. So much for turning a new leaf and extending a long-overdue olive branch. The large black coffee sat on the edge of the front desk, his name scrawled on the side. I took a sip of my own and stared at the cup. The order was a guess because I'd never actually seen him drink coffee.

Before I responded to his text, I picked up the cup, walked over to the drinking fountain, and slowly poured it out. The dark liquid swirling around the drain had me smiling a little at the irony that I now found myself dumping coffee that I'd meant for him.

I tossed the empty cup into the small trash can against the wall and went back to the front desk. I picked up my phone and tapped out the phone numbers for his clients because even though I could call them and offer to cover, I'd quickly learned that the people who wanted to train with Aiden only wanted to train with Aiden.

Not that I could blame them.

Me: Here you go. You don't have anyone on the schedule tomorrow, so take whatever time you need.

Aiden: I appreciate it. If you don't mind, there's a piece of paper on my desk next to the computer. I forgot to add that client onto the calendar for the end of this week.

Me: No problem.

The three dots on the screen bounced, then disappeared. One day at a time. No matter how impatient I could be, no solid relationship—regardless of the type—was built out of thin air.

Me: We'll take care of everything here. Tell Anya I hope she feels better.

Aiden: I will.

Aiden: Thank you again.

Me: Just doing my job.

Aiden: Glad to hear it, Ward. Even if my back still hurts.

I was still smiling when I let myself into his office a couple of hours later. The piece of paper was easy to find, and my eyes widened when I saw the name of his new client. The gym already boasted a number of former athlete clients, simply because of my connection to the Wolves and Amy's reputation.

Current elite athletes—including the one I'd watched play US Women's soccer for the past few years—was new.

The connection clearly came from Aiden, and it sent my wheels spinning about what his plans might be for the gym. The day went by in a blink. As did the next.

It wasn't easier without him there because I felt a strange

urgency to see if I could act normal around him now. Or as normal as I was capable of after our sexually charged sparring match.

On day three, I came in to work with another drink holder in my hands. One for me, one for Emily, and another black coffee for Aiden.

When his typical arrival time came and went without a sign of him, I set the coffee on the corner of my desk as I got to work. Emily popped her head through the door.

"Call for you," she said. "And the delivery guy is here with a huge delivery. Where should they go?"

"How many boxes?"

"Probably twelve or so."

I glanced at my office. "Stick them right outside my door. I don't want to crowd the front. I'll see what they are."

She left with a nod, and I tapped the button on my desk phone to pick up the call.

"This is Isabel."

"Ward."

My eyes closed briefly at the sound of his voice. So maybe I wasn't doing so hot keeping that reaction in check. "Hey, boss. How's Anya?"

He sighed. "A bit better, still not back to normal, though. Her fever's gone but …"

Leaning back in my chair, I tucked the phone between my ear and shoulder. "We can hold down the fort here if you're worried about that."

"I'm not. I trust you." He paused. "The new merchandise should arrive today or tomorrow."

"So that's what's getting stacked outside my door right now," I said.

"It came?"

"Just now."

"Good." But he sounded disappointed. I probably would've been too, if I'd bought the gym and was putting my name on everything.

"Want me to leave them for you to open?" I asked carefully. "It's a big deal."

He was quiet. "Would you mind?"

"Not at all."

"Thank you, Ward." Aiden sighed. "I wish I could sneak out and do it today, but I can't leave."

My eyebrows lowered. "She's still that sick?"

He hesitated before answering. "Anya hasn't really been sick like this since ... since Beth. She doesn't really want anyone but me right now."

There was a strange fist closing around my heart at how carefully he said it. Like he didn't want to divulge too much. Like it gave something away.

I licked my lips. "My brother used to buy us these special sticker books when we got sick. He'd put them on a tray with a big glass of 7 Up with a fancy straw and a little bowl of saltine crackers." My skin felt hot sharing the story, and I rubbed absently at the side of my neck. "I didn't even like stickers that much, but we never got them because my twin sisters once put hundreds of them all over his bed frame, and he couldn't get them off."

Aiden made a sound that could've been a laugh, but I wasn't quite sure. "How old were you?"

"Twelve." I shook my head. "Maybe it won't work for Anya. But I know, for us, it was just enough of a distraction."

"From what?" he asked quietly.

"Everything."

Aiden was quiet, and in that quiet, I felt naked.

"I'll see if my mom can find one," he said after a moment. "Thank you."

"Do you drink coffee?" I asked suddenly. My eyes pinched shut in mortification.

"I don't," he answered, and I heard the confusion clear in his voice.

My hand found the bottom of the cup, still sitting on my desk. "I was … I got you coffee on my way in this morning."

Again, Aiden was silent. Oh, silence was bad for me when I wasn't sure how to proceed. It made for all sorts of awkward babbling impulses.

"I mean, I got some for me and Emily too," I said. "I just … I wanted to repay the favor. Because I shouldn't have dumped the one you got me. That was rude."

He hummed, low in his throat. I found that I liked the sound. A lot.

"Forgiven," he replied. There was a smile in his voice, and I wished I could see it.

But that was it. Nothing further. It wasn't the first time that Aiden didn't react the way that I expected him to. Maybe, like Paige said, he was just as much of a mystery to me as I was to him.

I exhaled lightly. "Good luck with the stickers."

He said my name by way of a goodbye, and even if it wasn't much of an olive branch … it was something.

The next morning, I had an iced tea sitting on the edge of the front desk when his truck pulled in. There was no way I was capable of breathing normally when he approached.

Maybe it was because I'd only known him—the real him—for such a short amount of time, but the four days without seeing him seemed like a month. In his absence, the old gym signage had been removed from the building, and watching him pause to stare up at the blank space with an inscrutable expression on his face, I desperately wished to know what was going on in his head.

With one last look at the area where the new lighted sign would go, he pulled open the door.

"Ward," he said in greeting. But he was slower to speak, his voice lower in pitch, and his eye contact was … a vibe all of its own.

The phone call had been such meager practice. This was the real test after our sparring match.

His eyes landed on the cup, and one side of his lips quirked up.

Slowly, Aiden picked it up, studying the contents before he took a sip.

"Still not it," he said. "Good guess, though."

Not a single word came out of my mouth when he finally severed that eye contact and walked back to his office.

Not coffee. Not iced tea.

I caught myself watching him throughout the day. Sometimes his gaze tangled with mine, and sometimes it seemed like he was oblivious to my attention.

Like when he opened the first box of new merch and he held up one of the T-shirts for a long minute and just stared at it.

My head tilted from where I absently wiped down some bags with Kelly after her class.

"He really likes that shirt," she whispered.

I smiled. "Seems so."

"You know," she said, "for as much crap as I gave him at the beginning, he's an awesome boss. I figured he'd be … I don't know … one of those asshole prima donna fighters."

"He's definitely not that," I murmured.

He bought sticker books for his sick daughter and kept a low profile. He got in my face when he thought I was being reckless with my safety and didn't flinch at my anger. He bought coffees and wiped down weight benches. One moment, he looked like he was going to back me up against a wall, and the next, he was maintaining a polite professional distance.

"If you stare any harder, you're going to burn a hole in his skin," Kelly commented lightly.

"Just trying to figure him out."

"Uh-huh."

I rolled my eyes.

"You two have been circling each other since the day he started. It's like watching the two most flirt-avoidant people in the universe trying to figure out how to speak to each other."

I tossed a used wipe at her, and she laughed.

Aiden's attention moved in our direction, and with the T-shirt folded in his hand, I felt a little like he was studying me in the same way I was studying him.

The next day, I was off.

And the one after that, I added Kombucha to the list of drinks that Aiden did not drink in the morning.

It wasn't matcha either, which tasted like dirt, according to him.

The routine we settled into over the next week held a strange sort of tension, different than it had been at the beginning. Maybe because we were on more equal footing, or maybe because I wasn't doing my very best to avoid him anymore.

And what I found, as I watched him interact with his growing list of clients, with the new trainers we hired, with the rest of us, was that I liked him as much as I wanted him.

His sense of humor was there, hidden underneath the reserve.

"Lemon water?" he asked. He held the cup up and gave it a dirty look.

"Apparently I'm not very good at this." I watched him over the edge of the computer monitor.

"Tastes like I'm drinking Pledge."

I rolled my eyes, and Aiden watched me carefully.

"Do you want some help with that?" he asked, nodding at all the boxes I was still unpacking. We'd ordered new shelves, new racks to match the new branding, and it was taking longer than I thought while I trained the new hires.

I shook my head. "It's okay. Besides, you've got a new client coming at nine. All her paperwork is on your desk."

"The soccer player?" he asked.

With a nod, I turned to grab another stack of shirts. They were just out of my reach, and he leaned down to push the stack closer to me. I smiled.

"How do you know her?" I asked.

"Same agent. Or my former agent, at least."

I slid a neatly folded stack of shirts into the correct bin for their size. "You don't need an agent anymore?"

Aiden shook his head. A lot of athletes, especially if they were high-profile enough, maintained a steady stream of endorsement income after retiring. He was watching me, eyes considering, like he somehow knew how hard this was for me. But he also didn't share anything further.

I took a deep breath and glanced up at him. "You'd probably make easier money than what you're doing here, if you still had one."

Aiden's mouth softened, but he didn't smile.

He glanced at the gym, and I liked the way his eyes warmed when he looked at the space, the equipment. Like it was something more. "I probably would, Ward."

When he disappeared into his office, I buried my face into the shirt and tried to calm the racing of my heart.

Normal twenty-five-year-old women could flirt and laugh and ask a handsome man questions without triggering an anxiety attack, but not me.

Not Isabel Ward, the girl who could handle *anything in the entire world* except those three things.

His new client came, and I did very well not fangirling when she introduced herself.

"Welcome to Hennessy's," I told her, handing her a membership card. "Aiden will meet you back by the treadmills in just a minute."

As I approached his office, I shook the jitters out of my hands.

One day at a time. Even if he was only ever my boss, even if we never repeated what happened in the open space in the middle of the gym, this was how relationships of any kind were built.

Gently, I knocked on the open door.

"Come in," he said.

Aiden was sitting in front of his monitor, and my throat went dry because he'd slid black-framed glasses over his face. Not once in my entire life had I found glasses appealing, but apparently, I had a new fetish.

Former fighter turned businessman was a whole mood, and I really, *really* liked it.

His eyebrows raised expectantly.

"Right." I cleared my throat. "She's here for her session."

Aiden stood and tossed the glasses onto the desk. I stepped back so he could leave his office, but he paused in the doorway, his frame filling the space. His client stood over by the treadmill, stretching her legs, knee wrapped in a black brace. When she hurt it in the last World Cup, I almost cried.

"It's a big deal," I heard myself say.

He wasn't a world-famous trainer. He wasn't a loud social media presence or someone whose name was mentioned often anymore. But still, she was here to become stronger.

He didn't ask what I meant. "It is."

My gaze lingered on his profile. And when he turned, eyes locked on mine, I didn't look away.

"That's why," he said quietly. "This isn't easy money. But at this point in my life, I want to build something that matters."

Then he walked away, and I was left wondering if I wasn't completely making things worse by trying to understand him better.

He was in the middle of his session when the twins showed up, gym bags slung over their shoulders.

"I didn't know you two were coming today," I told them.

Lia hooked a thumb at Claire. "Her idea."

I glanced at Claire. "It's never your idea to work out."

Claire held up her hands. "Not for that."

My eyebrows rose. "For what then?"

Lia held up two fingers. "We wanted a glimpse at him because you're still being awfully cagey, and two, Molly told us about your fight."

"It wasn't a fight, per se," I hedged.

Claire set a hand on Lia's arm. "We get it. And we're not taking sides. I just wanted to check on you because we haven't seen much of you lately."

Standing from the stool, I joined them as they walked back toward the bags. "No taking sides, huh? You're saying I'm the only one not thrilled at the prospect of seeing her."

"If I thought she'd actually come, I'd probably need to medicate," Lia said.

Claire smiled. "I could go either way. But I tend to agree."

Aiden glanced over while I sat on the ground with them as they began stretching. But his client started a new rep, and he pulled his gaze from me and the twins.

"I'd just rather not think about her coming or not coming," I told them. "I hate that hanging over the day."

Claire wrapped her hands around the bottom of her shoe and leaned forward. "Just don't fight that discomfort, you know? Ignoring your feelings about it will only make it worse."

"Thank you, Miss Future Therapist."

She smiled. "Plus, even if she does come, no one says you have to engage with her at all."

Lia pressed her arm over her chest and stretched. "She's not gonna show. No way she has the guts."

When I shifted on the floor, Claire gave her twin a look. "We've got plenty of time to figure it out."

Apparently, my desire to talk about Brooke was stamped pretty clearly on my face.

Lia snuck a look over her shoulder, where Aiden was guiding his client in some lunges. He pointed out something in her form, and she nodded, immediately adjusting. "Holy shit, is that Allie Catalano?"

I nodded.

She whistled. "I can't wait to tell Jude."

"How's it going with him?" Claire asked carefully.

I gave her a look. "Perfectly fine, thank you."

Claire smiled. "Has he talked about his wife much? I can't imagine how hard it must be to start over like that."

"Just once," I said, watching him again. His eyes found mine and held.

Instead of looking away, like I might have before, I took a deep breath and gave him a small smile.

"Not really the kind of topic you can push if someone doesn't want to discuss it," Lia said. "Imagine if Logan lost Paige. He wouldn't be able to talk easily about her either."

The three of us went quiet. My heart went a little pinched, a little achy at the thought of it. He'd never be ready. Never.

Maybe that was the kind of marriage Aiden had too. The kind he'd never get over.

One day at a time, I reminded myself.

The twins left.

His client left.

A class started and ended while I continued to work.

And I found myself unable to stop thinking about what Lia had said. What this fresh start might mean to him.

As I thought it, a giant truck pulled up in front of the building and I hopped up off the floor to go to Aiden's office.

"Got a minute?" I asked, popping my head around the corner.

He sighed, pinching the bridge of his nose. "For you, yeah."

My cheeks went warm, and in the light of his office, I thought maybe his did too.

"The guys are here to install the new sign." I gave him a tiny smile. "Want to watch?"

He studied me. "If you'll join me."

Carefully, I nodded, and left his office while he followed.

CHAPTER 14

Aiden

I'D ALMOST CONVINCED MYSELF THAT THE INVITATION FOR HER to join me meant nothing. Almost. Because as we walked side by side, a low, humming awareness arced between her body and mine even though we didn't touch.

Nothing more would ever be possible with her, I'd come to realize. But it was tolerable, at least for my own sanity, as long as it didn't progress past this.

It was that awareness that had me stepping just a little farther away from her, because the last thing I needed was to ruin the ease we'd found in the recent stretch of days.

"Lemonade?" she asked.

In my head, I laughed out loud. But I kept my face even as I answered. "Nope."

When I glanced in her direction, she was frowning.

"It's not fair, you know," she said lightly. "I know you asked Amy what to get us."

I pushed open the gym door and gestured for her to exit the building in front of me. "Life never is fair, is it, Ward?"

She snorted.

The men standing in the cherry picker affixed the sign with precision as Isabel and I found a spot to stand and watch. The edges of the H appeared, a vivid blue that would glow brightly when the lights turned on at night.

Next to me, Isabel shaded her eyes and watched them work.

Her frame expanded on a deep inhale, and I found myself waiting to see if she'd speak, what she'd say.

"Before I came here for the first time, I had no idea how to handle all the things I'd shoved down. At fourteen, I didn't know it was just … anger waiting to get out." She licked her lips as more of the sign appeared. "Fear too, I guess. I ended my first workout a sobbing mess." She paused, a rueful expression on her beautiful face, and I couldn't tear my eyes from her. "I hate crying. But this place gave me something safe. Somewhere safe to put all the things that were too big for my body."

It was easy to imagine her at that age, blazing eyes and emotions exploding out of her.

The workers moved to the other side, half of the sign now visible.

"I have never loved a place more than the home where my brother raised us," she continued. "Until I walked through those doors." Isabel turned to me, eyes soft and solemn. "I'm really proud to be a part of what you're building here, Aiden. You're taking something I love, and you're treating it with the same care that I would if it were mine."

My reaction to her words, her admission, wasn't peaceful or soothing, and it took everything in me to hold still, not to reach for her hand, simply to find an anchor in the moment. "Thank you," I said in a gruff voice.

Through the sound of the drills they used, the loud tinkering of metal on metal, Isabel and I fell into a comfortable silence.

I closed my eyes as the sun warmed my skin, and I imagined Beth seeing this. She'd be proud, in this home I'd found, this haven I was building.

The workers pulled the last of the protective coverings down, and as the cherry picker lowered, I finally saw the name in full.

"Looks good," she said quietly.

The words were slow to crawl up my throat, past the hard-edges of emotion crowding the space. "It does."

Somehow, it felt right that it was just her and I witnessing this moment, and I refused to dig into why.

"You didn't want to have a big ribbon-cutting or anything?" she asked.

I shook my head.

"You know, you keep surprising me."

Glancing at her, I found her attention still focused on the sign. "Yeah?"

"I've known a lot of athletes, current and former. Even if they don't love the spotlight, they know how to use it to their advantage when necessary. I figured you'd do that here."

I hummed, folding my arms over my chest. "A few years ago, I think I might've."

Isabel gave me a quick look, then turned back to the front of the building.

"It might not be like this for everyone," I continued, "but when my wife died, I hated the attention that came with it. With my decision to leave the sport. Being the center of everyone's focus at the worst time in your life changed everything. Nothing about it appealed to me anymore." I stared at the letters in blue. "I know it sounds crazy."

"Not crazy." She gave me a look, wisps of her almost-black hair slipping across her face in the breeze. "But you deserve to celebrate this. Your family and friends do too."

My hands itched to slide the hair behind her ears. I left them where they were. "You think so?"

Her lips pulled at the edges, the start of a sly grin. "Well, if someone were to plan a party, they should have plenty of notice."

"Ahh. If *someone* were to agree, I'll let you know." I raised an eyebrow. "Nothing big though, if we do. I've got someone I can reach out to for a little press though."

"Okay." She bit down on her bottom lip, sent a quick glance in my direction. "Hot chocolate?"

"Nope," I murmured.

Isabel huffed quietly, and as she walked back into the gym, I found myself smiling.

☙

Isabel

The next morning, Aiden looked tired and a little grumpy when he came in, but at the sight of an empty glass filled with ice on the front desk, his eyes warmed.

"So close."

"Well, I'm running out of options."

"Maybe you just need to try harder, Ward."

I allowed a tiny eye roll and turned back to the computer screen, where an email popped up and had me smiling.

"Good news?" Aiden asked.

"Yeah." I scrolled down the email. "It's from the dean of student life at UDub. She's going to work with us on spreading the news about our self-defense class. She thought it was a great idea, and if we get enough people to sign up, we could offer a few different sessions so we don't overload the space."

Aiden glanced at the gym, and I could tell he was trying to picture it.

I stood, gesturing beyond the ring. "We could push some of the equipment to the far side, and remove a few bags to temporarily open some space. But I think for the first class, we should cap the sign-ups at twenty to make sure we have enough room to move around."

He nodded. "Sounds good."

I sucked in a slow breath. "We charging for the class?"

His eyes were bright and clear when he moved his gaze back to me. "What do you think?"

My lips twitched at his perfectly even, perfectly annoyed that I'd even ask tone. "In general? Or about this?"

"Ward," he growled.

I felt like I was poking a giant bear, but hell if I didn't practically feel high being able to get just a little mouthy with him. We'd come far, I realized with no small amount of pride. "I assumed I knew the answer, but I didn't want to do anything without your permission."

His eyes flared. "You mean like when you tried to kick me in the head a couple of weeks ago?"

Heart hammering at the warmth in his tone, I was very proud of myself when I coolly, *so coolly* raised an eyebrow. "Not my fault you weren't paying attention."

He gave me a long look, and it stretched just long enough that my belly flipped dangerously. Sitting back down on the stool, I cursed the warmth in my cheeks.

Aiden was quiet for a few moments, and I found myself holding my breath for what he'd say next.

It was the first mention of that night, and he'd been the one to bring it up. That had to be significant, right?

"Electrician should be here in about thirty to start setting up the scanning system for the door," he said. "Feel free to send him back to my office when he gets here."

141

I kept my tone light. "You got it, boss."

My hand had a slight tremble as I clicked on another email, and he was still behind me.

But when he walked away, I let out a slow breath and got back to work.

The rest of the day went smoothly. I taught a class and had a training session. The electrician installed our new system, and Emily and I worked for the next two days to figure out the distribution of the new card system to all members.

I set a carton of milk on Aiden's desk when I returned after a day off, and his lips twitched.

"Oh, come on," I said.

He leaned back in his chair, hands braced behind his head. "Eventually, you'll get it because you'll run out of options."

I narrowed my eyes in a glare, and as I walked out of his office, I heard a low husky laugh that had goosebumps popping along my arms.

It was that sound that had me sliding into vivid imagery, Aiden kissing along the back of my neck, laughing when I turned and tried to capture his mouth.

Just as I contemplated how long it had been since I'd allowed myself into that headspace, the sound of someone swiping a key card at the door registered, and I blinked a few times to clear my face.

With my polite smile affixed, I looked up, only to see Anya smashing her face against the perfectly clean glass. She waved frantically, and I smiled. Behind her was a tall, handsome guy with Aiden's eyes and jaw, but his hair was almost black.

I hated how immediately I cataloged all the ways he was *less* than Aiden.

He was younger, to be sure. If I had to guess, he was probably closer to my age.

He wasn't quite as tall, though when he pushed open the door for Anya, I knew he was still a solid six-one.

He wasn't quite as big, even though he looked strong and muscular.

And he didn't wear that constant broody, grump face that Aiden did, because as he saw me behind the desk, his face spread with a broad, handsome, white-toothed smile.

"Wonder Woman!" Anya yelled, running around the desk to hurtle her small body into my arms.

Emitting a shocked laugh at her effusive greeting, I gave her a quick hug and set her back to study her. "No tricks on the beams today, right?"

She nodded. "Uncle Beckham made me promise too. Only he gave me a giant candy bar."

"I see the evidence of it." I gestured to her chocolate streaked cheeks.

"Anya Hennessy," the man said in a scandalized voice, "that was supposed to be our secret. How quickly you turn on me."

Her giggle had me smiling again. "Miss Isabel won't tell daddy."

He leaned against the wall and gave me a quick study. "Miss Isabel won't, huh?"

His tone was undeniably flirty, his green eyes were warm and friendly, and honestly, this was the problem. Why 'going on dates' was about as far down my priority list as a full body wax. Because that undeniably flirty tone and warm eyes had my hackles up immediately. I felt like a dog who just spotted another dog far off, and instead of waiting to see how they'd act toward me, my instinct was raised hair along my back and the beginnings of a growl in the back of my throat.

This guy didn't even know me. I'd done nothing to warrant flirty eyes and a flirty tone.

This, ladies and gentlemen, was why I was still in full possession of a hymen.

Why only untouchable, emotionally unavailable men seemed to appeal to me, because things like this didn't happen.

Anya scampered off to find her dad, leaving the two of us alone by the front desk.

He stuck a big hand out. "Beckham Hennessy."

I cleared my throat to make sure that an actual growl didn't emerge. "Isabel Ward."

"The manager," he clarified.

I nodded.

"Hmmm."

My eyes narrowed. "What does *that* mean?"

At first, he did nothing but smile, but then he snapped his fingers like I wasn't sitting there glaring. "Logan Ward is your brother, right?"

"He is."

"He's a defensive genius," Beckham said.

"He is," I repeated, this time injecting a little warmth into my voice. "Though, I never saw him that way growing up. He was just the guy who forced me to do my homework and told me I couldn't torture my little sisters."

That had him grinning. "I had a picture of him on my wall when he used to play."

My face was on fire when I thought about the fact that I had pictures of Beckham's brother on my wall around the same time, but boy, did my mouth stay shut.

Beckham strode closer to the desk and dropped his elbows on the bar height counter along the front. Like a weirdo, I pushed backward in the chair so he wasn't so close.

"You and I could probably trade some absolutely killer stories," he said.

One eyebrow rose. "Could we?" I murmured. Please, not about posters on walls, I thought frantically.

He leaned in a little farther and dropped his voice. "Just imagine how much we have in common."

My head tilted. I couldn't peg this guy, because his eyes—up close—didn't hold anything except polite friendliness.

"Beckham," a deep voice snapped.

My back straightened. Because Aiden appeared around the corner, jaw tight and eyes very not-flirty.

Beckham didn't move from his position, with the leaning and the closeness. His smile spread. "Aiden. Lovely to see you. I was just telling your manager here that we have a lot in common."

Aiden's face was stormy. "Maybe you should let her get back to work."

"Maybe she wants to talk to me," Beckham said.

"Maybe you should pay attention to how she's leaning away from you," Aiden replied.

"Maybe," I interjected smoothly, "she can speak for herself."

Aiden's eyes locked onto mine, and even though all the normal 'Aiden-induced' physical reactions immediately kicked off, with the stuttering heartbeat and tingly hands and butterfly-filled belly, I refused to look away.

Beckham whistled. "I really like her."

My eyes dropped and I took a deep breath.

Beckham leaned back and smacked a hand on the counter of the desk. "See? We could write a book, you and me."

"On what?" Aiden ground out.

"How to deal with overbearing, athletically-gifted, pain-in-the-ass big brothers."

The laugh burst out of me so fast, so loud, there was no stopping it.

And the two men had very, very different reactions. As I slapped a hand over my mouth to stem the hysterical sounds trying to escape, Beckham smiled just a little too smugly.

And Aiden ... he looked like a thundercloud.

In fact, I'd never seen him look like that, and as my laughter subsided, I tried desperately to ignore the growing feeling that he looked ... he looked jealous.

"Beckham," he said, "thank you for dropping off Anya. Don't you have to go to work?"

"Nope, I have plenty of time."

My eyes flipped between them.

Aiden glared.

Beckham smiled. "I was having an interesting conversation with Eloise the other day when she was home from school."

When Aiden made a growling noise, deep from within his chest, my eyes widened. "Beckham," he ground out.

Beckham leaned toward me again. "Eloise is our youngest sister. She's a little nosy sometimes, but we all adore her."

"Debatable at the moment," Aiden interjected.

"How many of there are you?" I asked.

"Five," they said in unison.

My lips curled in a smile. "I have a big family too."

At that, Aiden's face finally lost its hard edge, and he nodded.

Beckham glanced at his watch, and like he hadn't instigated this entire conversation, he twirled his car keys on his pointer finger. "Well, I better get going." He held out his hand to me again, and I took it. "Isabel, it was a *pleasure* to meet you."

My brows lowered. "I think I'll withhold judgment until I'm not stuck in a verbal sparring match between you two."

He laughed. "Aiden, I'll see you later."

Aiden rubbed his forehead. "Thanks for watching Anya."

Her head popped around the corner. "Bye Uncle Beckham, thanks for the huge chocolate bar!"

Beckham winked at her. "Anytime, munchkin."

Aiden glared at his retreating back, and I tried to smother my smile.

What a strange, unexpected exchange to completely change

the trajectory of my mood. I'd seen so many different sides of him now, and none of them—not a single one—were any less appealing.

I liked grumpy, older brother Aiden. And I wished I didn't.

With Beckham gone, and Anya running back to her dad's office, it was just me and Aiden. I found myself holding my breath to see if he'd say anything. Praying he wouldn't. I wasn't entirely sure.

And wasn't that the problem?

I was in a constant state of push and pull over what I wanted, and what I needed from him.

He opened his mouth to talk, closed it, then shook his head slightly. "You're off this weekend," he commented.

I nodded slowly. "I'm watching my nephew while my brother and his wife are out of town." I gestured behind us at the main portion of the gym. "Kelly is covering for me."

He hummed in assent. "Have a good weekend then."

Aiden started to walk away, and I watched him carefully. I wanted him to be jealous over his brother flirting with me.

Like he heard me think it, Aiden paused and faced me again. "I shouldn't have assumed you didn't want to talk to Beckham. I'm sorry."

My eyebrows popped up. "It's fine."

He nodded.

I took a deep breath, steadily held his gaze, and lifted my chin a touch. "I'm not interested in your brother."

Aiden went stock-still, and I cursed myself up, down, and sideways for feeling like I needed to explain it to him.

In the moment we locked gazes after I said it, I imagined all sorts of things.

Me saying that I was interested in him.

That he was quickly becoming my favorite person to spend time with.

That I wanted him.

Imagined Aiden striding toward me, gripping my face in both

hands and slanting his mouth over mine. My hands snaking under his shirt so I could memorize the muscles with my fingertips. I imagined the way he'd be able to lift me easily, the way he'd be able to move and press and push my body into a knotted tangle of pleasure. Not once, in my entire life, had I fantasized about someone having the strength to hold me down, pin me in place, but sitting in that chair, I knew that I'd let him.

Let had nothing to do with it. I'd beg him to.

I'd give up all control to Aiden, and I had a feeling that he'd know exactly what to do with it.

"Good," he murmured, eyes holding mine for just a second longer. And then he turned back toward his office.

It was only when he did that I finally started breathing normally. For a while, it seemed like he and I might have found steady ground, a foothold into a new place that I was enjoying.

Maybe I was kidding myself to think that getting to know him better would ever lead to me wanting him less. Because as he walked away, I knew I wasn't doing so hot getting my feelings for him under control.

And when he glanced back in my direction, I had to wonder if I wasn't the only one.

CHAPTER 15

Isabel

"I THINK WE SHOULD GO OUT FOR BREAKFAST," EMMETT SAID.

We stood side by side, staring into the fridge. Amazingly, our staring did not magically make food appear.

I winced. "We can make *something*. There's like … eggs. And bread. And cheese. That's enough, right?"

He looked up at me. "You're asking *me* what to do with those two things? I'm a kid."

"You're almost ten."

"You're like … twenty-five. If anyone should be able to cook breakfast, it's you."

I stared at the shelves with a heavy sigh. "Everyone has talents in this life, Emmett. Cooking is not one of mine."

"No shit."

With a determined lift of my chin, I started pulling things out. "I'm going to ignore that."

He took the eggs when I handed them to him, setting them

on the counter with a skeptical look. "Mom's gonna be pissed if you poison me with your cooking before they get home."

"Nah, she'll forgive me."

Emmett grinned.

This poor kid. He had no choice but to speak fluent sarcasm considering the family he was born into.

A minute later, the kitchen counter was covered in an array of things that should've equaled out to a pretty epic breakfast.

"Don't they have like, fancy cooking gadgets that make this stuff easy?"

His eyes lit up. "They have one of those air fryer things. And a toaster."

I pinched the bridge of my nose. "I know what a toaster is, Emmett."

"Are you sure we can't just go out to breakfast?"

"Tomorrow," I insisted. "It'll be our reward for not killing each other after all this unsupervised time together."

"If your breakfast doesn't kill me first," he muttered.

I shoved him sideways. "Get out of here with that bad attitude."

Emmett sighed. "Just don't use the microwave and toaster at the same time. Mom said a really bad word yesterday when she did that."

Rolling my eyes, I said, "I know how to work appliances, Emmett. Go watch those awful cartoons."

After anchoring my hair in a bun at the top of my head, I mentally rolled up my sleeves and got to work. I managed to crack some eggs in a sizzling skillet, with only a few chunks of the shell that I scooped out. Bread went into the toaster, and I jammed the button down.

Pulling a bag of sausage links up closer to my face, I tried to read the reheating directions. The eggs took up the whole skillet, so I ripped a piece of paper towel off the roll and stuck a few links into the microwave.

For a moment, I eyed the two appliances. I'd never heard Paige complain about running them simultaneously, and even though I hadn't lived under their roof for four years, I would've remembered if it was an issue.

With a shrug, I pressed the start button on the microwave.

The whole kitchen went dark.

"Shit sticks," I whispered.

"Told you that would happen!" he yelled from the couch.

With my hands on my hips, I let out a deep sigh. "It'll be fine. I can just go flip the fuse. Can you yell when the lights go back on?"

"As long as you didn't blow the fuse," he said, sounding so much like Logan I almost rolled my eyes. "Dad said if Mom did that one more time, he was going to let her change it herself."

I smiled. "And what did she say to that?"

"That he could shove his fuse up his ass because she'd be just fine if she had to."

I was still laughing when I walked down the hallway and opened the utility closet. But when I opened the gray metal door, my laughter died a horrible death.

Note to self: listen to the ten-year-old when he tells you not to run the appliances at the same time.

Emmett eyed me when I came back to the family room. "What's wrong?"

"Fuse is blown."

"Are you going to call someone to come fix it?"

My thumb tapped furiously on my thigh as I thought about my options. "I may not have to."

I yanked out my phone and sent a text.

Me: You at the gym yet?

Kelly: Probably not for another hour, why?

Me: Nothing. Just trying to remember if I had a box of fuses in my office. Remember when Amy was having all those issues last year?

Kelly: Someone blew the fuse on the stereo in the middle of a Sunday afternoon class. YEAH, I REMEMBER. You ever tried to teach with only sound of your heavy breathing to motivate people?

Me: Thankfully, no.

With a glance at the dark kitchen, I decided that the very last thing I felt like doing was to wait around all day for an electrician. I went to find Emmett.

"If you don't mind a road trip to the gym, we actually have some spare fuses in my office. There's no point in paying someone to do this if I can figure it out myself."

"Yeah, except if you blow the house up because you put the wrong fuse in."

"Do you have that little faith in me?" I asked.

"You don't know how to scramble eggs without burning them, Iz." Emmett gave me a wide-eyed *duh* look.

I motioned to the front door. "Let's go, punk. I'll buy you breakfast on the way."

Twenty minutes later, he was still inhaling the rest of his breakfast sandwich when we pulled into the parking lot at the gym.

The sight of a familiar black truck at the end of the lot had me utter a curse word under my breath.

Emmett held out his hand. I tossed my entire wallet at him. "Take a twenty, then I'm covered all weekend."

His eyes were the size of the tires on Aiden's truck. "Deal."

I slid the car in park and turned to Emmett. "Okay, so my boss is in there. Be nice, be respectful, and don't tell him anything embarrassing, okay?"

He shrugged. "What would I tell him that's embarrassing?"

When we approached the front door, I glanced inside before I slid my new card in front of the scanner. Some lights were on, but not enough for me to see Aiden right off the bat.

As soon as we turned the corner around the half wall separating the front entry from the main gym area, I saw a small body lying like a starfish in the middle of the boxing ring. She was singing a song at the top of her lungs, completely unaware of our presence.

Emmett nudged me with his elbow. "Who's that?"

Anya jumped up with a startled shriek, white-blond hair flying in all directions. But when she saw me, she smiled. "Miss Isabel!"

"Hey, kid. Nice singing," I told her.

Aiden's frame filled the doorway of his office.

Emmett climbed up into the ring with Anya, and they started running in circles. I sighed quietly. Now that there was someone to play with, this would not be a quick trip.

I jangled my keys against my leg as I approached Aiden. "Didn't think anyone would be here."

"I could say the same." His eyes assessed me, head to toe, and I struggled not to fidget. It wasn't like I got dolled up for work, but this was the first time he was seeing me bare-faced, hair a mess, and wearing the black joggers I'd slid on when I woke up. My white shirt was loose and comfortable, and it constantly slid off my shoulder, so it was *painfully* apparent that I wasn't wearing a bra.

"Iz!" Emmett yelled from the ring. He'd stuck his body between the ropes and had his knees balancing on the lower one.

"Yeah?"

"Is that the guy Molly was teasing you about because you had his picture on your wall when you were little?"

My eyelids slammed shut, my heart actually stopped beating in my chest, and at that moment, I imagined just how possible it was to travel back in time and not turn on that fucking microwave.

When I opened my eyes, I glared at him so mightily that his mouth popped open. "Ohhh, is that the kind of embarrassing thing you didn't want me to say? Sorry, Iz." He hopped off the ropes and went back to running.

Like he hadn't just embarrassed the ever-loving shit out of me.

I covered my mouth with one hand when I heard a sound of choked amusement behind me.

I wanted to die.

When I turned, Aiden was still leaning up against the door, but oh, I couldn't believe it.

He was smiling at me.

This was no wide smile that showed all his teeth or made a surprise dimple appear on either side of his mouth. But it was so, so much worse. Because this smile absolutely devastated me.

I dropped my hand, pointing a finger at him. "It's not funny."

"It's a little funny," he teased.

Instead of answering him, I strode to my office, head held as high as I could manage when I wanted to crawl under my desk and hide.

With his eyes on me, I unlocked my office and started searching in the corner cabinet where I shoved all the shit I never felt like organizing. My mental peptalk while I ripped through boxes was something like, *it's fine. It'll be fine. A poster is not a big deal, and he won't care because he was a world-class athlete, so he probably won't even really remember.*

"Which poster?" he asked.

I straightened slowly, clutching a small box in my hands. He was behind me, perched on the edge of my desk.

"I don't even really remember," I answered, very *easy breezy, I don't have sex fantasies about you every day of the week.* I swept a lock of hair behind my ear before I turned to face him. "I had a lot of athletes on my wall when I was younger."

"Okay." He didn't believe me, but I couldn't have cared less as long as he didn't push it. My heart rate slowed a bit when he lifted his chin, eyes on the box in my hands. "What are you looking for?"

"Umm, a box of fuses."

His eyebrows lifted.

"I … sort of blew one out at the house. Didn't really feel like waiting for an electrician."

Emmett ran into the office. "She exploded it trying to make us breakfast."

Remember how much you love him, I chanted in my head.

"Did she?" Aiden asked.

"Yeah," Emmett said. "Isabel *sucks* at cooking."

Aiden smothered another smile.

"Okay," I interjected. "That's enough out of you, or you don't get your screen time later."

He sighed heavily. "Can Anya come over and play? I told her about the treehouse in the backyard, and she wants to see it."

"Oh, umm"—I glanced at Aiden—"I don't know if today is a good day. I have to get this fixed, and Mr. Hennessy is working."

Aiden stood from the desk. "You've replaced fuses before?"

I slicked my tongue over my teeth. "Not exactly, but I can figure it out."

"You know how many amps that box is for?"

Glancing down, I caught sight of the edge of the box. "Twenty."

"And that's the kind you need? If you replace the bad one with something that's got too many amps, you'll do even more damage to the wiring."

My eyes narrowed slightly, and immediately, Aiden returned the look.

Something dangerous kindled like a lit match under my skin.

"I don't know," I admitted.

"I have a bunch of stuff in my truck, including some fifteen amp fuses," he said. "I'd be happy to come over and do it. If it's not the right one, I'll run to the store."

"Please say yes," Emmett whispered. "I don't want the house to explode. Mom and Dad would be so pissed at you."

The only reason I had to say no was my pride, not to borrow trouble. Inviting him to our house felt very, very troublesome.

Unfortunately, that wasn't a reason to say no. Not with this.

"I would appreciate your help," I told him. "I'll text you the address."

He wasn't smiling anymore, and it had no less of an effect on me when he jerked his chin in assent.

All of my moments alone with Aiden had been accidental. Until now.

CHAPTER 16

Isabel

EMMETT EYED MY HANDS TAPPING FRANTICALLY ON THE steering wheel.

"Not a word, punk."

He rolled his eyes. "I wasn't going to say anything."

I turned the wheel and pulled the car into the driveway of the house. "You mean like you weren't going to say anything about having a poster of Aiden on my wall? I should take my twenty bucks back."

Emmett sighed. "I have a poster of Noah on my wall, and you don't see me going around calling people names if they tell him about it." Then he shrugged. "I don't understand why you'd be embarrassed about it. I'll fight him if he makes fun of you."

I smiled because as much as he drove me crazy, moments like this reminded me why I'd die for him so fast.

"You're going to fight Aiden Hennessy?"

"Yeah. It's not like he actually won the heavyweight title." He puffed up his skinny chest. "Besides, I hear Mom say all the time that one good fit of righteous rage makes you stronger than someone twice your size."

"*Why* is she telling you that?"

He thought about that. "One of my friends was getting bullied at school."

"And she told you to attack them in a fit of righteous rage?" I asked, smiling widely.

Emmett shook his head. "No. But the house rule is you ask them to stop. If they don't stop, you tell a teacher. If they still don't stop, you punch 'em, and even if I get in trouble at school, I'll *never, ever* get in trouble at home." His eyes got wide. "She has a violent streak, though, you know?"

"Yes, she does." I turned in his direction, carefully smoothing his hair back from his face. "Your hair is getting darker. Who said you're allowed to start looking like a teenager?"

Emmett's cheeks went pink. "How old do you think I look?"

"At least thirteen."

He grinned widely, unbuckling his seat belt and tearing out of the car like I'd just handed him a check for a million dollars. "I'm gonna go make sure the treehouse is all cleaned up!" he yelled over his shoulder. I waved, slowly getting out of the car after he sprinted around the side of the house.

It was fine.

This was fine.

The kids would play outside while Aiden helped me fix the fuse. It would take two minutes, they'd be on their way, and I could go about my day relaxing with Emmett. I'd planned absolutely nothing, hence the pajama-chic look I'd thrown on.

I glanced down and groaned.

Without a bra.

If I hurried, I might have time. A glance down the street showed that it was empty, so I jogged into the house and fidgeted with the key in the front door. Just as I heard the turn of the deadbolt, the sound of Aiden's truck came rumbling into the driveway. I allowed myself one brief fortifying exhale, then I slid the key out and turned, bracing my back against the door with a smile on my face.

Emmett must have heard the truck because he ran back around into the front yard, skidding to a halt when Aiden unfolded his great big body from the great big vehicle.

Would there ever be a time that seeing him wasn't like a hole being punched through my chest?

He didn't even have to do anything but *get out of his truck*, and I wanted to strip naked, stretch over his body like a blanket, and kiss him until I saw stars. It was confusing. And annoying. And I was starting to have just a little sympathy for why my sisters had all been such headcases at one point over the past couple of years.

Aiden was wearing dark aviator frames that hid his eyes. Even though I couldn't see his eyes, I knew he was staring at me as he waited for Anya to hop out of her booster seat. He opened the rear cab door of his truck and helped her down.

"Hi, Anya," Emmett yelled like they hadn't just seen each other.

"Hi!" She stopped in front of the house and stared up at the brick-front exterior. "You have a way bigger house than we do."

Aiden rubbed the back of his neck, dropped his chin to his chest, and sighed audibly.

At least I wasn't the only one with a filter-free chatterbox in this scenario.

I smiled at Anya. "Well, there were five of us when my brother bought the house. He had to have enough space for me *and* my three sisters. That's a lot of bedrooms."

Aiden lifted his head, and again, I got the feeling he was studying me.

Anya's eyes got wide. "You lived with your *brother?* Cool."

I nodded.

That was when my chatterbox nephew decided to interject. "Really, he's her half-brother. They had the same dad. He had a heart attack. But when their mom left, my dad bought a bigger house so they could all live together."

"Thank you, Emmett." I sighed. Aiden's mouth twitched like he was fighting a smile. "Anything else you want to share?" I asked the little person next to me.

"Yes."

I gave him a look.

"Well, you asked!" He took a deep breath and turned to Aiden. "You shouldn't feel too special that Iz had your picture on her wall when she was fifteen. She had a lot of people on her wall, and there was probably a whole section of athletes she *didn't* like too, you know, just to remind her who they were."

"Emmett," I ground out, "stop talking."

"Fine, geez," he murmured.

I raked my fingers into my hair and blew out a breath. "Why don't you show Anya either your video games or the backyard or … something."

"The treehouse!" Anya yelled, then she looked up at Aiden. "Can I?"

He crouched down to her height, sliding off his sunglasses. "Yes, but you treat their things respectfully, and what's the other rule?"

She sighed. "No climbing up too high."

"Go ahead," he said softly. He held out his fist, and she bumped it before running off with Emmett. They whooped and hollered like little savages, and I smiled as the sound disappeared into the backyard.

Aiden straightened.

And we were alone.

"I'll grab the fuses I have," he said. "Hopefully, one will work."

With a nod, I watched him open a steel-plated toolbox in the bed of his truck. Watched the stretch of his back, the way the muscles in his arms bunched as he moved items that I couldn't see. And his ass in the jeans he was wearing. I almost whimpered.

So yes, if I was guilty of anything, it was my complete physical objectification of this man. Yes, he was so much more than a beautiful body, but holy hell, his body was so, so nice to look at.

I wanted to *do things* to that body and let it do even more to me.

I opened the door when he reached the front step and followed him into the entryway. Head tipped, he took in the staircase curving up to the second floor, the wall of framed pictures that covered the wall leading to the kitchen, dining, and family room.

At the end of the display, there was one that made him pause—me, my sisters, and Emmett when Lia and Claire finished their undergrad. The twins in their cap and gown were flanked by Molly and me as Emmett stood front and center, sticking his tongue out at the camera.

"He's your nephew, you said?"

"Yeah." Then I laughed under my breath. "But sometimes it feels like he's our little brother. We have a"—I paused—"unique family tree."

He hummed. "All that teenage anger you mentioned."

Slowly, I nodded. "Yeah."

Aiden studied the line of pictures, and I wondered what he was thinking. His gaze landed on one of me, Logan, and Paige when I was sixteen.

"Your mom left the four of you."

He stated it so simply, without any inflection, that it didn't knock the breath out of me. Again, I nodded.

When he turned, his eyes held a dangerous edge. "I'd be pretty fucking angry too."

My smile was wide, my laughter unexpected. But it felt really good. Aiden's expression softened.

I stood next to him and looked at the picture. "That's the anger you caught"—I glanced sideways at him—"a couple of weeks ago. My sister invited her to their wedding, and I ... didn't handle it well," I said wryly. "Maybe I'm still not handling it well."

Aiden watched me with heavy-lidded eyes. Something about my honesty seemed to affect him the most.

"So I don't need to expect attacks like that often?" he asked. "I'll keep my guard up if I should."

"No," I answered around a small smile. "You don't." At his nod, I breathed just a little easier. "I'll show you where the utility closet is."

I brushed past Aiden, my arm grazing his where my shirt had slid off my shoulder, and I felt the small touch down to my toes because his skin was warm and firm. As he followed me, he was quiet, but I got the sense he was studying our home. Studying me.

We passed the guest room and a bathroom, turning by the doorway that led to Logan's office. Aiden paused, glancing inside. Over my shoulder, I saw him peering at the Washington Wolves paraphernalia lining the walls. Two framed jerseys hung centered over the couch along the back wall from Logan's professional career and college. Photos of him and Paige, the sisters, and Emmett adorned the wall behind his desk. On the dark wood surface were two massive computer monitors and neat stacks of books and binders.

"No trophies out," Aiden commented.

I smiled. "I think they're in a box in the closet."

His eyebrows popped up briefly. "Mine will probably end up there too. I can never figure out how to display them without seeming pompous."

"The burden of greatness?" I teased lightly.

One edge of his mouth hooked up in a wry smile. "Something like that. I haven't set up my home office yet."

"Probably because you never leave the one at the gym," I said.

His gaze moved from the office to my face. "If that's not the pot calling the kettle black."

"Touche." I lifted my chin at a nondescript door. "Fuse box is in there. I can go check on the kids so I'm not in your hair."

"Oh no, you're going to help." He was so nonchalant as he said it, opening the door and setting his toolbox down to hold it in place.

One of my eyebrows rose at the evenly spoken command. "Am I?"

He hit me with the full force of those eyes when he turned. "Yeah. Because if this ever happens again, you'll know what to do." Aiden jerked his head for me to join him in the utility room.

The small, not at all spacious utility room. The fuse box was on the middle of the wall, flanked on one side by the furnace, the water heater was in the corner, and on the opposite wall was some floor-to-ceiling metal shelving Logan had stacked with tools, light bulbs, and a bunch of other shit I'd never looked at.

All I knew now, as I stood next to Aiden, was that that shelving took up a shit ton of space in that room, and we were forced to stand with our arms brushing as he flipped open the door.

"It's that one," I told him.

He nodded. "Can you grab those two boxes on the top of the bag, the small red-handled voltage check next to them, and a flat-head screwdriver? Please," he added when I shot him a look.

Bending over to find the items he asked for, I couldn't help my grin.

When I handed him the fuse boxes, he started explaining what he was doing, checking the part numbers, and where to check that the main breaker was shut off. Then he unscrewed the cover and set it on the ground by his feet.

"You still have power coming through," he said, pointing for me to hold the gauge just beyond the wires to see how it lit up. "Now that we know the circuit breakers I had match up, we can replace the old one. But we have to turn off the main breaker first, so go ahead and turn on the flashlight on your phone. There's not enough natural light in the hallway to be able to see."

Yes, please, I thought. Just what I need. To stand side by side with Aiden in a dark closet. In a house by ourselves.

It wouldn't surprise me in the slightest if he could hear my heart hammering behind my rib cage. After all, the only thing covering it was one thin layer of white cotton and the flimsy protection of my skin, which hummed like a live wire at his nearness.

If someone held that voltage checker in the scant space separating our bodies, it would have lit up like the Fourth of freaking July.

Aiden flipped the main power off, and we were plunged into darkness.

I let out an audible breath as he shifted slightly, the skin of his arm brushing my shoulder. He smelled like a soapy pine forest which sounded so much less sexy than it smelled. I wanted to crush that scent into crystals and snort it.

"Can you, uh"—he paused—"the flashlight?"

"Right," I exhaled. I pulled my phone from where it was tucked into the pocket of my joggers, almost dropping it when my hands shook a little.

The light was garish and harsh, and when I glanced up at him, a muscle tightened ominously in his jaw as his eyes were straightforward on the fuse box.

"See that screw there on the far right of the blown fuse?"

I moved the flashlight but had to shift closer to get a clear view of it. "Mm-hmm."

"That's what you unscrew to remove the wire," he explained. "Do you have the flathead?"

Nodding, I lowered the phone so I could reach my other hand into my pocket.

"I'll take the phone," he said.

Passing it to him, I willed myself to stop thinking about anything except replacing that motherfucking fuse because the things running through my head were positively indecent.

They got worse when he extended his arm behind me to angle the light so I could see more clearly.

In my head, I had an image of myself as a marionette doll, and he could pull and tug me into the right position simply by plucking a single string. Each corresponding body part would bend to his will. What I wanted was to slide closer and see what would happen if I moved in front of him.

Would he curl one of those big hands around my hip and yank me back against him?

Would he drop the phone, wrap his arm around the front of me, slide it down the opening in my shirt?

Would he slide his arm around my waist? Pluck at the tie of my joggers and shove them out of his way?

In the light, my hand visibly shook when I lifted it to unscrew the fuse.

"Hey," he said quietly.

My hand froze midair. "What?"

"Take a deep breath." I did as he asked. "If you're nervous to do this, I can take over."

Take over.

I wanted him to take over.

Why was this happening to me? And with this man? I was always the strong one. The together one. The take-charge one.

And in that tiny, dark closet, I wanted him to absolutely dominate me.

Aiden and I were talking about two entirely different things, of that I was certain.

But still, I slid to the side so that my back was to his chest, and when he inhaled, a sharp quick pull of breath, I felt something powerful course under my skin.

"Please," I whispered. I wanted to turn around and face him, whirl in his arms and press myself against his body. "Please take over," I begged quietly.

For a beat, the air between us was so thick I couldn't breathe.

If this was all in my head, I could hardly imagine facing him again.

"Shit," he grumbled, a delicious vibration of sound at my back.

I felt his nose next to my hair, and he inhaled. His chest brushed my back, not accidentally, and not quickly.

The hand holding the screwdriver planted against the wall next to the fuse box, and I arched my neck. His breath hit hot against the skin of my neck. And then, oh, and then, his lips coasted against the shell of my ear. I shivered, and against my ass, he pushed closer.

Not in my head.

Not alone in this.

Because I *felt* him.

"Is—" Whatever he was going to say next didn't matter.

"Isabel?" Emmett yelled. "I can't turn any of the lights on!"

Aiden backed up. The screwdriver fell out of my hand with a noisy clatter, and I moved away from him. I couldn't even make eye contact as I frantically picked up the screwdriver and held it out to him. He took it.

I called out to Emmett, "Hang on, bud. We're working on it."

"I'll finish up," Aiden said, his voice rough.

I nodded, escaping into the safety of the hallway. I'd just lifted my eyes to look at him when Emmet slid around the corner with Anya right behind him.

"Iz? Can Anya stay and play when he's done?"

I could hardly even focus on what he said, but I saw Aiden blink rapidly. He might have had shaking hands as he unscrewed the circuit and yanked out the attached wire, but his jaw was tight, his entire frame looked like a string about to break. He was just as rattled as I was.

"Please, Daddy," she begged. "I don't want to hang out at the gym again."

Aiden's eyes briefly flicked to mine, then moved to his daughter. "They might have plans, gingersnap."

"We don't," Emmett said. "We were just going to hang out here all day."

The kids turned their pleading gazes to me, and I tried to force

166

a smile. "It's fine with me, but I'm leaving the decision up to your daddy, Anya."

Aiden fitted the new circuit into the slot, attached the wire, and quickly tightened the screw. When he flipped the main breaker into the on position, the hallway flooded with light. Along with it, some of my tension seemed to ebb naturally. If I hadn't felt the way he wanted me, I'd have thought I imagined the whole thing. Because when Aiden tossed the tools back into the bag and turned to us, he looked perfectly normal again.

"You sure she wouldn't be an imposition?" he asked.

I shook my head. "If she doesn't mind frozen pizza for lunch, she's more than welcome."

He ruffled his daughter's hair. "You win, kiddo." The kids whooped loudly as Aiden returned his attention to me. "Thank you. I shouldn't be more than a couple of hours."

"She's doing me a favor," I told him. "Now I don't have to entertain Emmett."

Emmett rolled his eyes. "Come on, Anya. Lemme show you the trampoline we have in the gym room."

They darted into the room to my left, and Aiden watched with a slight smile on his face.

"You're sure?" he asked now that they were out of earshot, though his gaze stayed firmly on the kids.

For that, I was thankful.

I kept my tone light and even. "Now I don't owe you for the circuit breaker."

His eyes found mine.

"Thank you," I told him.

Aiden didn't answer. But he must have clenched his teeth because that muscle popped again. As I walked him out, neither of us speaking, I knew that I had to pull my shit together. Because the more this happened, the wilder I felt anytime I was around him.

At the front door, he paused. "I'll be here no later than one," he promised.

I nodded.

With the door firmly closed behind him, I sank against the wall and let out a deep breath.

CHAPTER 17

Isabel

APPARENTLY, IF I'D EVER WANTED TO DELVE INTO THE Hennessy family history, all I needed to do was hang out with Anya for a few hours.

Over frozen pizza hot from a working oven, she told me all about her uncles (Beckham, Clark, and Deacon) and her aunt (Eloise). She told me about her grandparents and their favorite foods and how Eloise bought her pretty princess things.

She was a sweet girl and shared information in the way that only a girl well and truly loved could. There was no moment of pause as she talked about how she wished she had cousins, and how she slept with a picture of her mommy by her bed.

"What happened to your mom?" Emmett asked.

I watched them carefully but didn't chastise Emmett for asking. I'd learned, from my own experience, that it was something worse when people avoided the reality you'd grown up in.

Anya finished chewing her pizza. "She's in heaven. She got cancer."

Emmett glanced at me, wide-eyed, and I nodded in encouragement.

"I'm sorry she died," he told her.

"Me too. I only kinda remember her, though." She shrugged. "My daddy tells me stories about her a lot. So I don't forget."

"That's a good thing for a dad to do," I told her. I picked at the piece of crust on my plate. Anya and I shared many commonalities, but the way they played out was very different. Brooke never really talked to us about our dad after he died. Only that his absence left her alone and short of funds. My own memories of him were spotty and certainly nothing that would be told as a bedtime story.

"He's the best dad," she asserted. "He tries to bake her cookies for me even though he can't get them right."

I smiled. "She made good cookies?"

Anya nodded, then studied my face carefully. "Do you bake?"

Emmett laughed. "No way, Isabel is the worst baker in the world."

"Hey," I argued.

Anya's face scrunched in thought. "I don't really remember her baking. My grandma told me my mom was sweet as sugar and twice as nice. And *everyone* loved her because she was nice to every person she met."

Her words were so innocent, and no matter how much I was feeling for her dad, I felt the pang of what they'd lost. The absence of Aiden's wife left a ragged hole he was trying to fill by moving here.

Who was I to think that I could ever attempt to fill it? He'd married this person. Had a child with her. Quit his career at the very peak in order to care for them both, and from what I knew, didn't hold an ounce of regret in leaving all of it behind.

"Your mom sounds like she was an amazing person," I told her gently. "I wish I could've met her."

Anya smiled, but her eyes were a little sad.

Emmett pushed his plate away. "Wanna go in the treehouse?"

"I'll clean up," I said when Anya nodded.

The two scampered outside, and as I loaded the dishwasher and wiped down counters, I tried to untangle everything I was feeling. My tendency under normal circumstances would be to hit the bag. To push my body to sweaty exhaustion until I could make sense of what was tumbling through my head. At the moment, it wasn't an option, and it made me feel twitchy and uncomfortable.

Anya's words about her mom had me feeling twitchy for an entirely different reason.

Memories of the one who raised us, they were murky, not all good. But not all bad either. Briefly, I thought of the bracelet in the metal box.

I set the plate of leftover pizza in the fridge, and when the door closed, I found myself staring at a photo of Molly and me at a Wolves game. Suddenly, I couldn't call my sister fast enough, after weeks of not really knowing what to say.

Hopping up on the kitchen island, I brought up her name and started a FaceTime.

It was her last couple of days on a work trip, but when she got home, she'd be in the final stretch before the wedding. I held my breath when she connected the call.

She smiled, but it was restrained, her eyes a little wary.

I'd done that.

I started tearing up immediately. "I'm sorry," I said in a wobbly voice.

"Oh, Iz," she sighed. "I'm sorry too. I dumped it on you. I should have known better."

"Did I ruin your wedding planning?"

She laughed. "No. That's the beauty of having a wedding planner. She's taking care of almost everything."

I nodded. "Good."

"You at home?"

Still, even though none of us lived here anymore, we called it home. I nodded again. "Watching Emmett for a couple of days because everyone has a life except me. How's work?"

"Good." She tucked a piece of hair behind her ear. "Are you okay, Iz?"

I took a deep breath. "It shouldn't have taken me this long to reach out to you."

"You say that like I'm surprised it did," she teased.

I exhaled a laugh. "I'm a little slow to process things sometimes. The twins stopped by the gym, but I think they could tell I wasn't really ready to talk about it."

"Well, if it helps, Logan wasn't exactly jumping up and down for joy about it either," she admitted. "But he said that as long as he still gets to walk me down the aisle, he doesn't care who's sitting in that church."

"For as much as he and I are alike," I said, "he's way more levelheaded than I am."

"True," Molly agreed easily.

I glared at the screen, and my sister laughed.

"You know what knocked some sense into me today?"

"*So* hard to say."

I rolled my eyes but couldn't help but smile. "So much of what I remember about Brooke is just … muddled. When I actually try to remember what it was like when she was our mom, most of my memories are fuzzy." I exhaled. "And I was listening to a seven-year-old girl talking about memories of her own mom, and I realized that so much of what scares me about Brooke showing up isn't even based on what I remember of her."

Molly's brow furrowed as she listened, but she didn't interrupt.

"I cannot predict, no matter how much I try to imagine it, what she might say or do. And there is nothing more terrifying to me," I admitted quietly.

"Brooke is something you can't control."

Eventually, I nodded. "Maybe it doesn't make sense, but even hearing you, or Claire, or Lia say that I don't have to talk to her if I don't want to made it even worse. Because what if she is awful?" I paused. "What if she's awful to *you*? Or the twins? I will never forgive myself if I wasn't right next to you for that."

Molly smiled. "Even if she comes, and even if she's not a perfect guest, we'd handle it." She shrugged. "That's what we do, you know?"

"I would shank her ass if she ruined your wedding day."

She laughed. "I know."

Emmett ran into the house, breathless and red-faced. "Iz? Umm, we have a problem."

"What is it?"

"Hi, Emmett," Molly called.

He ignored her, and a pit yawned wide and dark in my belly. "Anya and I were playing in the treehouse, and umm, she wanted to show me something, and ..." He paused, his hands wringing nervously. "She kinda ... climbed out on one of the branches, and now she can't get down."

"Oh, shit," I breathed. "Molly, hang on."

Her face bent in concern. "Can I call someone to come help?"

I threw the slider into the backyard open. "Everyone's gone," I hissed. "That's why I'm here."

"Who's on the branch?" Molly asked.

I gave her a look. "Aiden's daughter."

"Oh, shit."

I walked around the tree and saw her. Anya was on a branch even higher than the roof of the treehouse. She was gripping it tightly, her legs dangling on either side.

"Can you help me get down, Miss Isabel?" she asked, voice wobbly with nerves.

"Yeah, sweetie, I will be *right* there, okay? You are doing great sitting there like that," I answered with way more fucking calm than I was feeling.

"What can I do?" I heard Molly ask.

I blinked, my hand rubbing my forehead as I thought. "Umm, I need to hang up, but … listen, if you don't hear back from me in like, ten minutes, can you call Aiden at the gym?"

"Of course. Love you, Iz."

Eyes trained on Anya, I replied, "Love you too."

I hung up and handed the phone to Emmett. Studying Anya's position, and the size of the branch, I spoke quietly to her as I moved directly beneath where she was. "Have you tried scooting backward, sweetie?"

She nodded frantically. "It made the branch wobble, and I got scared."

"That's okay. Being scared is totally normal, Anya." I sucked in a deep breath. "Even if we're afraid, we can still do brave things when it counts."

Anya looked down at me, and I saw tears in her eyes. My heart absolutely turned inside out at the sight of those big eyes.

"If I climb up there, do you think you'd be able to try again?"

Anya swallowed, then nodded slowly.

Emmett looked nervous, and I crouched in front of him. "Okay, here's the game plan. You hold the phone and keep your eyes on her while I climb up. I think I can reach her where she's sitting." I took a deep breath. "Just talk to her normally, okay?"

He nodded, face pale, cheeks red. "I can do that."

I dropped a kiss on the top of his head and then whispered in his ear. "You remember how to make an emergency call, right? We won't need it, but I need to know just in case."

Emmett exhaled. "Yeah. I know how."

"Okay, good."

I blew out a hard breath as I climbed up into the treehouse. "How the hell did she do this?" I muttered as I reached the entrance. Using the railing around the edge, I braced my foot on the edge of one window, clutched the line of the roof with both hands, and boosted myself up. The treehouse made an ominous creak as

I moved carefully over the roof and found the branch she was on. There was one lower than her, and I pressed my foot against it to test the weight-bearing.

"Okay, Anya, remember when you said I looked like Wonder Woman?" At her nod, I exhaled steadily. "Well, we're both going to channel her. I'm going to keep my feet on this lower branch right here and hold onto the one you're on. Once I'm a few feet out, can you try to scoot back a little? I'll be able to grab your arm and help you come back all the way."

I kept my movements slow and steady, but each inch I moved felt like a mile. Anya watched me with huge eyes, and I made sure to smile encouragingly as I inched closer. Now that I was closer, I did not really like the look of the branch she was on, which swayed as she shifted her weight. Every time she did, her hands gripped even more tightly.

"Here we go," I said as I got closer. How I was standing put my head about level with her chest. It wasn't perfect positioning, but I trusted this branch a lot more than the one she was on. "I'm going to grab your arm, Anya. Keep holding tight to the branch just like you're doing and slowly start backing up. It's okay if it's teeny tiny little movements. Once you're back far enough, I'll scoop you right up, okay?"

A tear slipped down her face, and she hiccupped. "O-okay."

"I want you to look at me." When she did, I held her gaze. "You can do this, sweetheart. You are strong and brave, and once we get down, we will have whatever treat you can find in the pantry, all right?"

"Even your Pop-Tarts?" Emmett asked. "She really likes you if she's willing to share those."

I managed a strained laugh. "I'll give you the whole box, kiddo."

Anya nodded. "Okay."

I took one more shuffle sideways and the branch creaked. With a slow exhale, I extended my hand and gripped her upper arm.

But instead of holding onto the branch, like she was supposed to, Anya turned her weight and grasped frantically at my arm with her other hand.

"Okay, okay," I breathed, "move slow, sweetie. You're just fine."

But then she swung her leg over, like she was going to try to clamber into my arms exactly as I stood. The last thing I heard before we fell was the violent snap of the branch, and Anya screaming my name.

CHAPTER 18

Aiden

"Thanks, Aiden," my client said. "Best sparring session I've ever had."

There was a reason I'd worked him so hard, but it wasn't like I was going to explain it to him.

I nodded. "Glad to hear it. Next time we'll focus on your footwork. You still have a tendency to want to square up in front of me, you're leaving too much of your body open."

He grinned. "After today, that's the last thing I want. Felt like I was facing you back in your fighting days."

Somehow I managed a polite smile. There was a reason for that. In that tiny closet, I'd almost descended on Isabel like a ravenous fucking beast. One more second, and without the interruption that had stopped me, I would've torn clothes, knocked over shelves, held her still while I lost my mind from want.

It wouldn't have been slow or sweet or respectful. And if I was expected to share space with her, even for five minutes, I needed to sweat all of it out.

"I'll see you next week," I told him.

"Sounds good." He hooked his gym bag over his shoulder, smiling at Emily as she approached with the gym phone in hand.

Judging by the look in her eye, I was not going to get out of here like I wanted. I was already itching to go get Anya.

"Phone's for you," Emily said. "You can take it on the cordless or in your office."

I sighed. "Did they say who it was?"

"It's Molly Ward. Isabel's sister."

Brows lowered in confusion, I took the cordless from her outstretched hand.

"This is Aiden." It was still loud in the gym, and I pressed my free hand to my other ear to hear her better. And as soon as I did, my stomach dropped out of my feet. "Shit," I barked. "And you haven't heard back from her?"

"No, I'm so sorry. And I don't want to distract her by trying to call if she's right in the middle of climbing down with Anya."

I jogged back to my office and snagged my keys and cell phone. "Unfortunately this doesn't surprise me. My daughter has a tendency to do this whenever she wants a little extra attention."

"I'm sure she's okay," Molly insisted. "Isabel would never let anything happen to her."

Words stuck in my throat, because even if I knew Molly was probably right, and the likelihood that Anya was hurt was slim, even the idea of it had my body going cold with terror.

Losing Beth had been awful. Exhausting. Heartbreaking.

But if anything happened to Anya … I wasn't sure I could survive it.

"I'm leaving the gym now, but this is my cell," I rattled off my number and Molly repeated it. "Call me if you hear anything."

"I promise, I will." Molly said my name quietly. "Just take a deep breath, okay? Especially before you get behind the wheel."

I clenched my teeth, but somehow her voice was comforting enough, kind enough, that I was able to do as she said.

Disconnecting the call after thanking Molly, I shoved my phone in my pocket and yelled for one of the trainers. He looked exactly like one of the other guys, and they were both in college, and I still couldn't remember their fucking names.

"I need you to stay and help Emily close up. If you can't, ask the other one." I snapped my fingers. "What's his name again?"

He grinned. "He's Grady, I'm Gavin."

"No fucking wonder," I mumbled.

"What?"

"Nothing. You can stay?"

"Yeah, no problem."

I jogged out of the building with a shove to the front door, my feet pounding on the pavement.

The peel of my tires drew a few dirty looks as I turned out of the parking lot, as did my driving abilities as I broke just about every land speed record from the gym back to the house.

She was probably fine. My daughter, the little shit, climbed everywhere. This was hardly the first time she'd bitten off more than she could chew. But I was used to it. My family was used to it.

Isabel wasn't.

And that was probably why Anya did it in the first place, to gain her notice. My hands tightened uselessly on the steering wheel. Of course she'd want Isabel's notice.

I was no better than my daughter because Isabel's notice was turning me into an animal. At least in my head.

That was something to deal with later, as my foot pressed just a little bit harder on the gas, the roar of the engine matching the energy under my skin.

By the time I pulled onto their street, I felt the same kind of tense, rolling motion in my stomach that I used to get before my fights. It wasn't nerves, not exactly. It was not knowing the outcome of a short, specific window of time. No outlet of the energy making my feet bounce, no way to take control of the situation yet.

That's when I saw the red and white of the ambulance in the driveway.

"Oh, God," I breathed. I wasn't sure if it was a plea or a prayer or a way to prepare myself for the absolute worst.

The back of the ambulance was open, no one was in sight. I saw a few neighbors standing in their front yard trying to get a glimpse of what was happening.

I yanked the truck up onto the curb and threw the gear shift into park, sprinting around the side of the house into the backyard.

I saw the back of the paramedics first, Emmett standing to the side next. He was wiping tears.

"Anya?" I shouted.

A male paramedic turned and I saw Isabel reclining on the gurney, her arm in the hand of the other medic, blood on her temple, and my daughter wrapped tight in her arms. Anya turned her face to me with a smile, and my panic eased immediately. Her grip never lessened on Isabel.

"What happened?" I asked, running my hand over Anya's back.

"We fell," Anya said.

My heart stopped when I saw the broken branch on the grass.

"Your daughter is fine," the paramedic assured me.

Isabel's eyes finally met mine, and I saw her apology before she even opened her mouth. "I should've been watching them more closely."

I held up my hand to stop her. "It's okay, I promise."

The sight of the cut at her hairline, the way she winced when the female paramedic pressed onto her wrist, it was almost too much.

"Is it broken?" I asked.

The woman turned to me and shook her head. "I don't think

so. But it's almost impossible to know without getting it checked out at the hospital."

Isabel's eyes closed tightly. "I *don't* need to go to the hospital."

Judging by the look the paramedics shared, this was not the first time she'd said it.

Instead of arguing with the bleeding woman on the gurney, like I wanted to, I turned and set my hand on Emmett's shoulder. "You okay, buddy?"

He nodded, but I could tell he'd been crying.

The guy tending to Isabel's forehead gave Emmett a smile. "He was the one who called nine-one-one as soon as they fell." Isabel hissed when he cleaned around the cut. "I don't think it needs stitches, but Miss Ward, you very well might have a concussion, I'd strongly advise you to let us take you in."

Isabel glanced at me, but her eyes didn't hold mine for very long. "I don't feel nauseous, I never lost consciousness—"

"That you know of," the woman wrapping her wrist interjected.

Anya snuggled her face into Isabel's neck, her arms tightening to the point that Isabel winced.

"Gingersnap," I said quietly, "can we give the paramedics a little room to finish checking her out?"

When Anya didn't immediately get off Isabel's lap, Isabel turned her head and whispered something I couldn't make out. Her good hand smoothed soothing circles on my daughter's back, and Anya nodded at whatever she heard.

The sight of it almost knocked me to my knees. I couldn't breathe through it, couldn't even name it if I tried.

"She's okay," Isabel said quietly. "I don't mind."

Through the roaring in my head, my heart, all I could manage was a slight nod.

The woman finished wrapping Isabel's wrist and gestured for me to step away from the gurney with her. I swiped a hand over my mouth and tried to gather my racing thoughts.

"Your daughter is very lucky," she said quietly.

"You sure she's okay?"

She nodded. "From what the boy said, Miss Ward took the entire impact with how she turned her body. Her side is going to have a nasty bruise, but it seems like her wrist hit first."

My jaw tightened dangerously. "You think she should go in?"

With a sigh, she shrugged her shoulders. "We can't force her. Emmett agreed that she never passed out when she fell. Her wrist and hip took the brunt of her fall, but there's no telling exactly where or how hard she hit her head."

Isabel smiled at something Anya told her, even as the guy finished cleaning the cut, and when he covered it with a butterfly bandage, she never took her eyes off my daughter.

The way my heart raced took on a dangerous edge, a hazardous speed that I couldn't quite pin down.

Too soon.

Too soon.

Too soon.

Isabel as a temptation for me alone was one thing, hidden in quiet moments between the two of us where it was about greedy hands and whispered desires. But Isabel showing me glimpses of a future I'd mourned was something I wasn't prepared for.

"She can't be alone tonight," the paramedic said, interrupting the speeding train of my thoughts. "She mentioned her family is out of town, but I don't know how soon someone could be here. She didn't want to worry them if she could avoid it."

"I'll talk to her," I replied.

Like she heard me, or heard the hard-edged tone of my voice, Isabel's eyes locked onto mine.

No longer did she look apologetic or pale.

Instantly, I was transported back to the night we were in the gym, she had that same combative look in her eye.

As I approached the gurney, Isabel sat up and my daughter

finally unfolded herself. Anya held out her arms to me, and I gathered her into a tight hug. Her small body clutched in my arms, I finally let out a full breath.

"Am I in trouble?" she whispered.

I smiled a little. "No. But no more climbing tall trees, okay, gingersnap?"

"Okay, daddysnap." She leaned back to smile at me, and my stomach turned over when I saw a smudge of dirt on her cheek.

"Can you go watch some TV with Emmett while I talk to Miss Isabel?"

She nodded.

I set her down, and gave a manly nod to Emmett. "Thanks for taking good care of her, bud."

He smiled, the color in his face looking better. "You're welcome."

The paramedic helped Isabel stand from the gurney, and she winced when she brought her full weight to her feet. Both medics watched her carefully as she walked toward me, but her balance seemed fine, even if her progress was slow. I snagged a chair from the patio table next to me and slid it closer to her.

She smiled gratefully, bracing her hand on the back. "I should probably get some coverage for class tomorrow, huh?"

I exhaled in a sharp burst. "I'd say so."

"I'll call Kelly," she sighed. "She owes me. But I'll be back on Monday."

Tilting my head, I regarded her steadily. "If you're making a call right now, it's going to be someone in your family to see who can come back and stay with you."

She swore. "I need to call Molly."

"How long until she can be here?" I asked.

Isabel wouldn't meet my eyes. "I'll just … text her real quick."

"How long until anyone can be here?" I amended.

She ignored me, pulling her phone out of her pocket and tapping out a text. After she hit send, I snagged it from her hand.

"Hey," she protested.

"*All good here. Sore wrist and a scratch on my forehead. No need to worry,*" I read out loud. I pinned her with an incredulous look, and she set her jaw. "Are you out of your fucking mind?"

The paramedics were still within earshot, and the guy approached us immediately. "Sir, she cannot be left alone tonight. Someone has to wake her up every three to four hours, and I'd strongly advise against leaving her alone."

With a lift of my chin, I handed her the phone back. "You have one chance to call someone over here."

Isabel swallowed visibly but tucked her phone in her pocket. "I am not forcing them home from their jobs, or their trips because I bumped my head. I am fine. I'll ice my wrist and take some Tylenol and set an alarm."

I folded my arms over my chest. "You're going to wake yourself up if you've got a concussion?"

She shifted on her feet. "I can ask a neighbor."

"To stay with you all night?"

Isabel rolled her lips between her teeth and stared past me. "Mmmhmm."

The paramedic shook his head.

"It's fine," I told him. "I'll handle it."

Isabel's eyes narrowed. The paramedic went back to the gurney to help his partner load up their equipment.

"You can do all those things if you want to. The ice, the Tylenol, the rest," I said evenly. She eyed me suspiciously. I leaned in until less than an inch separated our faces. "But you will do it at my house, and if you argue with me right now, I'll load you up and drop your stubborn ass off at the hospital myself, do you understand?"

Tense silence stretched like a rubber band, and she opened her mouth to argue. I saw the heat of it in her blue, blue eyes.

"I get it," I said before she could disagree. "I hate it when people need to take care of me. Nothing makes me feel more powerless."

Isabel huffed out an annoyed breath.

"This is not just about you, okay?" I gentled my tone. "I owe you, Isabel."

At the sound of her name, her eyes softened.

I'd never said her first name out loud before, or not to her, at least.

Something switched in her head, maybe I'd never know what, because she pinched her eyelids closed, let out a slow, deep breath, and then nodded.

"Good," I said quietly. "Do you want to pack your bag or should I?"

CHAPTER 19

Aiden

THE INSIDE OF MY TRUCK WAS SEPARATED INTO TWO VERY distinct moods on the drive back to my and Anya's house. The back seat, holding Emmett and Anya, was giggles and laughter, her telling him all the toys she had, all the things they could do during their sleepover.

The front seat was a bit quieter. Isabel stared out the window, her black backpack at her feet. From the corner of my eye, I could see the dried blood on her temple, and my hands tightened on the steering wheel.

Her silence didn't bother me, because I wasn't sure what to say either.

Guess what? Six hours ago, I imagined screwing you against the closet door, and here we are, on the way to my house, so you can spend the night.

The words didn't exactly flow naturally off the tongue.

I opened my mouth to say … something … and I stopped myself. That indecision rankled. Nails on a chalkboard type discomfort.

I never second-guessed my decisions, never doubted what my next move would be.

But this position I found myself in—one of my own making—had me on unsteady ground.

Isabel shifted in the passenger seat, and I caught the way she tried to hide her wince.

"Did you take anything yet?" I asked.

She glanced at me, her eyes holding that same wariness as when we first met. Eventually, she shook her head. "I feel like I got hit by a car," she admitted. "I think the adrenaline is wearing off."

"Tomorrow's going to be even worse."

Her head angled back, she sighed heavily. "I know."

I pulled the truck into our neighborhood, and Emmett pressed his face closer to the window. "Cool! You guys are right by the lake."

"Pretty close," I told him. "We can walk there after dinner if your aunt wants to take a nap."

"What are we having for dinner?" Anya asked. "I'm starving."

"Please don't let Isabel cook," Emmett begged.

Isabel turned her head and smiled. "Hey, I didn't let you starve this weekend, did I?"

"Not technically," he muttered under his breath.

I caught myself smiling a little at the exchange.

Our house came into view, and her head tilted with interest when I slowed. It looked small, from the front, with the pine trees towering over the top of it. But inside, it opened to the kind of space and view I never could've provided for Anya in California. She had a yard to play in. Mountains and water practically in our backyard. It was as idyllic of a childhood as I could give her, as the sole person responsible for her upbringing.

And for the first time since Beth died—no matter what the circumstances were—I was going to walk into the front door with another woman so that she could sleep under our roof.

As I hit the garage door button, I couldn't help wondering what the fuck I was doing, bringing her here like this. The instinct to do so, standing in her backyard, had been overwhelming and impossible to ignore. I never would've been able to walk out of that door if I'd known she was alone.

This, however, was different. Because now, there was no going back from it.

Denying that I was attracted to her was a fool's errand. I could lie to myself about a lot of things, but not this, no matter what had grown between us the last couple of weeks.

But having her in my home, the place I shared with my daughter, after the experience they'd just shared, felt like I was tempting fate.

I parked the truck and let the kids out, watching carefully to make sure Isabel was walking steadily as she waited for me to unlock the door into the house. Her progress was slow, her hip clearly bothering her more as time passed.

As soon as I opened the door, she gave me a subdued smile as she passed into the kitchen through the laundry room.

"Come on," Anya yelled, sprinting for the stairs, "I'll show you my room. I have a pink canopy!"

"Uhh, okay."

Isabel exhaled a soft laugh. "I don't think he'll act suitably impressed." As she walked slowly into the family room, her gaze lit on the wall of windows, pitched in an A-frame, overlooking the sprawling view of Lake Sammamish. "It's beautiful," she said.

"Thanks," I replied. "Do you want to go straight to bed? Or rest on the couch?"

Her eyes flew to mine, her cheeks becoming a shade of pink. "Which room should I use? I wouldn't mind a nap."

I blew out a hard breath because I hadn't thought this piece through. The guest room, which I'd assumed Emmett would use, was across the hall from Anya's room on the second floor. The third bedroom—my own—was on the main floor, along the back of the house with the same view as the family room. I gestured in that direction. "You can sleep back there. I don't want to make you do stairs."

Without argument, Isabel walked in that direction, and when I pulled the Tylenol out of the cabinet in the kitchen, I had to take a moment. Hands braced on the kitchen counter, I pushed through the feeling that I'd made a massive mistake by doing this.

As soon as I strode through the living room, painkillers in one hand and an ice pack in the other, and caught sight of her sitting on the edge of my bed, I knew I had.

She took the pain meds without complaint, allowing me to pull back the covers so she could slide in. Not a word was spoken as she settled herself onto my pillow, let me set the ice pack on her hip. For that, I was glad because I didn't even know what to say.

Isabel Ward was the blood-red apple, tempting just by being herself. She was the thing I shouldn't want but might wreck the world around me in order to try.

One taste, even the smallest indulgence, and I'd know exactly what I was missing.

If I allowed myself to, I'd want to devour her whole. Because there were no half measures, not with her. There might be a hundred things I didn't know about her. What her favorite food was. If she was a good dancer. If she liked action movies or romances or stories that made her cry. If she liked to read or if ice cream in the winter sounded good to her.

The frantic urge to uncover each and every thing took me by surprise. Because I'd never felt anything like it.

It was impossible not to compare it to Beth, and I hated that too. Beth had been slow, sweet growth. And this ... this was not in the same universe.

I walked out of the bedroom and took a deep breath because I didn't need to figure it out immediately.

While she slept soundly in my bed, I fed the kids dinner, and we walked down to the lake for a little bit.

After we got back to the house, I quietly pushed the door open. She was on her back now, her wrapped wrist laying on her chest, which rose and fell evenly.

"Are you going to wake her up?" Anya whispered.

I ushered her away from the door. "Soon. She's only been asleep for a couple of hours. I'll give her another hour and then see if I can wake her up."

Emmett gave me a nervous look from where he sat on the couch. "And if you can't?"

"I'll be able to," I promised him. "She'll be okay, bud. You said she never passed out when she … when they fell?" I almost stuttered over the question because it sparked a dangerous, violent reaction in my head if I tried to imagine her and Anya crashing to the ground. Something volatile.

He shook his head. "No, she said way too many bad words when she hit the ground."

Reluctantly, I smiled. "That's a good sign." I tilted my head toward the bedroom. "Your parents gonna be mad when they find out about this?"

His eyes got huge. "Oh yeah. I was actually supposed to FaceTime with my mom tonight, but maybe I'll just ignore it so she doesn't find out and try to get a flight home. My dad has to coach tomorrow."

If I had to guess, missing a game would be an easy sacrifice for both of them, but I didn't tell him that.

"Is Isabel's phone in her backpack?"

He shrugged. "Probably."

Her pack was still sitting on the floor by the door, right where she'd left it when she walked in. After turning on a movie for the kids, I picked it up, pausing before I unzipped the front pocket.

The phone was right there, and when I touched the screen, I saw a few texts and two missed calls from Paige.

"Do you know her passcode?" I asked Emmett.

"You're breaking into her phone? Cool." He motioned for it. "I know the pattern. Up, middle, down, then middle."

He tapped the screen, the phone unlocking immediately.

"You're not going to throw me under the bus if she kicks my ass for this, are you?"

Emmett laughed. "No. I'll tell her I did it."

With a nod, I walked out onto the back deck and pulled up the missed call. I hit the name of her sister-in-law and took a deep breath.

Paige answered on the first ring. "Holy shit, Isabel, I've been freaking out since Molly texted me. You *fell out of a tree?*"

I winced. "This is Aiden, actually. Her ... boss."

Deafening silence met my announcement.

"You're ..." She paused again. "Aiden Hennessy?"

"Yeah. I'm sorry to call you like this."

"Is she okay? Why do you have her phone?" Paige asked, the concern in her voice loud and clear.

"She's asleep, and I think she'll be fine. Sore, but nothing broken or seriously injured."

She exhaled heavily, then I heard her cover the microphone and repeat what I said to her husband. "I'm going to put you on speaker, Aiden. Logan wants to know what's going on. Is Emmett okay?"

"Yeah, he was a little rattled when I showed up at the house, but he's the one who called 911 when the branch broke. He's a brave kid."

Logan spoke next. "What happened exactly?"

I told them what I knew and what the paramedics relayed to me.

Paige made a tsking noise. "Why am I not surprised she'd be so damn stubborn about this?" Her voice wavered on the end. Then she sniffed, and I heard Logan murmur something quietly to her.

She sniffed again. "Sorry, Aiden, I just hate being away when something happens to my babies."

I smiled a little, imagining the woman in my bed as anyone's baby. "No apology necessary."

"You're sure she shouldn't go to the hospital?" Logan asked. "How do you know she doesn't have a concussion?"

"I don't," I answered honestly. "But I've had a couple myself, so I know what to look for. She's steady on her feet, she never passed out, no nausea, no confusion." I sat in a chair and stared out at the water, thought about the night in front of me. "I'll wake her every three to four hours, and if I have even the slightest worry, I promise I'll take her in."

"What about the kids?" Paige asked.

"My parents live about five minutes away. I can call my mom to come over here if it comes down to it."

She exhaled audibly. "Okay. Before we even talked to you, I decided to switch my flight to the first one out tomorrow. Logan is going to talk to his head coach, not sure if he'll be with me or not."

"I'll text you my address."

Paige paused. "She's going to hate that you called us. Like, a lot."

"Yeah, I figured as much," I answered wryly. "But I'm a parent. I'd want to know if it was me."

"We appreciate you telling us," Logan said.

"Gimme a second, honey," Paige said to her husband, and I heard the sound of a door closing a second later. "Just ... a word of advice, Aiden. If you're open to it."

My brow furrowed at the change in her tone. "Of course."

"Isabel is the most stubborn of the four girls, and that's ... a pretty impressive feat if you've met her sisters." She took a deep breath. "And underneath that is the kindest, biggest heart of anyone I know."

My face went hot. "Paige, I—"

She ignored me. "She will argue with you helping her. She will fight you every step of the way tonight, and I need you to promise me that you will ignore her when she says she can handle it herself or she doesn't need anything. Because knowing someone is there to take care of her is the only thing keeping me from losing my mind right now."

"I promise," I told her.

"But also," she continued, her tone perfectly polite, perfectly sweet, "if you upset her in any way, I'll make you wish you were never born."

My eyebrows popped up. "Umm, okay?"

"Good talk, Aiden. We'll see you in the morning."

Despite the warning, I walked back into the house with a smile on my face.

The kids were fully engrossed in their movie, and I walked quietly past the family room and down the hall to my bedroom.

The light from the hallway spilled into the opening, and Isabel hadn't moved from the last time I checked on her.

I crouched next to the bed and said her name quietly. Her eyelids fluttered, but she didn't wake.

Even as I held my breath before I raised my hand, I wondered at the intelligence of allowing myself even this slight touch.

Even before Paige had finished saying what she said, even before I recognized the deep swell of emotion in the words, I knew exactly what Paige was going to say about Isabel.

Because somehow, in the midst of all the mundane, I knew exactly who this woman was.

That was why the details didn't matter to me.

Carefully, I slid my fingertips along her cheekbone and let out a slow, shaky exhale. Her skin was so soft.

"Isabel," I said again. "Time to wake up."

She hummed. Her head turned toward my touch. "Wha—" she murmured sleepily.

My fingers trailed the hairline at the back of her neck, and I said her name again. My palm laid gently along her neck, my entire hand now framing her face.

Slowly, her eyelids fluttered, and she woke. "Aiden," she whispered.

"You know who I am. That's good."

"Mm-hmm." She inhaled, and I saw the slow trickle of awareness in her face at the way I was touching her.

I pulled my hand back even though that awareness told me it was a welcome touch. "You remember why you're here?"

"That fucking tree," she said, stifling a yawn.

I smiled. "What about the year?"

She told me. With a dry look, she also told me the president and what kind of car she drove.

"Are you hungry?" I asked.

"A little." She used her good hand to brace on the mattress and sit up. Her hair was a tangled mess, and it was a good thing she was injured. A good thing there were children in the other room. Because she looked so fucking irresistible, I had to step back from the bed.

"I'll go heat some lasagna," I told her.

With a slight shake of her head, Isabel opened her mouth, and like an idiot, I laid a finger over her petal-soft lips.

"No arguments," I said in a gruff voice. My finger slipped away from her mouth slowly, and her eyes were huge when she looked up at me.

"No arguments," she agreed quietly.

Paige's words swam through my head as I fixed her a plate and brought it to where she was propped up against my headboard. With perfect clarity, I understood her protective instincts toward Isabel. Not because she wasn't strong or because she couldn't handle herself. But because there was some soul-deep recognition that she was mine to protect.

That if anyone upset her, I'd make them wish they were never born.

Only once in my life had I ever felt like that. I'd married her. Loved her. And when I'd lost her, I mourned ever feeling that way again.

But as I watched Isabel eat, drink some water, and as I watched her hug my daughter good night like she was something precious, I already knew that somehow, by some magic, some miracle, it was happening again.

Nothing, absolutely nothing, could have terrified me more.

CHAPTER 20

Isabel

I MANAGED EVERY WAKE-UP JUST FINE.

Every three hours, Aiden pulled me from a deep sleep, surrounded in sheets that smelled like him. He never touched my face again, simply called my name or laid a gentle hand on top of the covers over my shoulder. His questions were innocuous—the year, my middle name, where I worked. At one point, he gave me more painkillers and a new ice pack for my wrist, and even with the frigid cold against my skin, I fell right back asleep.

Each time, I managed fine. So did he.

Until the last one.

No dreams were happening because I was too exhausted, too sore. But the last time he woke me up, it was still pitch-black in the room with only a weak path of light coming from the hallway. I'd hardly moved on the king-size mattress, sticking to one side and my back because my hip was too sore to roll to the other side.

His voice, low and quiet, pierced through the haze of sleep, and I found myself humming contentedly. My name on his lips made me want to curl up like a cat in his lap and arch my body into the sound, roll my back into his hands.

"Isabel, come on, you gotta wake up for me."

This time, his hand was skimming down my upper arm in small circles, and the calluses on his palms felt delicious on my skin.

"Hmm, that feels nice," I heard myself say.

His hand only froze for a moment but then continued. "Does it?" he asked quietly.

I pressed my face into his pillow and inhaled. I kept my eyes firmly shut because if I was dreaming this, I refused to wake up. I wanted to allow myself this moment of a loose, sleepy tongue, where I could say the things in my head without fear of embarrassment.

"Everything you do feels nice," I murmured. "I wish you'd do more."

Aiden was quiet for a moment, and cautiously, I opened my eyes in narrow slits to see his face in the dim light of the room. It was so terribly intimate, how closely he crouched down by the bed. He didn't sit on the mattress to possibly cause me discomfort. He'd given up his bed so I could get better sleep.

His profile was visible as I studied him, but I couldn't tell where he was looking. Maybe he was watching his hand on my arm because he moved from my upper arm, down around the curve of my elbow, allowing his fingertips to drag softly over my forearm, stopping just shy of the wrapping of my wrist. Then back up.

"Where did you sleep?" I asked him.

"The couch."

My lips curled up slightly. "You fit on that thing?"

"Not very well," he admitted. "But I've slept in much worse places."

I adjusted my head and stared openly at him. "Thank you for doing that for me."

The thick column of his throat moved in a heavy swallow, but he nodded. "I told you, I owe you, Isabel."

"No, you don't." I paused. "I did what anyone would've—"

The pressure of his hand increased as it coasted back up over my shoulder, and that was where it came to rest, the blunt edges of his fingertips tangling with my hair.

"I'm not talking about what anyone else would've done. I'm talking about what you did for Anya. And me." He shifted his weight, and I finally got a clearer look at his eyes. He wasn't looking at his hand; he was looking at me. "Thank you, Isabel. I need you to hear me say that."

I'd never had anyone look at me like Aiden was, and I had no clue what to make of it.

This wasn't reality, this tiny moment in his bedroom. And if I thought too hard about how little we knew about each other, I'd question my sanity. But he was looking at me like I was unexpected, and he wasn't sure how to handle me the right way. Aiden was looking at me like I belonged in his home, in his bed, and he just might be okay with that.

I let out a shaky breath. "You're welcome."

"What's your favorite food?" he asked suddenly.

I blinked at the change in topic, the change in tone. It was the only reason I answered honestly. "Strawberry Pop-Tarts."

Now it was Aiden's turn to blink. "No, it's not."

"You don't get to argue with me about it."

"No one's favorite food is Pop-Tarts after the age of seven."

"Well, mine is," I said indignantly. "They're delicious, and maybe you just haven't had one in a long time so you don't remember."

The smile that spread over his face was warm, and it made me all gooey inside, and I pressed my now-hot face back into the pillow that smelled like him. His warm smile turned into a low, amused chuckle.

"I had no idea you were this judgmental," I teased. "You better tell me your favorite food now."

"You're very demanding when you wake up."

That was because my filter was gone. That process had been a slow one, pushing through embarrassment, pushing through the first unsteady weeks, then the tiptoeing into a more balanced relationship. He didn't even realize that this was me, wide open.

But I did. And that was why it mattered, these quiet moments.

"Cranberry juice?" I asked.

He laughed, eyes tracing my features. "Getting warmer."

I had to bury my face into his pillow to hide my pleased smile.

Aiden moved from a crouching position to sitting on the floor, his back braced against the nightstand, and he turned his head to face me. I tucked my good hand up under the pillow and imagined that this was just … normal. The two of us trading whispered questions in bed. He grimaced, sending a glare over his shoulder at the table.

"What?" I asked.

"Nothing. Just the handle digging into my back." His eyes traced my face. "I'm too old to be sitting in places like this."

I pulled in a deep breath and decided not to weigh the wisdom of what was about to come out of my mouth. "You can lay up here," I whispered. "On top of the blanket," I rushed to add when his gaze sharpened.

After a weighty silence, Aiden finally answered. "You know I can't."

My lips pursed thoughtfully. "What if I draw an invisible line you're not allowed to cross?"

His eyelids fell closed, his chest rose and fell on a slow, steady inhale and exhale. "You are dangerous to my mental health, Isabel Ward."

I smiled even though he couldn't see me. I liked knowing that. I liked that he'd said it out loud. Maybe Aiden was just as aware that this wasn't reality, and we were allowed to make whispered admissions that might never see the light of day.

There were a million things I could've said to him, could've told him, in this last conversation of our long, sleepless night to-gether. Things no one knew about me, or things I wanted him to know about me. But I kept all those words inside because some-how, I knew this wasn't the time.

When Aiden opened his eyes and studied me, he seemed to be pondering the same depth of thoughts, judging by the thought-ful look on his face.

"It would confuse Anya," he said after a few seconds. My eye-brows lowered. "If she walked in here," Aiden explained.

Right.

I didn't have to make all my decisions through the lens of a child. And it was a timely reminder that he did.

"You're right."

"She already thinks you're a superhero, especially after today. No matter what invisible line is up"—he paused meaningfully—"if she saw us in bed together ..."

I nodded. "I get it."

My eyes burned hot, though, because it very much seemed like an hourglass had been turned over when I crawled into his bed, and I was watching the last few grains of sand slip through the opening.

"How do you feel?" he asked.

Carefully rolling onto my back, I took a quick assessment of my body. "My head doesn't hurt as bad as it did last night."

He held a hand out. "Let me see your wrist."

I turned again and laid my taped wrist gently in his palm. His face held no expression while he turned it, smoothed his fingers over the area.

"Swelling isn't too much worse, so that's a good sign." He glanced up at me. "No tingling in your fingers?"

I shook my head.

When his fingertip traced the edge of the tape and brushed the skin over my knuckles, I made a discovery that maybe no woman in history had ever discovered: if the right man, with the right fingers, touched the skin on your knuckles, you could feel it spread warm and slow over your entire body.

I couldn't breathe, let alone answer his question.

My lack of speaking didn't seem to draw his notice because his eyes stayed trained on our hands. Slowly, so slowly, and so gently, he found the edge of the tape and started unraveling it.

Over the years, I'd seen him inflict incredible violence. Leave his opponents bleeding and sweat-drenched on the mat.

And watching his hands slowly peel away the medical tape like he was unwrapping a priceless gift almost made me burst into tears.

I hated when people took care of me. The last time I had the flu, I crawled my ass into bed with a veritable drugstore set up on my nightstand and told everyone to give me forty-eight hours to ride out the plague in peace.

All anyone had to do was ask the paramedics who helped me what kind of patient I was.

The worst. I was the worst patient in the world.

What was it about Aiden that made me feel safe to be in this position?

I shifted, bringing my arm to a better position for him, and he glanced up with a tiny smile.

It was easily four o'clock in the morning, and he didn't seem to be in a hurry.

"What's *your* favorite food?" I whispered.

His hands paused in their unwrapping to check the bruising on the underside of my wrist with only the slightest brush of his fingers.

I shivered.

He noticed.

Before he answered, he went back to removing the wrap. "Not strawberry Pop-Tarts."

I laughed.

His eyes landed on my mouth. "You don't laugh very often."

"Neither do you."

"My brother made you laugh," he said casually.

Oh, my heart. It wouldn't surprise me if Aiden heard it thrashing wildly where he sat.

"He said something funny." When Aiden pinned me with a searching look, I simply raised my eyebrows. "What?"

"Nothing."

"You still haven't told me your favorite food."

His smile was slight and sexy. "I called Paige when you were sleeping."

As a distraction technique, it was really effective. My mouth fell open. "You what?"

Aiden finished unwrapping my wrist and turned it carefully. But he had no choice but to release my hand when I sat up. My legs swung in front of him on the floor, so I tucked them up criss-cross underneath me.

"Why would you call her? The whole point of coming here was so no one knew."

"No," he countered, "the point of coming here was so that you didn't have to go to the hospital. She heard about the tree from Molly and called you multiple times."

"So you unlocked my phone and called her back?"

An eyebrow rose on his forehead imperiously. "Technically, Emmett unlocked your phone."

I gave him a withering look. Amazing how knuckle-stroking-al-most-orgasms only went so far when he took it upon himself to tell Paige about something without asking. My chin rose a notch. "You had no right to do that."

"I didn't have your permission, no." He got on his knees, hands braced on the edge of the mattress, bringing his face closer to mine. "But whether I had the right is debatable. You are in my home with a head injury, and the worst thing I could imagine as a parent is if something awful happened and I didn't know."

My withering look softened into something a little less ... withery because he wasn't wrong.

"She wasn't mad," he told me. "They switched to the first flight out this morning. I think they'll be here after breakfast."

My shoulders slumped. "I didn't want to worry anyone."

"I know."

Carefully, I flexed my fingers, turning my hand back and forth so I could see it in the light. It was swollen but not terribly. The bruising would be ugly, but I was so fortunate. Anya was so fortunate.

"But maybe," he said, "it's okay to let people worry about you every once in a while. It doesn't mean you're a burden. It sure as hell doesn't mean you're weak because that is the last thing you are."

I almost swayed in his direction. Once Logan and Paige got me and Emmett, once we pulled out of his driveway, I probably wouldn't see him for a few days. Certainly not like this.

In general, I wasn't an impulsive person. I was decisive, and that was different. It didn't take me long to decide about ... anything, really, because I always had the sense of which course of action made the most sense.

At this moment, I knew I was going to touch Aiden because I couldn't not touch him.

"I think I'm done sleeping," I said quietly. I inhaled slowly, and he was *so* close—even though I was staring at my hand, and he was staring at me. It felt safer that way, to keep my gaze off his. With my good hand, I slid my fingers over his, and relished in the way he breathed out. Aiden's hand was so much bigger than my own. It would span so much of my body with those fingers fanned out.

As I moved my fingertips over his knuckles, I couldn't help but wonder if it had the same effect on him as it had on me.

Instead of fighting the impulse that tugged my body toward him, I let it flow through me. A hot sweep of power had me turning my head and resting my forehead against his temple. Underneath my palm, his fingers curled up into a tight fist. The muscles in his forearms flexed, and he breathed out of his nose, a short puff of air that sounded loud in my ears.

And that big man, who caused such big feelings, he didn't move away. Neither did I.

I slid my hand up his forearm, curled my fingers around his shifting muscle and sinew, until I felt the hard knot of his elbow, the tight, hot curve of his bicep underneath his skin. My teeth dug into my bottom lip when I saw, through heavily weighted eyes, the way his jaw flexed and bunched.

Grab me.

Touch me.

Kiss me.

My demands almost fell past my lips, but I yanked the words back in because I didn't dare break the spell.

Maybe it wasn't a spell, I wondered, as my fingers curled, the tips of my nails digging slightly into the surface of his skin. Maybe this was me sticking my hand willingly into the fire, just to see if it would burn the way I imagined.

His whole body trembled when—with the slightest lift to my chin—my lips swept over his cheekbone. If he ever unleashed the full force of himself on me, I'd probably snap in half from the impact.

Aiden sank in, just an inch, his own forehead resting now on my bare shoulder. His exhale, heavy and hot, snaked down the gap in my shirt, and when it hit my breast, a sound escaped from the back of my throat.

His hand, still fisted on the bed, shot forward, and with a hard press of his hand on my good hip, my legs unfolded like he flipped a switch. He curled that big hand along my lower back, under my shirt, and tugged me forward on the bed. My hand slid the rest of the way up his arm, over his shoulder, and my fingers curled around the back of his neck.

And then nothing.

Our heads stayed just as they were—his pressed into my shoulder, mine tucked against his—like neither of us dared to move.

We'd both taken one step up to the invisible line because a touch could be ignored, but the second his lips hit mine, the second I knew what his tongue felt like slick and sliding against my own, the line would be obliterated.

Obliterated.

Such a good word for what he was capable of doing to me. Aiden Hennessy was *huge*, and my toes curled helplessly at the feel of him pressed between my legs. All it would take is a tip backward, a tug of a few meaningless scraps of material, and I'd be his.

Please, I mouthed against his cheek.

"Fuck," he whispered, a tortured whisper that made my thighs clench around his hips. "I can't," he hissed.

Aiden shoved away from the bed and stood, striding out of the room before I could take my next breath.

I fell back on the bed, hand pressed over my hammering chest, and wondered if it was possible to die from built-up sexual tension.

Even though the door was open, and I heard the bang of a kitchen cabinet, I stayed right where I was. There was nothing to be gained from following him out of the bedroom, from pushing him on why he held up this imaginary line.

Or not now.

This night felt like a crossroads. The moment we just shared was a road diverging into two distinct paths in front of us.

Admittedly, his was even bigger than mine. He was moving on from a love he'd lost. I was simply taking a first step toward something that large.

Wearily, I rose from the bed and walked into the massive bathroom attached to his room. The sunken white tub looked pretty amazing, along with stretches of gleaming tile and a glass-enclosed shower. My whole body ached, and I couldn't even tell how much of it came from what just happened with Aiden, a letdown of energy that had propped me up for that moment in time.

In the mirror over the double vanity, I leaned in and studied the cut on my forehead. There was minimal bruising around it, which was good. Maybe Paige wouldn't lose her shit too badly when she saw me.

Everything about the past twenty-four hours was hitting me at the same time. The entire roller coaster almost too much for my body to process.

I just wanted … to float. Feel warm and clean and good.

Decision made, I walked over to the tub and flipped the water on, testing the water when it got to the right temperature. There was no fancy bath soap in his bathroom, but I found some good old-fashioned Epsom salt in the linen closet, which I poured under the running water. It dissolved in the water as I swept my hand around the crystals.

There was no more banging in the kitchen, and I walked back into the bedroom to grab the clean clothes out of my backpack. As I straightened, I caught sight of Aiden sitting on the couch, his head in his hands.

When I paused in the doorway, he lifted his head, and our eyes met.

"If it's okay with you, I'm going to take a bath," I said.

His eyes burned bright, but he didn't answer.

"Unless you feel like explaining to me why you can't," I added. "Because I'd love to understand it."

Aiden dropped his chin to his chest, shielding his gaze from view. "You're injured, Isabel," he said quietly.

I shook my head. "That's not it."

His head snapped up, but he didn't argue.

The specter of his wife hung between us. I knew it.

"I know that's not it." My voice gained strength. "And I wish you'd explain it to me."

Those eyes of his, I'd never seen any quite like them. A wordless answer hit me straight in the heart as he stared at me. *I can't.* It was as clear as if he'd spoken the words out loud.

"Don't tell me you can't," I told him quietly. "You won't, and there's a difference."

My lungs didn't work quite right as I gripped the knob on the bedroom door, and he disappeared from view, jagged bursts of oxygen making my whole chest ache. The door closed with a quiet click, and I sank against it for a moment.

I pushed off the door and walked into the bathroom, stripping off my clothes and letting them fall haphazardly onto the floor. As I slid into the water, I knew he wouldn't come in. I wasn't willing to pretend anymore, like I didn't have big, scary feelings for this man. Twice now, I'd begged him to do something. And he hadn't.

I had a feeling I knew why.

But I needed him to open up a little too. Not all the way, and not all at once. But if he was unwilling to give me anything, then I had to decide if I could make peace with that.

CHAPTER 21

Isabel

A FEW HOURS LATER, EMMETT AND I WERE READY TO GET
home.

Well … Emmett wasn't.

I sure was. My bath had revived me, and with the help of one
more dose of Tylenol, even though my body was still sore, I could
manage more easily. And as I'd moved around the kitchen after packing my backpack and making his bed, Aiden acted like there was a
six-foot force field surrounding me that he wasn't allowed to breach.

Breakfast was bagels (for the adults) and cereal (for the kids)
because it wasn't like Aiden had prepared for guests.

"I'm hungry," Emmett told me, tossing a pine cone into the air
and catching it. Logan and Paige would be there any minute.

"I told you you should've had a bagel."

Tongue trapped between his teeth, he tossed the pine cone
higher and darted to the side to catch it, but his hand-eye coordi-
nation was off, so it bounced off my head.

"Sorry," he said with a grimace.

I brushed flecks of the pine cone off my hair, slicked back in a braid going down my back. "Hey, what's one more head injury."

Anya flew out of the front door and scrambled on my lap, where I sat on a white Adirondack chair that overlooked the front yard. She studied my face, her mouth twisting up in a thoughtful grimace when she looked at the bandage at my hairline.

"Does it hurt?" she asked.

"Not too bad." I gently touched the bottom of the butterfly bandage. "Itches a little, but I need to leave it on here for a few days."

Her eyes, bright blue, and an entirely different size and shade as her father's, met mine. Her mother's eyes. My eyes came from my mother too, and I couldn't help but think about how differently I might've felt if I liked seeing that reminder of her in the mirror. Anya would. And Aiden, every time he looked at his daughter, would see glimpses of the woman they lost.

Gently, I brushed her hair behind her ears.

"You don't laugh a lot, do you?" she asked.

Her father had asked me something similar, and I struggled not to feel like I'd done something wrong by the repeated question.

I tapped her chin with my thumb, and it drew a smile. "I laugh more once you get to know me," I told her.

My answer made her happy, and my heart struggled to work past the sweet melancholy ache she brought out in me. If I was already falling in love with her dad, then Anya might have beaten him to the finish line.

I loved her serious questions. I loved her daredevil streak, even if my wrist throbbed in protest. I loved that she laid in the middle of a boxing ring singing at the top of her lungs.

"I went to sleep right away last night," she told me in a serious tone.

"That's ... good." My brow furrowed because it certainly seemed like she was telling me something important. "Is it usually hard for you to get to sleep?"

She shrugged. "Sometimes."

Her eyes moved from my face down to the letters on my Wolves T-shirt. The worn black fabric wasn't something I would've packed had I known anyone outside of Emmett would be privileged to see me in all my morning glory. There were holes in the hem. I'd ripped the arms off years earlier because I hated sleeves on my shirts when I worked out.

"What keeps you up, sweetheart?" I asked. As I watched her, it was impossible not to think about the nights I'd stared at the ceiling of my bedroom when I was younger.

"I don't know." Her answer was honest and simply spoken, but still … it wedged something raw and vulnerable into my heart. "But I liked that Emmett was across the hall. I pretended he was my big brother." Her eyes met mine again. "And you were downstairs. Daddy wasn't alone either. I think it was easier to sleep because I was happy."

It was almost impossible to swallow past whatever was lodged in my throat. I thought of what Aiden said the night before, about confusing her.

"Your daddy was very nice to let us stay because I was hurt," I said gently.

Anya nodded. I found myself studying her more closely than I ever had.

I'd probably seen pictures of Aiden's wife in the past, but if I had, there was no recollection of her face. Nor had I searched the house for her picture the night before, but I had no doubt there were images of her around the space where they lived.

Behind me, I felt him approach, his presence something akin to its own force field. Since I closed the door to take my bath, he hadn't spoken a word to me.

He simply watched, studied me with a wariness that I hadn't seen in him before, like I did him harm in some way that I didn't understand.

Didn't he know? I didn't want to do any unseen damage. I'd love them so easily if he'd let me.

"Will you bring Emmett to play again sometime?" Anya asked, now fiddling with the edge of my braid. "You didn't get to walk to the lake with us and see me skip rocks. I'm really good at it."

Aiden came to stand next to the chair, and carefully, I glanced up, but his attention was on his daughter.

"We'll talk about it later, okay, gingersnap?" he said.

She pouted. "You only say that when you don't want to say no in front of people."

I smothered a smile. "I'll tell you what, Anya, maybe your dad can drop you off at Emmett's house someday when I'm there." I tapped her on the nose. "No climbing that tree, though."

"Can I, daddysnap?" she asked, bouncing excitedly on my lap.

Aiden gave a slight nod. "Why don't you hop off her lap? I think her brother is here."

Logan's SUV pulled into the driveway, and I caught sight of their identical worried expressions.

"Here we go," I murmured.

"Mom looks pissed," Emmett whispered.

I gave him a look when Aiden sighed.

Emmett glanced up at Aiden, voice serious. "I don't know if you're ready for this, Mr. Hennessy."

Aiden's eyebrows lowered. "For what?"

Paige threw open her door, and in a flurry of red hair and long legs and motherly affection, she filled the entire front yard with her presence.

Her hands ran over my hair, my shoulders, and then tilted my chin to the side. "Oh my *gosh*, Isabel, we are going straight to the hospital. What is the matter with you?"

I stood, and when I grimaced at a twinge in my leg, she set her hands on her hips and glared at me.

"You told me her head was fine," she said to Aiden. Paige pointed at the bandage on my head. "You call that fine?"

His eyes were huge, and he glanced at me for help. "I—"

I shrugged because I'd had more than a decade to get used to her.

Logan approached at a normal speed, and with normal people skills, he held his hand out to Aiden. "Logan. Nice to meet you."

Aiden shook it, still casting wary looks at Paige as she clucked and cooed over my wrist, which was rewrapped in clean bandages after my bath. "Nice to meet you too."

"Paige," Logan said evenly.

She didn't so much as look at him. "Not the time to rein me in, buddy." Her eyes were pinned to me. "You're sure this isn't broken?"

I nodded. "Yeah. Trust me, if the pain or swelling was worse today, I'd let you take me. But I'm fine."

"Forgive me if I don't trust your opinion on that, Miss *I refused to get checked out at the hospital.*"

Anya came next to me and tugged on my good hand. "Is this your mom? She's pretty."

"Kinda," I explained. "I was fourteen when she married my brother, so even though she's my sister-in-law, she's my mom in all the ways that matter." Paige sniffled noisily, and I gave her a look. "Do not start crying right now."

Paige softened her posture, giving Anya a sweet smile. "You must be Anya."

Anya nodded. "I'm sorry I broke your tree branch."

"Oh honey, you don't need to apologize for that. I'm just happy you're all right."

Paige straightened, and Logan slid an arm around her waist. He eyed my wrist. "How bad's the sprain?"

"Grade two," Aiden interjected. "If I had to guess."

"I love when athletes make medical diagnoses like they're doctors," Paige said to me. "It's my favorite thing ever."

Logan ignored her. "I made you an appointment with the team chiropractor for an adjustment. He's coming to the house tomorrow." When I opened my mouth, he held up a hand. "You are staying with us for a couple of nights."

"I love it when the men in my life make decisions for me," I told Paige. "It's my favorite thing ever."

Aiden swiped a hand over his mouth, and Logan gave me a level look. "Isabel, my sister whom I love and respect greatly, would you be so kind as to stay at our house while you recover?"

I gestured for more.

"Please," he managed.

In answer, I gave him a magnanimous smile. "Of course. Thank you for asking so nicely."

"Aiden, it was nice to meet you. Thank you again," my brother said, then he walked back to the car, muttering something about sisters and gray hair.

Paige laughed. "Emmett, grab Iz's backpack. She's injured."

"I can carry it."

"No way, let him be useful. It's good for him."

Emmett slung it over his shoulder and waved goodbye to our hosts. "Thanks for letting us stay over."

Aiden nodded. Anya ran up to Emmett just before he climbed into the back seat and squeezed him in a tight hug. Emmett's face went bright red, and Paige grinned. "I love that kid."

Anya ran back in our direction and flung herself around my legs. I smoothed a hand along her downy soft hair. "I hope you feel better soon," she told me. "Thanks for catching me."

Paige waved a hand in front of her face, and her eyes were suspiciously bright. Mine probably were too. Aiden was staring at the ground.

"Anytime," I told her. "I'll see you later, okay?"

When Anya disappeared back into the house, Aiden finally,

finally made eye contact with me. My stomach flipped featherlight at what I saw.

I blew out a slow breath because we both seemed to have lost the ability to pretend anything after what happened in his bedroom.

Paige glanced between us, her eyebrows popping up. "I'm, uhh, just going to get in the car. Aiden," she said, waiting until he looked at her to continue, "thank you for taking care of my girl."

He nodded. "You're welcome."

"I'll be right there," I told Paige.

She squeezed my hand, eyes warm and understanding. Honestly, there was no conceivable way she could understand shit because I'd told her so little. That was always my problem. Hold it just long enough that it pressed the seams of my skin to bursting.

I'd done it with my mom leaving.

I'd done it with Paige showing up.

And now I was doing it with Aiden.

All the big things, the changes that I hadn't seen coming, the pieces that made me who I was. And now, I knew, he was part of that. Even if he may not be able to say the same.

Neither one of us spoke for a moment after Paige left us alone. "I'll probably take a day or two off work," I said quietly.

His brows lowered.

"I'll go crazy sitting at home."

Aiden sighed, briefly moving his gaze to the car where Logan and Paige weren't even pretending not to watch us. "I'd feel better if you took the whole week. Definitely no teaching."

"I've already got my classes covered." I fidgeted with the hem of my shirt because I had nothing to do with my hands. "If I take this whole week off, that means I miss most of the next two weeks."

He tilted his head. "Why?"

"My sister's wedding. It's on the calendar." I sighed. "And the—" My voice cut off because it wasn't like I owned the self-defense class. But it was important to me. To him, too.

I saw in his face that he wanted to ask, in the way he opened his mouth, in the searching way he watched me. But no words came out, and the searching stopped when he turned his attention to the car again.

Standing in the silence with him no longer felt tolerable, and that realization could so easily turn to frustration, to anger, if I let it.

He wanted me. I knew he did.

"Thank you, Aiden," I said.

His jaw clenched. And nothing.

Right.

"You're welcome."

There was so much I wanted to scream at him in the wake of that. In the wake of those bullshit, politely spoken phrases. I wanted the Aiden who sat in the dark with me. But instead, I chose to protect what was left of my energy after a really draining twenty-four hours, and I walked to the car with my head high.

Once I was buckled in, Paige turned around and gave me a look.

"Holy shit, girl, you and I are *going to talk* when we get home."

Logan sighed, pulling the gear shift so he could back the vehicle out of the driveway. "I don't have to be a part of that conversation, do I?"

"No," Paige and I answered in unison.

"Excellent." He caught my eye in the rearview mirror and winked. "Ready to go home?"

I sank back against the seat and sighed. "You have no idea."

CHAPTER 22

Isabel

"**P**LEASE?"

"No."

"Paige, I'm so bored." I pushed my lip out, but all she did was roll her eyes. I'd never pouted in my life, but this seemed as good a time as any. "I have been doing nothing for the last three days. You can't keep me here. You heard the Wolves' chiro, he said if I feel fine, I can do light desk work. Kelly texted me that the schedule is a mess."

She finished putting away the groceries. "Yeah, I also heard him say you needed to be careful because of how out of whack your hip was. He said ice and stretch and rest, nothing strenuous for a few days."

"It's *been* a few days."

"He was here yesterday, Iz."

My breath came out in an angry puff, moving into the family room so I could sit on the couch. Emmett tossed me a controller, and I shook my head. "No thanks, bud, I've played enough video games to last me for ten years."

"You know," Paige said from the kitchen, "this just shows how badly you need to find a hobby. Only workaholics freak out after three days off."

"I have hobbies."

She laughed. "Name one."

"I—" My jaw set mulishly when nothing sprang to mind. "I love hanging out with my family. And … sports. I love sports."

"That doesn't count, Iz." She pulled a box of Pop-Tarts out of the paper bag. "Admit it or I won't toss you one of these."

"That's emotional warfare," I told her. "And I'm not admitting anything. There is nothing wrong with loving my job and wanting to be there. I've always been like this. It doesn't mean I don't have hobbies."

"Falling out of trees to rescue your hot boss's daughter doesn't count, kid."

Eyes wide, I gestured at Emmett.

"He's not listening," Paige said.

"Yes, I am." He hit buttons on the controller. "You think Mr. Hennessy is hot?"

I gave Paige a look. "Answer that carefully."

The only way I could describe her smile was *pure evil*. "My, my, someone sounds possessive. You never did tell me what happened."

"Nothing happened." Again, I pointed at Emmett.

"*Liar*," she mouthed.

"So, the wedding," I said. "Getting close, huh?"

"What an inconspicuous subject change." But Paige smiled as she glanced down at her watch. "I actually have to go. I'm meeting Molly at her and Noah's place to go over the last details for the rehearsal dinner. If you're so bored, you could come."

I tilted my head to Emmett. "What about him?"

"I'm going to my friend's house," he said, eyes still glued to the TV. "His mom is picking me up in a little bit."

My wheels started turning immediately. "Nah, you go ahead," I told Paige. "I might nap."

Her eyes narrowed slightly, so I yawned for effect.

"Okay."

"Still nothing from … her?" I asked.

Even after so many years, I didn't love saying Brooke's name, and Paige knew it.

Paige shook her head. "Not yet." Paige knew about my phone call with Molly, but I still hated feeling like I wasn't sure what to expect. "I wouldn't worry about it. If she was going to come, she would've sent in her RSVP."

I laughed humorlessly. "You guys give her more credit for manners than I do."

Paige walked around and dropped a kiss on the top of Emmett's head, then mine. Carefully, she traced her thumb by the butterfly bandage. "It's starting to peel up a bit. How long until you can take it off?"

"Paramedic said probably seven to ten days. Once the wound is totally closed."

She nodded, then tilted her head. "You going to sneak out to work as soon as I leave?"

I held her eyes. "Maybe."

"Aiden know you're coming?"

"It's his day off, so no. I just want to fix the schedule and check that he did payroll right." I paused. "And make sure he didn't mess up my storage closet."

Paige sighed. "No kicking or running or punching or *anything* other than a sedate walk, okay?"

I smiled. "Okay."

Fifteen minutes later, I was behind the wheel of my car with the warm September air blowing through my hair. It wasn't like I wasn't enjoying some extra time with Logan and Paige and Emmett, but it had been so long since I'd had to account for my time to anyone. And after the night at Aiden's, I found myself craving a little solitude to process it.

It was the only reason I felt sort of okay with the agreed-upon four days off work, tacked in front of my usual day off. Seeing him, thinking about what I'd say or how to act, I was still tiptoeing around it.

The last thing I wanted to do was make the work environment impossible for either of us, but I was no good at faking. I never had been. My thoughts, for better or worse, had always been stamped clearly on my face.

It was probably why most men didn't even really try with me.

And now—wasn't it so freaking ironic—I found a man I wanted, and his lack of trying stemmed from something entirely different. I just wasn't sure if he'd ever trust me with the truth of why.

After parking my car, and making sure I didn't see Aiden's big black truck, I let myself into the gym and smiled at Gavin, who was on the phone behind the front desk. He mouthed something, but I couldn't make it out.

I pointed back to my office. "Tell me later," I said.

He gave me a thumbs-up.

But as soon as I cleared the front area, I knew what he was trying to tell me.

Aiden was standing in front of a small news crew, an attractively dressed woman holding a microphone in his face. He hadn't seen me yet because he was angled away from the front door.

"And what's the biggest problem you see facing young fighters today, Aiden?"

With his hands propped on his hips, a black shirt bearing the gym's new logo tight across his chest, Aiden looked so serious, so handsome. He shook his head. "No doubt about it, it's the way the weight classes are set up. If they don't add more, you'll just see more and more big guys dehydrating themselves going into a fight so they can make a lower weight class."

She nodded. "And why do you see that as an issue?"

"If you've got someone who weighs in at one ninety before the match, but normally weighs two fifteen, and he's going against a guy who's a healthy one seventy-five, you will have more injuries. Serious ones too. Not just the injuries that can come from a fair fight. It's one of the reasons I was ready to be done when I retired."

She smiled. "No chance you'd ever return?"

"No, my fighting days are over. I'm excited about what we can accomplish here."

I shifted my weight, and Aiden noticed.

He did a quick double-take, and his countenance went as dark as a thundercloud. Head down, I walked back to my office and hoped it would be a very, very long interview.

The newscaster started speaking again, and I closed my office door.

"Well, shit," I whispered.

I got to work because I had a feeling my door would burst open, and a very tall, very angry man would be behind it as soon as it did.

As I was staring at the computer screen and clicking through a few things, my phone buzzed.

Molly: Oooooooooooh, PAIGE TOLD ME ABOUT THE LINGERING EYE CONTACT. You owe me stories.

Molly: I need something to distract me from wedding stress. Why didn't we just elope on a beach with our families??

Me: It's not too late, Mol. You still can.

Molly: Don't think I don't notice how you deflect.

Me: See? Wedding isn't getting you down. Still sharp as a tack.

The phone got tucked back into my bag, and when I heard someone knock on the door, I froze.

"Come in," I said.

Gavin popped his head in. "Got a minute?"

"Of course. What's up?"

He nodded at the clunky black wrist brace I was wearing. "How long until you can ditch that?"

"Another week probably. Thanks for covering for me this afternoon."

"Sure." He pulled his phone out. "I wasn't sure if I was supposed to take any pictures or videos for our social media with that news crew showing up, so this is all I got."

I flipped through a couple of shots, stopped to watch a quick video he'd snagged of Aiden demonstrating a few moves in the ring with one of our regulars. "These are great, Gav. Can you text them to me?"

"Sure."

Gavin was only a couple of years younger than I was, one of our college students working toward a kinesiology degree. Once he had that piece of paper, and whatever else he decided to add to his education, he'd be far more qualified for this job than I was. But moments like this made me even more thankful Amy had taken a chance on me.

Now I just needed the big, angry guy out in the main area to figure out his issues so I didn't have to worry about my place.

Or my heart.

Standing a few inches taller than my five-foot-ten, Gavin studied my forehead after sending the text. "You're gonna have a badass scar."

I smiled. "Totally my intention."

It was at the moment I was smiling up at him that a very large body stepped into the doorway of my office.

"A minute of your time, Ward," he all but growled.

Ahh. We were back to Ward.

I'd never had the sound of my last name spark such immediate and hot rage. My bones practically melted from the force of it.

Gavin's eyebrows lifted briefly. "You okay if I go?" he asked quietly.

Aiden's countenance darkened even further.

I gave Gavin a subdued smile. "Yes, thank you."

He nodded deferentially to Aiden as he left my office. I crossed my arms as Aiden closed the office door behind him.

It took him a second to say anything once we were blocked from prying eyes.

Oddly enough, it was the first time I felt no butterflies, no flutters, no walking-a-tight rope feel in the fact that he and I were alone.

No, I was too frustrated with him for that. So even when he walked closer and tilted his head to look at my bandage, I didn't move, didn't smile, didn't break the silence.

"Why are you here?" he asked.

"Fixing the schedule you messed up."

"I didn't …" He took in a deep breath. "Okay, I probably did."

My eyebrows lifted. "And making sure you didn't do the same thing to payroll. If you plan to keep your employees, you kinda need to pay them."

"They'd forgive me," he answered simply.

I exhaled a laugh. "Well, at least you're feeling more confident in your role."

"Because of you," he explained. "They'd forgive me because of you." At my silence, he took a step closer. "But none of that matters because you should not be here. You're supposed to be off work for at least four days."

"I'm done resting, but I appreciate your concern." I hooked a thumb at my desk. "Is that all? I'd like to get back to work."

My tone remained calm and even, but my heart started to race at his nearness. An unconscious reaction that I had no control over.

Born from the frustration of that, I turned my back to Aiden and walked to the storage cabinet in the corner. I wasn't even sure what I was looking for; I just needed space. I needed distance between his body and mine, and my desk didn't provide enough of that.

Aiden's response took a long moment to come, but when it did, it stopped me in my tracks. "You're mad at me."

In the middle of pulling a stack of shirts out of the cabinet, my hands froze.

"Is that it? You're mad about the other night."

Not in a million years did I expect him to push this. Push what had happened—or not happened—in his bedroom. Slowly, I slid the shirts back into place and closed the cabinet.

When I turned, his face was impossible to read. I'd need a chisel and crowbar to get this man's thoughts out of his head clearly. Leave it to me to find someone like this to finally light me up inside. Someone guarded and cagey. Someone who couldn't— or wouldn't—make things easy.

It was … poetic justice at its finest. I deserved someone like Aiden because this was how everyone, in my entire life, had always felt about me.

And it was the only reason I started laughing. Once I started, I couldn't stop.

Aiden looked at me like I'd lost my fucking mind because I kinda felt like I had.

He clenched his jaw, crossing his arms over his chest, but he didn't say a word as I tried to get a hold of myself. Eventually, I did, and as I wiped away tears underneath my eyes, he shook his head. "You done?"

"The hell if I know," I said around a few stray giggles. I never giggled. But this—him and me—it was too much. And if I didn't laugh about it, I'd probably cry. Finally, I took a deep breath. "You are … impossible, Aiden Hennessy."

His face went blank with shock. "Me?"

"I've always been that person," I told him. "The impossible one. Always. And now I understand what it must have been like for the people waiting for me."

Aiden's brow furrowed, his chest worked steadily as his breathing increased.

"I wish you'd trust me enough to tell me why this is so hard." I searched his face. "I want to know. But I won't keep putting myself in this position, where we *almost* do, we both *want* to, and then you pull back. I won't do it anymore."

&

Aiden

She was right.

And she was wrong.

I knew a whole lot standing in that office with her.

I wanted to grip the back of her neck and take her mouth, not gently, not sweetly.

I wanted to see what I'd find if I peeled her tiny shorts off her long, long legs.

And beyond all that, I wanted to wrap her in my arms because I knew why she was frustrated. Knew what I was doing to cause it.

But I didn't know how to stop. How to explain.

Never in my entire life had I felt this sort of barely leashed energy, and Isabel had no idea how close she was to shoving open the flood gates holding back the snarling beast inside me.

I didn't like that she was frustrated with me.

I didn't like that I'd walked away from her in my bedroom.

I didn't like that we forever seemed to walk this tightrope of soft, stolen touches or immediate combustion.

At my continued silence, she made a frustrated noise in the back of her throat.

"I'm sorry," I ground out. I unfolded my arms and set my hands on my hips. It was the only way to keep from grabbing her, tugging her to me like I wanted. "I'm sorry for the other night. I shouldn't have …"

But my words stopped there. Because I couldn't make myself apologize for touching her.

I couldn't make myself apologize for one moment where I felt the press of her body against mine. Imagined pushing her back onto my bed and finding slick, sweet comfort with her legs around mine. I'd thought of it a dozen times since she walked out of my house, each time, finding empty release with the shower pulsing hot over me, the bed empty next to me.

"You shouldn't have what?" she whispered. Isabel didn't back down an inch. "Even now, you can't say it."

My eyes held hers because of course she knew what I wasn't willing to say.

I held myself still because this precipice was dangerous, and it wasn't the place for us to fall over it. There was no way for me, not now, to explain how selfish it would be for me to go down this path with her.

How unprepared I was for someone like her.

Her blue eyes changed as I stood there silently, from anger-tinged desire to resignation, and it made me want to rage.

"Isabel," I said, shifting closer to her, my hands lifting toward her.

"No," she said firmly. Her hand came up, stopping just shy of my chest. I think she knew—we both knew—that if we touched right now, any good intentions would vanish. Not just vanish, they'd explode. "Don't call me by my first name, don't act like you're going to touch me right now, unless you know *exactly* what that means for you."

I backed up, hands dropping back by my side.

Her chin quivered dangerously, but she sucked in a sharp

breath. Watching her ability to get control of her emotions was incredible.

"I'm done being awed by you, Aiden Hennessy. I'm done acting like I don't want you because I do."

If a man could remain standing while feeling humbled to his core, without falling to his knees, then I'd just managed it. She was staggering in her strength, and I had my first flash of unease that I was fucking up something big ... something that might not happen to me again.

"And I think the part that makes me so mad," she continued, "is that I know you want me too."

I had to look away. I had to get myself under control. Remember why she was so wrong for me.

But even if she was, Isabel was right about this, and I respected her too much to lie to her.

My voice hardly worked when I spoke. It sounded rusty and rough, but the words came out clearly all the same. "You have no idea how difficult this is for me."

"Then tell me," she begged, stepping closer. "Tell me."

I swiped a hand over my mouth.

If I pinched my eyes closed, I could hear Beth talking to Anya. I could hear the words she said. Isabel represented every selfish desire I could've conjured for myself. So that was what I did. I tried to tug that memory front and center because it felt like the only way to make sense of this mess.

"I just need you to be patient with me," I told her, voice taking on a harsh, frustrated edge.

"I am being patient." Isabel swallowed. "But that doesn't mean I'm going to keep letting myself get whiplash until you decide this is okay. I've had a lot of things happen in my life that I had no choice but to push through." Her voice was unsteady, but her eyes were clear. "But this, I can choose. Until you're ready to do the same."

My feelings for Isabel were too big. At that moment, the worst thing I could've done was tell her that.

That she was too much.

Too young.

Too beautiful.

Too guarded. I wanted nothing more than to break down her walls and let her do the same to me.

That together, we were too intense, in a time of my life when all I'd been seeking was peace.

The last thing I'd ever do was make her feel that way. And I didn't trust myself to speak.

Isabel swallowed roughly, her eyes suddenly bright. "Please let me get back to work."

She turned away, the long sweep of her dark hair making a hushed sound in the quiet of the office, and as she sat at the desk again, I saw her hands trembling.

It was the tremble that had me walking away as she asked.

CHAPTER 23

Isabel

ONE THING I COULDN'T HOLD AGAINST AIDEN WAS HOW WELL he listened.

Like I'd asked, he stayed away.

Like I'd asked, he let me get back to work.

Even though I wasn't teaching, I did just about everything else simply to stay busy. If I slowed, I would scream, just to have an outlet for my frustration. Not that he could've known the type of restless energy this distance caused in me.

Because the worst feeling in the world was falling in love with someone who wasn't capable of returning that love in the way you needed. As I made the finishing touches on setting up for the self-defense class on my last day of work before Molly's wedding, I kept thinking about Brooke.

I thought of the look I'd seen on her face the night before she left.

There was a resolve there that still made my stomach curl up unpleasantly when I thought of it. The love of Logan and Paige couldn't erase it entirely, though it helped as much as anything could.

Telling Aiden how I felt about him was the closest I could come to baring myself to him completely. Standing naked in front of him would feel less vulnerable than this silence did. Because I had no guarantees that he'd ever love me like I wanted him to. Like I knew he was capable.

I'd never had the chance to beg Brooke to stay. So many years later, I knew I wouldn't, even given the chance. But it still triggered the same uncomfortable edginess as if I had.

Which was why I threw myself into the work I could do.

I sat at the front desk, the gym's pleasant sounds behind me filtering into my thoughts as I readied everything for the class. The front door opened, and Casey walked in, followed by three other girls.

"Morning," I told her. "You ready to beat people up?"

They laughed.

"Okay, we won't be beating anyone up, but go ahead and partner up. I marked out spots in the main open area. There should be two of you in each section."

Casey gave me a once-over. "What happened to you?"

I touched the bandage, which was soon to be removed, using the hand still in an ugly black brace. "I had a mishap with a tree branch that decided not to hold me any longer."

"Ouch." She winced. "You won't be teaching today then?"

"I'll be on the mic walking everyone through the moves, but I'll have some help from our trainers."

Kelly, Gavin, and Grady were already warming up, along with a couple of others, and I had a feeling Aiden would be helping too, even though he'd yet to come out of his office.

Casey went to join her friends, and I stayed busy, greeting the girls who came through the front door with their smiles and nervous energy. By the time everyone on the list had arrived, we had a full gym, and the vibe was different than a typical class, that I found myself feeling a little nervous.

Aiden stood in the doorway of his office, watching the energetic buzz in the room with a slight smile on his face. But when his eyes met mine, his smile fell. His gaze sharpened, and even with the distance between us, the intensity of it was like a knife blade. Completely lethal if you pressed on it hard enough.

So I looked down and finished hooking the mic up.

"All right, everyone. Welcome to Hennessy's Gym, for what is hopefully the first of many classes like this." The girls clapped excitedly. I motioned for Gavin and Kelly to join me in front of them. "These are my helpers. They'll be demonstrating all the basic self-defense moves we want to teach you today, and I'll be walking around helping you guys while you practice. So will Grady and Aiden." I made eye contact with everyone. "If you only want me or Kelly to help you, please just raise your hand at any point if you're struggling, and we'll be right over."

I held up my wrist. "Unfortunately, I won't be kicking anyone's ass today because I got in a fight with a tree and lost, but trust me … we'll be able to inflict some damage together, okay?"

The small ripple of laughter eased some of the excited tension.

Over the next hour, I found my new favorite part of my job. By the time we finished, there was yelling and cheering and more than one male trainer hitting the mat with a thud.

I laughed when Casey managed to push Gavin to his knee. "You guys are savage, I love it."

Some of them stayed afterward to keep practicing, and it was then I noticed Anya sitting on the edge of the center boxing ring. She waved at me, toothless grin bringing a smile onto my face.

I walked over to her. "When did you get here?"

She kicked her legs back and forth. "About halfway through. My uncle Clark dropped me off. He said I should learn how to beat the boys up for when I get older."

I laughed. "Well, we only use stuff like this if someone is trying to hurt us or one of our friends."

Anya's face pinched up thoughtfully. "Have you ever had to do that to someone?"

"Nope. And I'm very thankful for that."

Her eyebrows were still lowered.

"What is it?" I asked.

"Are you … gentle?"

My head tilted. "What do you mean, sweetheart?"

Anya's big blue eyes searched mine, and again, I got the feeling she was trying to figure out something that was much more serious than I could guess. "Do you sing lullabies even though you aren't a good singer?"

I blew out a breath, glancing over my shoulder to see if Aiden was anywhere in earshot, which he wasn't. "Not really," I admitted.

Anya nodded, still deep in thought.

"Why do you ask?" I asked gently.

Oh, her eyes when she looked up at me, I had the strangest sensation that she was about to rip my heart from my chest, and when she spoke, I wasn't wrong.

"You're different than I thought you'd be."

"What?" I whispered.

"My mommy told me she'd be sweet and gentle, and bake me cookies and sing me lullabies when I couldn't sleep, but you're different."

My heart skipped erratically as she spoke, and I wasn't sure which impulse was stronger—to cover my ears at what she said, or wrap her in my arms and let her know that love came in so many different forms.

At my back, Aiden approached without sound. But I felt him all the same.

"Anya," he said quietly. "Why don't you go play in my office."

She smiled up at me, then hopped off the edge of the ring, scampering off to his office.

I covered my mouth, my eyelids falling shut.

"Isabel …" he started.

I turned, and his voice faded at whatever he meant to say next.

"I cannot even imagine how hard it must be to think about moving on," I said quietly. "I've never …" I paused. "I've never been married or engaged. Never found someone who made me want any of that until now," I admitted. His eyes blazed. I forced the words out, and each one felt like glass in my throat. "Losing that"—I pressed a hand over my heart—"it must have been hell on earth."

His eyes darted away from mine, his jaw tight.

A group of girls said goodbye, and I waved. Aiden rubbed at the back of his neck, but when he lifted his head, I saw the truth buried in his guilty expression.

"And I'd never, ever expect you to leave the memory of your wife, and what she meant to you, behind. But I can't compete with the wishes of a ghost, Aiden." My eyes burned with unshed tears. "I won't."

"I didn't …" He paused, face bent in a grimace.

I rolled my lips between my teeth and begged him silently to give me something. Anything.

When he met my gaze again, his was untamed, unguarded.

"That's what makes this so fucking hard for me," he whispered fiercely. My mouth went dry because if we were alone, he would've grabbed me to him. I could see it in his eyes. "When it comes to you, Isabel, there is no competition, and I don't know how to make peace with that."

Without another word, he turned and marched to his office. Before anyone saw my face, I turned back to the ring and took a few deep breaths.

But my heart, oh my heart. I laid a hand over it, tried to calm its wild, furious drumming.

"Iz?" Kelly called from behind me.

I blew out one more breath and turned. "Yeah?"

"These two would love to sign up for a membership. Can you help them while I finish up here?"

At the two girls, I smiled. "Of course. Why don't you two follow me up to the desk? I'll get you some paperwork to fill out."

I went about my job for the next hour, and by the time I gathered my things to go, I still wasn't sure if I felt better or worse after his admission.

"That looked intense for a minute there," Kelly commented mildly, watching as I finished tidying my desk and shutting off my computer monitor.

"Did it?"

"My, my how far we've come from you hiding behind boxes." She nudged me as we walked toward the front. "I think our boss looks a little smitten with you, Isabel Ward."

I laughed, and the sound was tinged with the slightest edge of hysteria. His office door was still closed, and when I walked out of the building, I wasn't coming back until after Molly's wedding. I forced my attention back to Kelly. "Call me if you need anything this weekend. Saturday is the only day I can't really answer my phone."

She sighed at my obvious deflection. "It's not too late to invite me, you know."

I rolled my eyes. "Goodbye, Kelly."

"Have a fun weekend off," she called after me.

When I turned to wave, I saw Aiden watching from the doorway of his office. And just like it always seemed to with him, my heart responded like he'd touched bare wires to my skin.

It didn't slow until I'd driven away, and still ... I felt him. I was starting to realize that I probably always would.

CHAPTER 24

Aiden

THE DAYS SHE WAS GONE WERE EVEN MORE DIFFICULT THAN when she was in front of me because I couldn't even attempt to decipher what she was thinking.

Couldn't take the little bit I had of her, even if it was a pale, watered-down version of what I wanted. It made me want to break things, hit things, and put my rage and frustration somewhere. And my anger wasn't aimed at her. I could hardly look myself in the mirror because I hated what I saw when I did.

I was going through the motions in a way that I hadn't since Beth died. More than once, I caught my family watching me, caught Anya talking to me, when I'd only heard half of what she said.

What if you're wrong?

That was what I couldn't mute in my head, to distraction.

What if you're wrong?

This—Isabel—was the first time in my entire life that I questioned myself so much, and I hated how much anger it stirred up in its wake.

She was nothing Beth had talked about, nothing like I'd tried to imagine.

And maybe that was part of the problem. I'd never even attempted to imagine the person who would come after Beth. Never wanted to. Her description, her wishes were as good as any, because I had no desire to find someone else to take that space in my life or in Anya's.

Each day that Isabel upheld the invisible wall that she'd promised, one that I could've launched over with ease if I decided, I slipped a little further into questioning myself.

"You look like shit," Deacon told me when we all ate dinner at my parents'. They'd tiptoed around me all week.

"Didn't sleep well." Not that I planned on explaining why. When Isabel left work the day before, she was off for the next three because of her sister's wedding. And since she'd swept out of the building, I hadn't heard a thing from her. And why would I?

Isabel might've been the one to take longer to gain her footing around me, but there was only one person too chicken-shit to admit what they felt, and it wasn't her.

"You can borrow my special lamp," Anya told me. "It helps me sleep."

I gave her a tired smile. "Thanks, gingersnap. Maybe I'll try that tonight."

Clark stood from the table. "Come on, Anya. Want to help me fix something in the backyard?"

She shrieked when he scooped her up and tossed her over his shoulder. Wearily, I rubbed the back of my neck.

"Anything you wanna talk about?" my mom asked later as I helped her clear dishes before taking Anya home.

My dad set a hand on her back as he set his dish down on the counter. "Don't pry, honey."

She shooed him away. "Asking isn't prying."

He swatted her butt. "It is when you do it."

"Nothing to worry about, Mom." I handed her the dish towel.

Even if they all watched me carefully, no one else said a word. I got Anya loaded into the truck and made my way back home, weariness covering me like an iron blanket. It was different than losing Beth—so very different—but it still felt like grief.

Like I was mourning something that I'd never really had.

It was a startling realization, one that shook me more than I wanted to admit. But how was I supposed to reconcile everything I'd believed I might need someday to what I wanted when I looked at her.

Anya was drifting off to sleep in the back seat as I pulled into our neighborhood, and I caught sight of an unfamiliar car parked in front of our house. It wasn't Isabel's car, but when someone with her build and long dark hair got out of the driver's seat, my heart started hammering.

But when she lifted her head and smiled as I drove the truck into our driveway, I knew it was one of her sisters. From the pictures I'd seen in the entryway of the house, they all looked similar, and it calmed my nerves to know it wasn't her. Sort of.

Anya had fully drifted off, and I decided to let her stay where she was while I talked to whichever Ward sister was waiting for me.

She was walking up the driveway as I got out of the truck.

"Aiden?" She gave me a small wave, her features so similar to Isabel's that it was almost hard to look at her. "I'm Molly, Isabel's sister."

"What can I do for you?" I was too tired for pleasantries, too exhausted by cycling through this situation in my head to even attempt to manage them.

She held out a large envelope, edged in gold, and heavy in my hand when I took it from her. "I'd like to invite you to my wedding this weekend."

My head snapped up. "Why?"

Molly smiled. "Because my sister will never do it."

Immediately, I was shaking my head. "Trust me, she doesn't want me there."

"If she knew I was here," Molly said carefully, "she would be mad at me."

I extended the envelope back toward her. "Then maybe you shouldn't be."

Inexplicably, that made her smile widen. "I know you don't know Isabel as well as I do, but from the little bit I've heard, you've gotten really good glimpses of who she is." Molly tucked a piece of hair behind her ears, the massive diamond on her finger winking in the sun. "She'll never ask you to come to this wedding, even if she wants you there, because she is as stubborn as anyone I've ever met."

I exhaled a humorless laugh. "I feel like we're talking in circles."

"I know." She licked her lips before speaking again. "I don't know where your relationship stands with her," Molly continued. "Because even though she can dish out advice to us like it's her job, she rarely tells us anything she's going through. And I think it's because she's doing what she did when she was young, when Paige showed up. She'll give these tiny windows of opportunity, and if you don't take them, you won't get another chance. My sister is one of the strongest, most incredible people I know, but she will shut down anyone if she's afraid they'll hurt her."

I swiped a hand over my mouth, regarding Molly with unfiltered curiosity. "Why are you telling me all of this? You don't even know me."

Her smile was mysterious. "Because I know my sister. And if she's refusing to talk about you, then you've wedged a foot in the door, and that means you're important to her." She stepped closer. "What I'm giving you, Aiden, is a chance."

I glanced up at the sky and took a deep breath.

"But," she said carefully, "only take that chance if you can see her in your future. I'd never make that kind of dramatic statement for anyone other than her." She laid a hand on my arm. "I know you lost your wife, and that puts a lot of extra pressure on whatever relationship you have next. But if you think it could be her, then don't miss your chance."

If Molly Ward made me start crying in my own driveway, I'd never forgive her.

"I've … I've done all of this already, and I wasn't looking to do it again," I said quietly. "The big wedding and I have a child, and I don't know if it's even fair to ask her to walk into all of that, knowing the firsts that she should be experiencing with the person who loves her."

It was an oversimplification of the mental hurdles facing me, but enough that Molly gave me an encouraging smile.

"There is one thing I can tell you with a hundred percent certainty, Aiden." She held my eyes. "My sister could not care less about which firsts you experience together. What she wants is forever."

All I could manage was a short nod. "I hear you."

"Good." She studied me. "I hope I see you there. But if I don't, then you never deserved her to begin with."

Even though her parting shot was a gut-punch, Molly gave me a small smile and walked down my driveway like a queen.

With my head spinning, I transferred a sleeping Anya from my truck and into her bed. I walked back downstairs in a daze and sank onto the couch. Down the hallway, the door to my bedroom was open, and if I closed my eyes, it was so easy to imagine Isabel as she'd lain in my bed. Once more, I was struck with the complete pendulum of our interactions.

There was no lukewarm.

No shades of gray to dissect.

I stared at the wedding invitation, and imagined showing up for her there. I imagined staying home, knowing I'd think of her all evening.

Because I couldn't not, I imagined what Beth would say. What she'd tell me to do.

Before I knew what I was doing, I pulled out my phone and dialed my parents' number.

My mom picked up on the first ring.

"Miss me already?" she asked, smile evident in her voice.

"I lied. Earlier." I punched the button to put her on speaker and set my phone down, idly scrolling until I found a picture of Beth on my phone. From before she was sick, before her cheeks hollowed out and the skin shrank over her bones.

Her response took a few seconds in coming, "Okay. What about?"

"When I told you not to worry." I pinched the bridge of my nose. "I don't … I don't know what to do, Mom. And normally, I can imagine what Beth would tell me, what advice she'd give me, and I can't with this."

My wife's face smiled out at me from the phone, but for the first time in two years, I couldn't hear her voice in my head. My hands started tingling, my neck tight and chest as heavy as if an elephant sat squarely over my heart.

"Talk to me, son," she said gently.

There was no part of me that wanted to recap my relationship with Isabel, so I picked up the proverbial scalpel and cut straight to the heart of what was bothering me.

"What does it mean if my feelings for Isabel are … fuck, I don't know, bigger? More intense. More," my voice faltered, "everything, than what I had with Beth."

"Oh Aiden," she exhaled heavily, "there's no rule book for this. Nothing that says you can't love someone in a different way than you loved Beth."

"I did." My finger and thumb tightened on the bridge of my nose again until it hurt. "I *loved* her. She was kind and funny and a great mother, and I never wanted this to happen. I don't know what it says about me that Isabel is nothing—and I mean nothing—like the person I loved first." I dropped my hand and forced myself to stare at Beth's picture. The gold of her hair and the deep dimples on either side of her smile. I pinched my eyes shut. "Isabel scares the hell out of me, and I never had that with Beth."

She made a soft sound that I couldn't decipher.

"And I promised her," I said quietly, "I promised her and Anya, and I don't know how to break that promise without feeling like I've betrayed her memory."

"Aiden," she started cautiously, "I loved Beth too. But she never should've given Anya that list. I know she was just trying to make a scared little girl feel better, and maybe it made her feel better too, but I don't think she truly meant to box you into something you didn't really want."

A stray tear slipped down my cheek, and I wiped it away.

"You are not betraying Beth by finding happiness, son. It's horseshit, and if she was here, she'd tell you the same thing."

I exhaled a laugh.

"You are so honorable. You've always done right by the people in your life. It's what made you a good father, and husband, and son and brother. But the only thing that matters is that you find someone who loves you and loves Anya. That's it."

"It's so soon," I said quietly. "And when I moved here, I wanted calm. Peace. We'd had so much chaos, so much upheaval."

"Isabel doesn't bring you peace?" she asked.

I exhaled a laugh. "No. I don't think I've had a moment of peace since I laid eyes on her. She's too ... she's more than I expected."

My mom sniffled on the other end of the phone. "You know as well as anyone, there's no rule book you can follow, no plan that is guaranteed. And if this person can bring life into your heart, into Anya's, then you owe it to Beth to see where that leads."

It took me a second to find my voice, but when I did, it was hoarse. "You know, I think even if you'd told me to let her go, find someone ... else, I don't think I could've done it. But I'm glad you didn't say that."

"I can't wait to meet her," she said warmly. "Now how can I help?"

I picked up the wedding invitation, head clear and heart steadier than it had been in a long time.

"Would you be willing to take Anya tomorrow night?"

CHAPTER 25

Isabel

"I THINK I'M GOING TO PUKE."

I tucked a piece of hair back into the small diamond clip that held Molly's hair back. "No, you're not."

"I just want to see him." She waved a hand in front of her face, sweat misting her forehead, even though the day of her wedding had dawned perfectly clear and mild. "You've seen him, right?"

Crouching down to fluff the flowing organza of her dress, I hummed in assent. "He sounds about as worked up as you do."

"Really?" She smiled wide. My sister, as beautiful as she was in the every day, was the most gorgeous bride I'd ever seen. "Tell me. Gawd, I bet he looks so good in his tux. He shaved, right?"

"I believe he did, but I can't say I would notice if he hadn't."

The photographer moved around us, snapping away as I readied Molly to do some shots with Logan in the gardens outside of Cedarbrook Lodge. She'd risked an outdoor wedding at this venue of her dreams, and so far, Seattle was delivering. The hotel sprawled behind us, the indoor reception room already dimly lit and decorated in soft creams and gold.

Off to the side, Lia and Claire chattered happily, snapping pictures of their own. Paige stood between them, red hair swept up off her face, and peacock blue column dress making her look like a friggin goddess.

"It's not too late to see him now," Paige teased. "Spare the man the embarrassment of bursting into tears in front of a hundred people at the sight of you."

Molly laughed. "No way, I can't *wait* for someone to catch that on camera."

I stood back, and the photographer moved around Molly, directing her this way and that.

Paige slid an arm around my waist. "You four sure clean up all right."

"For as much time as we spent in a hair and makeup chair, we better," Claire said.

Because Molly allowed us freedom in choosing our dresses, Claire and Lia had opted for a dusty shade of blue, and in similar styles that flowed gently away from their hips, off the shoulder straps holding up a sweetheart neckline. All of us wore our hair down and curled, Molly was the only one who kept hers pulled back.

Her wedding dress, with impossibly thin straps holding it up over her shoulders, was fitted to the waist, covered in delicate floral lace before it flowed out dreamily toward the floor.

And after trying on dresses with far too many frills and embellishments, I found one in a deep navy that skimmed the length of my body, crisscrossing fabric covered my breasts, which left a small peekaboo cutout underneath. My back was completely bare.

I looked beautiful, felt beautiful, and so far, could breathe easily that the pre-wedding moments were going off without a hitch.

"Logan is on his way," the wedding planner told us, tapping her CIA-level earpiece and speaking to someone we couldn't see.

Nodding, I picked up my small clutch and walked to meet him, careful to miss the cracks in the path with my heels even though they were wedges. The last thing I needed was a rolled ankle. I'd just ditched the wrist brace the day before.

I stopped when I caught sight of my big brother walking my way. Hands tucked into his black tux pants, dark hair starting to show the slightest hint of silver at the temples, he looked handsome, and visibly nervous.

His smile was slow when he saw me. "Look at you."

"Wait until you see the bride," I told him.

Logan stopped in front of me and shook his head. "You look beautiful."

Instead of deflecting like I so desperately wanted, I let out a deep breath. "Thank you." I tilted my head back where Molly waited for him. "You ready for this?"

"Hell no," he answered feelingly.

I laughed.

But to my absolute horror, his eyes got bright as he stared over my shoulder. "Shit, I just saw her."

"Do not start crying." I glanced up at the sky and blinked. "If you had any idea how long this makeup took, you'd take pity on me."

Behind him, I saw guests starting to filter toward the adjacent garden, where the ceremony would take place. From where she stood, Molly was protected from view by a large hedge. I clutched my purse tightly, and Logan laid a hand on mine, squeezing gently.

"I don't think you have anything to worry about, Iz. She's not here."

I turned my hand and clutched his. "I know. I think I always knew she wasn't going to come."

His eyes, so capable of seeing through all of us, studied me carefully. "From the first day, it's been her loss. And my unbelievable gain."

When my eyes watered, I let out a deep breath. "Today is going to be great," I told him. "Even if you cry like a baby when you walk her down the aisle."

He chuckled.

"Who's crying like a baby?" Paige asked. She grinned at Logan when he stepped away from me and slid an arm around her waist. "Is it you, husband?"

"Maybe," he murmured.

"Ready to go see our girl?" Paige said gently. "She's waiting."

Logan nodded, his jaw tight.

I stood in place and watched them walk hand in hand toward Molly. My sister turned and saw Logan, and my big brother had to stop to rub suspiciously at his eyes. Paige rubbed his back, which heaved on a massive breath. He approached Molly, shaking his head. He reached out and swiped a thumb under her eyes, and when they embraced tightly, I had to look down at the grass so I didn't absolutely lose it.

No matter what happened for the rest of the day, I would be okay.

Or tomorrow, or the week after.

Even if I felt slightly hollowed out after what happened with Aiden, and his continued silence, days like today filled some of that void with pure joy.

It's the only reason I could smile as I turned toward the hotel.

But I stopped short, the breath knocked out of me like a punch.

Aiden.

He was at the end of the path, waiting for me. Hair slicked back neatly, jaw slightly dark with stubble, and his muscular frame covered in a deep navy suit that fit him so perfectly I could've wept. He wore no tie, his hands hanging loosely at his sides.

My hand fluttered to my stomach, and his eyes tracked the movement.

It must have been enough for him because he approached with long-legged strides, eyes confident, mouth slightly curved in a smile.

"Wh-what are you doing here?" I asked.

His eyes traced my face, but he said nothing until he held out his hand. "I'm here for you."

The sight of his arm outstretched blurred through the tears that filled my eyes until I willed them away. Taking in a slow breath, I slid my palm against his, only exhaling when he wove our fingers together.

Together, we walked down a short fork in the paved path, and he gave me a secretive smile over his shoulder when we turned around a large tiled wall to a small enclosed garden.

I was gripping his hand so tightly when he stopped, I wondered if he would pull away. Instead, he took my other hand in his, gently curled his fingers around my wrist, lifting it up to his mouth so he could press a kiss to where I'd worn the brace.

His eyes held fast to mine, and honestly, I wasn't sure how I was still standing.

I wasn't sure how my legs still worked or how my heart was still pounding blood to my body because it all rushed through my head.

Even with my heels, he towered over me, but Aiden gently tugged, pulling me into his arms.

His hands slid over the skin of my back, my arms curled around his middle, and I breathed out shakily when there was nothing but him. Nothing I could smell or see or feel except Aiden.

All the times we'd been alone, I'd imagined heat and the lighting of a bonfire, flames hitting the sky in a sharp whooshing sound.

But this, what a slow, gentle undoing of my heart. His fingers slid up the bumps on my spine, and I tucked my body closer to his. Those hands, they pushed underneath the veil of my hair until he cupped the back of my neck.

I pulled back to stare up at him. My smile was as easy as breathing, which was sort of how it felt to fall in love with him. It was simply the way I worked, I realized. It was the big picture that I hadn't been able to see until he was in front of me. Loving him was the thing I was born to do.

His big hand slid over the side of my face, thumb brushing the seam of my lips.

"I'm sorry I made you wait," he whispered.

My lips split in a happy smile. "You're worth it."

Aiden cupped my face in both hands and leaned down. But instead of brushing his lips over mine, he kissed my cheekbone. My forehead. The tip of my nose. My hands curled into the lapels of his jacket, helpless fists that did nothing to make him hurry up and kiss me already. Then I tugged, and he chuckled against my temple.

"Impatient," he said.

My nose brushing his, I angled my head so that our mouths were a hairsbreadth apart. "You have no idea," I told him.

"And beautiful." He kissed the edge of my lips. "So beautiful." The other side.

Every inch of my body vibrated dangerously, his lips hovering over mine for a beat. Our eyes met, locked together like that, and I saw the challenge he held in his.

Sliding my hands up his chest and around his neck, I curled my fingers around the curve of his skull and pushed up on the balls of my feet, mouth sealing over his.

It was the only moment I was in control.

Aiden wrapped an arm around my waist, sliding his tongue against mine, angling his head so he could take our kiss deeper. His fingers tangled in my hair, and I tried to scramble closer but couldn't.

He groaned, deep in his chest when I sucked on his tongue. His fingers dug into my flesh as our kiss went on and on.

Sipping at my lips, Aiden tested the way our lips moved together. Our bodies were so close, breath moving from me to him, and when he slid his tongue in a long swipe over mine, I hummed happily.

His body was so strong, so hard, and I stumbled backward,

my shoulder blades hitting against sun-warmed tile. He followed me, tilting his head to suck at my bottom lip.

My head dropped back, and his fingers found the curve of my ass through my dress, grabbing hard, tugging me closer to him. His mouth slid along the edge of my jaw, the edge of his teeth pulling at my earlobe until I moaned a curse.

"Iz?" Lia called from the other side of the wall.

Aiden and I froze.

"Hang on," I managed.

"Yeah, umm"—she sounded like she was grinning—"you're needed for some pictures."

Aiden stared down at me, looking very much like he wanted to devour me whole, and when I licked my lips, he clenched his jaw until a muscle ticked deliciously. He pulled his hand from my ass, sliding it up my waist, skirting the side of my breast, stopping briefly to drag his thumb along the small cutout on my midriff.

"I meant to take that a little slower," he said, speaking into the crown of my hair, dropping a kiss on the top of my head.

I blew out a hard breath. "I'm sure as hell not complaining."

Aiden burst out laughing, his smile broad and happy, his teeth white and straight, and he wrapped me up in his arms again.

When I pulled away, my cheeks felt hot. "Did you mess up all my makeup?"

"You look perfect."

With a skeptical lift of my eyebrows, I ran my fingers through my hair, then picked up my clutch where it had fallen onto the grass. I reapplied some ChapStick because not even on my sister's wedding day was I willing to wear lipstick.

I tucked my hair behind my ears and gave him a slight smile. "I'll find you after the ceremony."

He nodded. "I think I'm going to wait here and recite multiplication tables."

I glanced down, pursing my lips thoughtfully. "Probably a good idea."

When I rounded the corner, Lia was grinning like a loon.

"Shut up," I told her.

When I glanced over my shoulder, I saw him watching us. And the promise I saw in his eyes, I couldn't help but shiver.

"Ooooh, baby, Isabel's got a *boyfriend*," she sang. "It's about fricken time."

"I hate you."

With a happy sigh, she slid her arm around my waist. "No, you don't. Now come on, let's go get Molly married."

CHAPTER 26

Isabel

ANY ATTEMPT TO SAVE MY MAKEUP FROM LOGAN OR AIDEN or whatever man seemed destined to ruin it was a fool's errand.

Once I made my way down the aisle, clutching the small bouquet, it was the last dry moment my eyes experienced for the entirety of the twenty-minute ceremony.

Emmett, dressed in a tux to match Logan's, was pushing a stroller that we'd decorated in Molly and Noah's wedding colors. Strapped inside was Gabriel, wearing the cutest fricken baby tuxedo the world had ever seen, holding a small pillow that said, *Here comes my aunt.* At all of a few months old, he may have started my crying first.

Music cued up over the speakers, and I gave Noah an encouraging smile. The large man looked as nervous as I'd ever seen him, hands fidgeting in front of him while we waited for Molly and my brother to appear. I'd seen her all morning, witnessed her transformation to the bride he was about to see for the first time, so instead of watching the aisle, I watched Noah.

And I knew the moment she appeared because the scariest defensive end in the league, the one who grew up in the house behind ours, absolutely crumpled when he saw my sister walking toward him.

He held a hand over his mouth briefly, eyes shining with unshed tears. His friend and teammate, standing in the mirror position to mine, slapped him on the back and whispered something to Noah that had him dropping his hand, straightening so that he could watch Molly. A tear slid down the side of his cheek when he smiled at her.

Behind me was joint sniffling from the twins, and in the front row, Paige cried without even attempting to stop the flow of tears down her face as Logan walked Molly down the aisle. When they reached the front—as planned—Paige came from her seat and took her place on the other side of Molly, anchoring her arm around my sister's waist.

Logan kissed Molly's cheek and whispered something that made her emit a watery sob. With a brief glance up at the sky, I blinked rapidly. Claire tapped me on the shoulder and handed me a small tissue. I smiled, gently blotting underneath my eyes.

After a short greeting, the minister took his place with a smile, gesturing for Noah to get Molly. "And who gives this woman to be married today?"

Paige and Logan shared a meaningful look. "We do," they said in unison.

Noah and Logan exchanged a small, secret handshake that had the Wolves' teammates in the crowd chuckling audibly. And then my sister took Noah's hand, pausing so he could say something quietly, only audible to her, that had her looking up at him with so much love, the waterworks almost started anew.

It was difficult to stand still, especially in those freaking heels, but once I got Molly's flowers from her, that was kind of my job.

Only once—and I was very proud of myself—did I look out into the rows of seats.

Aiden's gaze was on me, and when our eyes locked, he sent me a subdued smile that had my palms going a little sweaty.

What a first date.

Bawling my eyes out in front of a hundred people, finally letting go of the emotional weight that had been pushing on my shoulders, and wearing the type of dress that made any type of undergarment outside of a G-string completely impossible.

Even if I had pictured my first date with Aiden, I never would've pictured this. A hike maybe. Wandering around downtown. Something simple and easy, nothing overdone or fussy.

This was as fussy as I'd ever get. And still, he was here.

Spinning down the mental path of what it meant or what it signified was pointless. Which was why I directed my attention back to the minister, and to Molly and Noah.

I couldn't see my sister's face, but I could see Noah's, and the way he gazed down at her was enough to turn me into a giant pile of mush.

Molly took a deep breath when it was her turn to say vows.

"Today, surrounded by all the people who love us best, I say the words I do, but I am really promising that I will." He smiled, lifting one of her hands for a soft kiss. "I will take your hand and stand by your side in the good and the bad. I will be your guiding light in the darkness, your shoulder to lean on when life is hard. As your wife, I will be your navigator and your best friend. I promise to honor, cherish, and love you through all of life's adventures." Her voice wobbled. "Today, Noah Griffin, and every day for as long as I live, I will choose you as my husband."

Noah grinned down at her.

"Today, surrounded by all the people who love us best," he rumbled in that deep voice of his, "I say the words *I do*, but I am really promising that *I will*. I will take your hand and stand by your side in the good and the bad. I will be the one who supports your dreams more than any other. I will shelter you from whatever storms hit us. As your husband, I will be your partner and your best friend. I promise to honor, cherish, and love you through all of life's adventures. Today, Molly Ward, and every day for as long as I live, I will choose you as my wife."

Rings were exchanged, they were pronounced husband and wife, and when he wrapped her in his arms for a shockingly passionate kiss, a cheer of Super Bowl proportions rang through the gardens. Laughing along with my sisters as it did, I couldn't help but sweep my gaze over the people sitting in the chairs.

I recognized most of the faces, but not all. Out of all those faces, I didn't see the one I was seeking.

It was a strange realization to have amid such overflowing happiness that still … Brooke hadn't come. Given the choice, extended with grace by someone who'd forgiven her, she'd stayed away.

Molly, I knew, would be fine. As her brand-new husband drew away from her, tucked her hand in the crook of his elbow, and escorted her down the carpet of lush emerald grass to the sound of cheers and whistles, I thought about all the different ways people moved on.

Maybe I held onto the past, held onto anger, or my reserve with men with white-knuckled hands because they were all something I could control, but Aiden showing up for me today was something I hadn't been in control of.

It was his way of moving on too, and I had to recognize the gesture, even if it hadn't come with any big speeches. Yet.

He couldn't have predicted how I'd react, but still, he showed up. Held his hand out to me, gave me a choice.

When I took the arm of Kareem, one of Noah's teammates, and we followed the happy couple down the aisle, I knew my choices would be unfolding in front of me all night.

I chose, as Aiden watched me with a steady, calm gaze, to set aside anything Brooke could've done—or not done—to this day. Like my brother said, it was—and always had been—her loss.

When Molly jumped into Noah's arms for another kiss, I felt lighter than I had in years. Happier.

The wedding planner hustled the wedding party back out to another garden for pictures, and when I glanced over my shoulder to catch Aiden's eye, he winked.

That wink held me over the eternal length of time it took us to take pictures with the whole wedding party. If what I needed to do was screw a smile on my face for a billion clicks of her camera, then that was what I would do.

Hovering at the edge of the side garden where we stood, I saw a glimpse of his navy suit. The wedding coordinator was talking to the photographer, and Molly and Noah whispered quietly to each other, so I decided to sneak in his direction.

I nudged Lia with my elbow. Both of the twins turned.

"I'll be right there if they need me," I said, tilting my head to where I'd seen him.

"I will make sure to give plenty of warning before I come around the corner to get you," she answered seriously.

As I walked to Aiden, I flipped her my middle finger, which had her and Claire laughing.

He turned as I approached, no smile on his face but warm, warm eyes. It was terrifying how much I wanted to dive into him and never resurface.

Aiden opened his arms, and I walked straight into his embrace. His hands smoothed along my bare back, and I curled into him, burrowing deeper into his warmth.

This cannot be normal, I thought.

When his broad chest started shaking on a laugh, I realized I'd spoken out loud.

Pulling back so I could see his face, I gave him an embarrassed smile. "You know what I mean."

"Yeah," he murmured.

"I didn't even ask earlier, but who invited you?"

"Molly," he said. He drew a hand from my back and smoothed it down the line of my arm, like he simply wanted to touch as much of me as possible. "She stopped by my house."

"Really?"

Aiden nodded.

But then he seemed to struggle to find the words, and I couldn't help but smile. "Okay, the big broody silent man routine is only sexy in certain situations, and this isn't one of them, Hennessy."

In response, he tugged me closer with a subdued laugh, and I played with the edge of his lapel. He smelled so good, but gawd, I'd stop sniffing like a crazy person if he came only because of this.

"Didn't you have time to practice what to say?" I teased.

His eyes held mine, his fingers sweeping into the ends of my hair. "I'm not ... I'm not good at speeches like this. I never know the right thing to say, or how to explain what I'm feeling."

Underneath my hand where it laid on his jacket, his heart was pounding. It was unbelievable how much peace that fed into me, knowing he was just as nervous about this as I used to be around him.

Aiden and I, this entire time, had been sitting on an invisible teeter-totter, and eventually, we'd even out into perfect balance. I had a feeling it would be tonight.

His hand smoothed along my face, and I turned my head to kiss his palm.

"I knew Beth for years," he started quietly. I willed myself not to react as he spoke, simply kept my hand over his heart and my body pressed close to his. "We were friends. She moved in down the street, and the first day I met her, she brought us a plate of gin-gersnap cookies to introduce herself."

I gave him a tiny smile. "Anya's nickname."

He nodded. "And my favorite food. It felt ... impossible to

explain that to you when you were in my bed," he said, voice rough with emotion.

My eyes closed for a moment. "Yeah, I can imagine."

"When we were eighteen, she announced to me that she was going to kiss me, and I would be her first boyfriend because she saw how I looked at her, and she was sick of waiting."

My smile widened. I had a feeling I would've liked Beth.

"She was my best friend," Aiden continued. "And I knew everything about her. Loving her, falling in love with her, was something slow and steady and gradual, until suddenly it was ... everything."

My eyes filled with tears as he spoke. "I'm so sorry you lost her," I told him.

His own eyes were bright when he leaned down to kiss my forehead. "I am too." When he pulled back, he studied my face. "She was my first love, and when I came here, I was not looking to replace that, Isabel."

My fingers fidgeted restlessly, but I refused to look away. "I know."

"You," he continued, eyes locked in on my lips, "did not come into my life slow or steady."

I smiled.

"Because of that," Aiden whispered, "it became something I felt like I needed to resist. Something too intense for what I was capable of in this second chance of my life."

Slowly, I nodded. All of that made sense. And my heart, it breathed just a bit easier understanding it.

We were on borrowed time in this conversation, and I didn't know how much longer I'd have. My fingers trailed the edge of his jaw and followed the line of his lips.

"My sister must've given one hell of a pep talk," I said lightly.

Those lips curled up at the edges, and Aiden kissed the tips of my fingers as he drew my hand away. "She just affirmed what I was a little slow in figuring out for myself."

"What's that?"

His eyes held mine, the intensity in them making my stomach weightless. All the butterflies from the first day I met him whooshed back into place. "That if I could see you in my future, I needed to take my chance."

The way he said it sounded so simple, so sure.

"She's very smart," I answered seriously.

Aiden wrapped his arms around me, and I did the same around his waist.

"Just making sure she didn't make this a pity date," I spoke into his chest. "Because if you are here because of my mommy issues, I will kick you in the balls."

Aiden pulled back in laughter. With a grin still playing over his lips, he slid his hand over my cheek, weaving his fingers through my hair until he cupped the back of my head. He lowered his mouth, his lips brushing mine in tantalizing slowness when he spoke. "The very last thing I feel for you is pity."

I might've said something like, *hey, that's wonderful.* But it was all I could do to keep from falling as he deepened the kiss into something brimming with unspent tension. His lips moved harder, and my breathing picked up when his hands slid over my body. He and I, we'd need a week locked in a hotel room to feel like the need was sated. It was all I could do to keep my feet planted, my legs holding me up as his tongue swirled around mine.

And right now, all I wanted to do was wrap those around his waist.

One of the twins called my name from the other garden, and I whimpered. Aiden pressed a hard kiss against my lips, then another one.

"Family pictures and then I'm done." I slid my hand under his jacket and sucked his bottom lip into my mouth. His fingers curled around my hip, and the hot press of him against my stomach had my toes curling up in my shoes.

"Okay." He pulled back and smiled.

"Don't smile at me like that," I said, staring at his mouth.

"Why not?"

My hand curled into his belt, the heat of his hard stomach coming through the material of his shirt when I pulled him closer and spoke against his neck. "Because I'll end up missing from my family pictures when I start ripping your clothes off."

Aiden hissed out a slow breath. "You are dangerous, woman."

I kissed the edge of his jaw. "Just wait."

"Go," he said in a rough voice.

Without a backward glance, I did. Because whoo, okay, I thought we were potent in that utility closet or in his bedroom. Apparently, we really found our stride at garden weddings.

Lia smirked as I approached. I gave her a look right back.

Jude was bouncing Gabriel in his arms, and I picked up his chubby hands and kissed each of them.

"How's my boy?" I cooed. His big blue eyes and shock of dark hair had me grinning as did his gummy little squeals. Dropping a kiss onto his cheek, I laughed when he yanked on a chunk of my hair. "A little help, please."

Jude carefully extricated Gabriel's fist from my hair. "Savage little child we've got."

"Then he fits right in," Bauer interjected as he approached. He kissed Claire on the top of the head.

"Hi," she said with a smile. "You were almost late to the wedding."

He grinned. "I was exactly on time, thank you very much. Traffic was a little heavy coming down from Vancouver. I got to sit next to Isabel's new boyfriend." Bauer paused thoughtfully. "He's huge and intimidating, and I find that I approve of him wholeheartedly on the basis that he could probably snap me in half."

The twins laughed, Jude smiled, and Bauer held out his fist for me to tap.

"Nice work, Iz," he said. "I think you finally found one who can keep up with you."

The photographer called us over, and I was saved from having to respond. Jude and Bauer stood off to the side while the four girls gathered around the couple, and we were shifted around Logan, Paige, and Emmett.

I found myself tapping my foot in anticipation while the photographer worked.

Gabriel cried and squawked in Jude's arms once the guys joined us, which made all of us laugh, but through all of it, I felt a push, an urgency to be by Aiden. The wedding planner pulled us out of the frame so she could set up some shots for Molly, Noah, Logan, and Paige.

Logan appeared next to me while the photographer's assistant fixed the back of Molly's dress. At first, he didn't say anything, and we watched together in silence.

"Looks like we had a surprise guest after all," he commented.

I smiled. "Looks like."

He glanced over at me. "Do I need to pull him aside and have a talk with him?"

A hysterical laugh almost burst out of me. If my big brother—the most protective man I'd ever known—knew that my first date with my older-by-a-decade boss would (fingers friggin crossed) end up with me losing my virginity, he'd have a coronary.

"Not to warn him off," Logan amended.

Turning slightly, I raised an eyebrow. "No?"

He wrapped an arm around me, and I let my head rest on his shoulder. "If you want this one, there's a reason."

That had my heart going all warm and gooey, and I tried to smother my pleased smile. "No *I can't believe another one of you picked an athlete* sermon?"

"Nope."

"Did Paige yell at you about that after you said it to Lia?"

"Yup."

I laughed. "What would you tell him in your little talk then?"

Logan took a deep breath and tightened his grip on me for a moment before turning me gently so we faced each other. "For better or worse, you're a lot like me, kid. You always have been." He smiled. "We hold back until we don't have a choice. Paige is the exact right person for me because she ripped through that reserve like a battering ram."

I laughed.

His face went serious. "But you, Isabel, you are braver than I ever was at your age. I hope he knows that you choosing him means he's getting one of the best gifts in the world because the way you love the people in your life ..." His voice trailed off. He cupped my face. "It's a *privilege* to be one of them."

My eyes burned hot, and the bridge of my nose tingled. "Thank you."

Logan cleared his throat, dropping a kiss on my forehead. "Love you."

"I love you too." I wrapped my arms around him and hugged him like I hadn't in a long time. Wasn't that funny? When you saw someone all the time, it became so easy to forget how much you might need their hugs. And nothing, at that moment, felt more like a blessing to move forward than a hug from my brother.

Paige approached with a tiny smile on her face. "You can go," she told me.

"Really?"

She nodded. "They're done with the family pictures. You have about thirty more minutes before we'll need you lined up for the reception."

Instantly, I kicked off my shoes, only stopping to scoop them up by the strap. I clutched the hem of my dress and ran across the grass to the sound of Paige's laughter.

CHAPTER 27

Isabel

IT DIDN'T TAKE ME LONG TO FIND HIM. I'D SLOWED TO A FAST walk, barefoot as I crossed the lobby of the hotel into the reception area. It was dimly lit, tall tables circling the perimeter of the room for guests to mingle and have a cocktail while they waited for the wedding party to arrive. Along the edges and in corners of the room were soft places to sit, some draped in white gauze, lending a magical atmosphere along with the hundreds of candles, the twinkle lights swooping down the ceiling.

Aiden stood toward the edge of the room talking to Luke Pierson, one of Logan's former teammates. Next to them, her arm curved around Luke's waist, was Allie Sutton-Pierson, the owner of the Wolves and one of Paige's best friends.

Allie said something that made the men laugh, and her face lit into a brilliant smile when she saw me. "Iz, you look gorgeous."

When I hugged her, I glanced quickly at Aiden. "Thank you. Did the girls come with you?"

Luke shook his head. "Faith and Lydia decided a weekend at Grandma's was a lot more fun than a wedding."

"How old are your kids?" Aiden asked. I slipped next to him, and my breath caught when he casually folded his hand through mine.

Allie noticed and gave me a pointed look. I had to bite down on my lip so as not to burst into laughter. None of these people had ever seen me in a relationship, and you could freaking tell by their absolute lack of chill.

"Faith is sixteen, Lydia is almost eleven, and I have never felt older in my life than I do when I say that out loud," Luke admitted.

Aiden smiled. "My daughter is seven, so I get it."

It was hard to focus on what they were saying because I was standing next to Aiden, holding his hand and chatting with family friends like absolutely nothing was strange about that. My impatience to be alone with him must've shown because Allie gave me a tiny wink and then tapped her husband's chest. "You know, my glass is empty. Buy me a drink?"

He smiled down at her. "Logan's buying. Hell yeah, I'll buy you a drink."

They wandered off, and I let out a deep breath. "Did you get something at the bar?" I asked.

Glancing at me with warm, humor-lit eyes, he tilted his head toward a table. "It's over there."

Aiden pulled us away from the milling groups of people to a corner that held a white couch just big enough for two. His jacket was hanging over the arm, like he made sure to stake a claim to this slightly private spot. He slid into the corner and stretched one arm over the back of the couch. Instead of joining him right away, I took a moment to study him like that, lounging like a great big cat.

His long legs were slightly spread, and it was so easy to imagine if we were alone. Judging by the look in his green eyes, he was doing some imagining of his own.

My skin heated under his perusal, tightening underneath the silky fabric of my dress where I wanted his hands. If we were alone, I'd slide the dress up over my thighs and climb into his lap, smooth my hands up his chest, let those large, capable hands hold me in place, and his mouth find the parts of me that tasted best.

Aiden exhaled a low chuckle, shaking his head slightly. "You keep looking at me like that, and we're going to cause trouble."

I blinked slowly, coming out of my stupor. Carefully, I took a seat next to him, tucking one leg underneath me so I could angle in his direction. His fingers slid over my shoulder blade and toyed with the ends of my hair.

Then he paused, reaching for a tall glass on a table next to the couch. My eyebrows bent in when he handed it to me.

"Screwdriver?" I asked. "I didn't peg you as a mixed drink guy."

Without a word, he motioned for me to take it. Our fingers brushed as I took the glass, and after I took a sip, his eyes warmed.

"Orange juice?" I asked, mouth widening into a massive smile.

Aiden retrieved the glass and took a drink. I licked my lips as he set the glass down. He leaned in, angling his back so he was blocking me from view, and he took my mouth in a voracious, toe-curling kiss that tasted like bright citrus and held the promise of sex. I was ready to *climb him* by the time he pulled away.

"Orange juice," he said.

"I'll make a note for work." This level of happiness should be illegal.

"You're okay with sitting in the corner with me at your sister's wedding?" he asked.

With a glance around, I saw only a few people who I probably should have been making small talk with. Finally, I looked back at Aiden and studied his handsome face.

"Completely okay," I told him. "I'd rather talk to you."

Because I could, I touched my thumb to the bottom curve of his lip and swept it softly over the stubble that lined his jaw. I loved that he hadn't shaved for this. It made him look a little dangerous, or maybe that was just how I felt being with him like this. The entire thing felt too big to be real, to be safe.

Could two people survive this level of sexual tension? Because I wasn't sure we could.

"What do you want to talk about?" he asked. He took my hand away from his mouth and kissed the tip of my thumb before settling it on his rock-hard thigh, fingers lightly entwined with mine.

So many questions I could ask. Some that could wait, a couple that couldn't.

I took a deep breath and asked the first thing on my mind. "Is this ... our first date?" I looked at him from under my lashes.

"You don't count changing the fuse?"

With a grin, I shook my head. "No."

"Your night at my house?"

I gave him a dry look.

Aiden hummed. "What about our first training session?"

Slowly, I raised my eyebrows. I know I'd felt like the slightest touch from him that night would've made me explode, but I was never certain if he'd felt the same.

"Maybe," I conceded.

"First dates are about figuring out the person you're with," he said. "I learned a lot about you that night."

"Like ...?" My voice trailed off.

His fingers dragged along my back, and I shivered. "You don't like to burden people with what's bothering you. Talking about it probably makes it worse." At the accurate statement, I lifted my chin slightly. He kept going. "You couldn't decide whether you loved it or hated it that I'd been watching you that closely and you didn't realize it. Normally you've always got a bead on what's happening."

"True," I conceded. "What else?"

"When it surfaces, you harness your anger into something

productive, something tangible, probably so that you don't lash out at the people around you."

I fidgeted on the couch, my breath coming a bit faster that he'd picked up all of that just from one night.

Aiden leaned in, our knees touching, and he angled his body so that we gained even more privacy. "And me saying this to you makes you want to run, just a little."

Undaunted by the flutterings of panic that his spot-on assessment caused, I met his gaze head-on. "I'm not going anywhere."

"No?" he asked in a rough, uneven voice. When I shook my head, he tipped his head down and slid his mouth over mine for a sweet, slow kiss. My tongue slipped to the seam of his lips, but he pulled back. "No more, woman. You're killing me."

My smile was full of satisfaction because he sounded like he was walking a razor edge of restraint.

"Second date then," I said.

"Deal." He sat back, allowing for a safer distance between us, given we were both feeling the need to mount each other in public.

"Where's Anya tonight?" I asked.

"My parents.'" He pulled out his phone and showed me a picture that had me laughing out loud.

"Is that your dad?"

"It is."

I took the phone from his hand and zoomed in on the image. Anya was standing on their kitchen counter behind a man who looked like Aiden might in about twenty years. They shared the same jaw, the same nose, the same build. And his dad, judging by the pleased smile on his face, was perfectly content to let his granddaughter put foam rollers into his slightly graying hair.

"May I?" I gestured to the picture. He nodded. I swiped through a few pictures, studied one of his mom. "Your parents look young, considering…" I stopped, not sure how to say, *considering how old you are.*

Aiden laughed softly. "You calling me old?"

I bit my lip to smother my grin. "No."

He took the phone out of my hand and found a shot of his whole family, then let me study it. Just like my family, they held such a strong resemblance to each other but still managed to be a perfect balance of his parents.

"My parents were fifteen when they met," he said. "Sixteen when my mom got pregnant with me."

My eyes lifted in surprise. "Seriously?"

He nodded. "They got married before I turned two but knew they were still too young to add more kids into the mix." Aiden pointed at the faces on the picture. "Beckham came when I was ten, then Clark, Deacon was next." And when he gestured to a woman who looked younger than me, I found that I liked her broad smile and the way she looked like she was laughing. "And because she could be nothing other than the youngest and spoiled rotten, Eloise was the Hennessy family grand finale."

"Wow," I breathed. Before I could say anything else, a gentle tap on my shoulder pulled my attention from Aiden. It was the wedding coordinator.

"Sorry to interrupt, Isabel. We're going to announce the wedding party, and then you can come back. Since Molly and Noah just have a table for the two of them, I only need to steal you away for a few minutes."

Aiden smiled, joining me as I stood. The perfect gentleman on an unconventional first date.

And that continued, once I was able to join him at the table we were sharing with my sisters and their men. He kept a hand curled around my thigh under the table, engaging in pleasant conversation with everyone as we ate. Occasionally, he'd lean in and ask me something random, switching his hand from resting on my thigh, to stretching out behind my back along my chair.

"Favorite movie?"

I hummed. "I rarely watch them, so it's hard to pick."

"Really?" he said, clearly surprised.

"But," I amended, "I love a good sports documentary."

"Me too." He leaned in for a sweet kiss.

It was so easy to forget other people were at the table when he looked at me that way. I didn't really care if my sisters were watching with unabashed interest because Lord knows I'd had to watch my fair share of mooning over the last couple of years.

I slid my hand over his, relishing the easy affection. "The questions Anya asked me," I started. He smiled sadly but didn't interrupt. "What were those about?"

His chest expanded on a deep breath. Then he told me the story, and I didn't even attempt to stop the tear that slid down my cheek. He brushed it away. "It was something she looked to for a long time as ... truth, I guess. That if anyone would know, it would be Beth."

"And you?" I asked carefully.

Aiden shook his head. "It was, I don't know how to say it right. I wasn't planning on using it as a checklist, if that's what you're asking, mainly because I had no intention of finding someone." He curled his fingers around my thigh, smoothing it up and down. He gave me a wry smile. "But it probably didn't help that you were the exact opposite of what she told Anya."

I smiled. "Probably not."

He studied me so intently.

"What?" I asked.

He shook his head. "Nothing."

The thing I loved was that I could wait to ask him more because we had the time, not because I feared the reaction.

People shifted around us, moving to the dance floor as he and I talked.

He preferred winter over summer and broke his leg when he was twelve.

He didn't drink often, and only one beer when he did.

When he went to college, his sister made him take a stuffed animal so he didn't get lonely, and he kept it on his bed his entire freshman year, no matter how much his roommates teased him.

He asked me why I decided not to go to college and how it was being raised by my brother.

When the cake was cut and passed around, he took a piece of coconut, and I chose the strawberry, which we shared. When he held his fork out to me for a bite of his cake, I absently wondered if I'd ever get sick of talking to him. Of hearing what he had to say.

His eyes darkened when I licked at a speck of frosting at the edge of my lip.

When our plates were cleaned of cake, I sat back in my seat and surveyed him carefully. "Not a bad date, Hennessy."

At the use of his last name, he quirked an eyebrow. "We're back there."

"Well," I drawled, uncrossing my leg so that I could turn fully to face him, "I think you still owe me a little bit."

"Do you?"

His dry tone had me smiling. "You didn't have to buy me dinner," I told him. "Or dessert."

He hummed, caging me in by setting an arm on the table, the other stretched along the back of my chair. "How would you normally end a date like this?"

There was no way for me to answer that without giving myself away completely. I had no idea where the night would lead, but I knew where I wanted it to. "I don't think I've ever had a date like this," I told him with complete honesty.

Based on the look in his eyes, he saw the truth of my answer.

"Me neither."

It knocked the breath from my lungs when he said it, and I didn't realize how badly I craved some sort of sign that this intensity wasn't one-sided, wasn't confined just to my inexperience.

Because I couldn't not, I leaned forward, cupping the side of his face in my hand, and I slid my lips over his in a soft kiss.

We left the kiss there, pulling back at the same time, content not to deepen it further.

Aiden turned, placing a kiss in the center of my palm. "Dance with me?" he asked.

Slowly, I nodded, and he stood, a firm hold on my hand as he led us to the dance floor crowded with people. We stood between a former defensive player of the year and his wife, and an executive from Molly's job at Amazon, and not once did his attention waver.

It didn't matter who surrounded us, I realized.

It didn't matter what he may have experienced in his past, or what I had yet to experience in my future. This was about us. Aiden gathered our joined hands against his chest, over his steadily beating heart, and his other arm curled low around my waist as he pulled me into his body. My free hand slid around his back, and I laid my head on his chest as we swayed.

His fingers strayed slowly, first to the edge of my dress where it wrapped around my body, but he dipped beneath the fabric to strum featherlight touches along the curve of my hip. With a restless exhale, I shifted closer, and he tightened his hand around mine.

The beat of the song was slow and sweet, but in his arms, it became something else entirely. It was foreplay.

All of it had been.

For days and weeks.

My fingers on his back curled, nails digging slightly into the hard, shifting muscles on his back and I lost the ability to breathe properly when I closed my eyes and imagined how they'd feel when he moved over me. He'd be relentless. He'd be brutal if I begged it of him.

Aiden's chest expanded on a deep inhale, his nose burying into my hair. When he made a restless shift of his own, I felt how much he wanted me. The noise that started in my throat was practically a purr. And he heard it.

"We either need to stop dancing or get the hell out of here," he rasped in my ear.

Tilting my head up so I could lock gazes with him, I licked my lips before speaking. His nostrils flared when I did. "What will you do to me if I choose option two?"

Somehow, he managed to tighten his grip on me, bring me even closer to him so that he could rest his lips against the shell of my ear. "I am going to do everything," he growled. "And trust me, my imagination has come up with a lot since you decided to climb into my bathtub without me."

I was panting when I stepped back, my hands shaking. At first, his face smoothed like he thought I might deny him.

"You have ten minutes to get a room," I told him in a remarkably even voice. "I will meet you by the elevator."

It took six minutes for me to hug and kiss Molly and Noah, who were swamped by people, and to inform the twins that I would be exiting the party early. No one argued with me, and Lia gave me an obnoxious high five.

I marched—shoes and clutch in hand—to the elevator, where I saw him waiting for me.

Calmly, he hit the button and slipped his hands into his pants pockets. I blew out a slow breath while the numbers descended.

In the quiet between us, I wondered a dozen things about how it would be between us, what waited when we opened the hotel room door to complete privacy.

But one thing I didn't wonder was whether I'd been stupid to wait for someone who made me feel like this. There wasn't an ounce of hesitation anywhere inside me. The doors opened, and we walked in side by side, silent as the grave.

Aiden pushed the button for the correct floor, and as soon as the doors closed, as soon as we were alone, he exploded into action.

Before I could breathe, I was against the wall, his mouth hard and demanding over mine, his hands ruthless as he strained the seams of my dress by pushing his grip underneath to fill his palms with my flesh.

His tongue was hot and slick, and I whimpered when it swept around mine in a tantalizing circle. My arms were around his neck so tightly that when he straightened, I could hardly find purchase on the floor. But I didn't need it. He wrenched my hip up and rolled himself between my legs.

This kiss was a dark prelude that we'd danced around the entire time we knew each other.

It was dirty, and everything I wanted, everything I'd dreamed of from him. He devoured my mouth, tilting his head to deepen it further, and I stole the breath from his lungs because I'd not be the one to pull away.

I'd live there, in that kiss, if he let me.

His body shook from the force of everything he was pouring into our embrace. If we stayed on that elevator much longer, I swear, I would've given it up to him right there.

We arrived at our floor, an inconspicuous ding heralding the gentle stop of the car, and Aiden pulled back, breathing hard, lips red from our kiss.

"Fucking finally," he said, tugging on my hand as I exhaled a laugh.

We rushed down the hall, and when he found the right door, he almost dropped the key in his haste to unlock the door.

Behind him, I couldn't help myself. I pressed my front to his back and started unfastening his belt. A hand shot out, bracing against the doorframe, and he muttered another foul curse word when I got the buckle undone.

"I'm going to tell you something before we walk in that room," I whispered against his heaving back. The muscles shifted against my forehead when he lifted his head. My nimble fingers pulled the leather belt from the metal buckle. "For reasons which we can discuss later, I need you to know that I've never done this before." When his whole frame, big and broad, went still as a statue, I smiled. It should have made me feel at a disadvantage that I couldn't see his face, but I'd never felt more powerful. Never felt so in control of what I wanted.

We were still in the hallway, and I tugged his shirt out of his loosened waistband and slid my hands over the ridges of his abdomen, which was all scalding skin and heavy muscle. When I tried to push my hand lower, Aiden growled my name. I stopped.

"You're a ...you've never—"

He couldn't say it.

"Never," I affirmed.

Aiden spun, gripping my face in his hands, eyes burning down at me. "Why?"

I gave him a coy smile, reaching behind his back to finish pushing the key card into the door. "I've never wanted anyone like I want you. No one's hands or mouth," I whispered, leaning up on my tiptoes to suck his bottom lip into my mouth, "and wasting time with someone who doesn't know how to handle me has never been appealing." I kissed down the strong column of his neck. "But I think you know exactly what to do."

With a tortured groan, he slanted his mouth over mine, fisting his hand into my hair. Our tongues dueled, and I felt him grapple with the doorknob. I exhaled a laugh when he still couldn't get it open.

Down the hall, we heard the ding of the elevator, and he tore his mouth from mine to face the entrance to the room again.

The door opened with a click, and he shoved it open so violently that it banged off the wall. Aiden turned, and the look in his eye had me breathless with anticipation, because I knew he was about to absolutely destroy whatever fantasy I'd had of him in the very best way. He reached forward, gathering a fistful of my dress, and tugged me forward as he walked backward into the room.

"You'll pay for that," he said, glancing down briefly at his opened belt.

"Promise?"

The door slammed shut behind me, and before he could move, I reached up behind my neck and unhooked the strap holding my dress up. Before it could fall, he stepped up to me, gripping the back of my neck.

"Nothing else comes off unless I do it," he whispered against my lips.

My eyelids fluttered shut. I wanted to say something cheeky like, *yes, boss,* or *maybe I'll do it myself.* But no words came. I'd lost the ability.

At my expression, he hissed in a breath through clenched teeth. "On the bed," he commanded.

I walked into the room, heart thrashing and legs quaking as he locked the door.

CHAPTER 28

Aiden

THE CLICK OF THE LOCK MAY AS WELL HAVE BEEN A GUNSHOT going off in the room. Red-hot tension coursed through my veins, angry at being pent-up for so long. Before I went to her, I pressed my forehead against the cool metal of the hotel door and attempted to steady my hands. They didn't tremble because I was nervous, but I did feel a slight tremor of apprehension at my ability to keep myself in check.

Maybe it was the way I'd wanted her, or how long I'd resisted something that felt irresistible.

Maybe it was that I'd gone so long without this type of desire—wild and untamed. I wasn't sure I'd ever felt it, and I needed this moment of pause to ensure that I wouldn't unleash a beast onto Isabel in my rib-crushing need to slake what she'd stirred in me.

Very little surprised me anymore.

The fact that she was a virgin almost made me fall to my knees in that sedately decorated hallway. Holding someone's past against them was the sort of hypocrisy that I hated, but the fact that hers brought her to me untouched by any other man humbled me enough that I managed to calmly unbutton my shirt as I turned to where she waited for me. The other option was ripping it open in my haste to touch her, taste her, lose myself in her.

I'd still do all those things.

Isabel sat on the foot of the bed, hands braced behind her, long legs crossed demurely.

The way she held my eyes, the way hers burned as she watched me approach, it was like no image of any virgin I could've conjured.

Again, I was reminded of the black panther I'd seen at the zoo. I might've held a bit more experience than her, but she was looking at me like I was her next meal. And as soon as the thought crossed my mind, her eyes tracked down the front of my chest, and she licked her bottom lip.

Instead of prowling over her and pinning her hands over her head onto the soft mattress, I stripped off my shirt and let it fall in a heap on the floor.

She blew out a slow breath, and I held out my hand for her to stand. Not once did she blink shyly away, did her gaze waver, not a word spoken between us when she smoothed the flat of her hand up over my chest. My nostrils flared at her touch, the wildfire it set off in my blood. It had been so long, and I wanted her so viscerally.

It dawned on me as I drew my fingertips down the graceful line of her neck and carefully tugged her dress forward, that she and I were the same, and that was why I never expected her, never anticipated finding a well of feeling like this. Because I'd never, not in my entire life, met a woman who was my exact counterpoint.

Some people found a soul mate in the one who filled in the gaps and closed in their pieces with one of their own. But she and I, we weren't like that. Isabel and I were the same in the heat that ran through us, and instead of tempering the flames, we burned that much brighter together.

The crisscrossing straps of her dress fell with a whisper, and I sucked in a breath as she was bared to me. Isabel needed no guidance from me as she tugged down the small hidden zipper on the side of her dress, and it slid quietly off her hips until she stood before me in nothing but a tiny scrap of fabric.

I drew the tip of my finger down the front of her throat, whisper-light between her breasts until my hand spanned her waist. She was panting just from that single touch.

"So beautiful," I murmured.

With the grace of a goddess, she sat back on the bed and quirked an eyebrow. "Your turn."

I shucked my pants off, and she rolled her lips between her teeth. Her body laid out like that, it was no sacrifice to fall to my knees in front of her. I filled my hands with her flesh and tugged her hips against my stomach, Isabel clutched my head to her as I used my lips and tongue and teeth until she threw her head back with a loud gasp. With a hand on her chest, I pushed gently until she laid back on the bed, and I crawled up and over her, licking a line over her hip bones, nibbling the curve of her ribs.

When I placed a sucking kiss just underneath her belly button, her skin shook with anticipation.

"Oh, please," she whispered.

"You've waited this long," I murmured against the sleek muscle on her thigh. "You can be patient a little bit longer."

Her head thrashed on the bed at the use of my fingers, back arching in a delicious curve. "I can't."

"Hands over your head," I instructed. "If you can manage this without laying a hand on me, I'll give you what you want."

Instantly, she complied, and I felt the snarling beast inside me shake dangerously.

And then I used my mouth, her legs snapped tight over my shoulders, but she kept her hands fisted in the comforter. When she finally broke, a low moan wracked her frame. Fists planted on either side of her, I slid up the length of her body until I covered her completely. My hand curled over hers where it stayed on the bed as we kissed. As she worked through the aftershocks of what I'd done with fierce, deep kisses, angling her head to take more and more and more from me.

Despite her inexperience, Isabel would take everything from me that I'd give her, and already, I knew I'd serve myself up on a platter just to keep her like this for the rest of my life.

"I don't know what I did to deserve this," I whispered against her mouth, and her eyelids fluttered open. One of her hands cupped the side of my face while I pulled one of her thighs close to my side. "To deserve you."

"It's not about deserving, Aiden." She kissed me. "It's not about being worthy or perfect. It's about finding the right person and choosing them."

Isabel moved under me impatiently, but I kissed her again, gathering her body to mine until there was no space, no room for a single breath between us.

"I am falling in love with you," I told her because I couldn't not tell her. "And I choose you, every stubborn," I pushed forward, and she gasped, "frustrating," forward, "sexy," more, "smart inch of you," with a final snap, I let my forehead rest on hers as I tried to catch my breath.

Isabel's breath escaped in a sob. Then she gripped my hips, fingernails digging into my skin.

"Are you okay?"

She grinned, looking more than a little drunk. "Yes. And just remember who fell in love with who first."

I exhaled a laugh, pulling at her lips with a kiss. It slid into something deeper, something that had her shifting, tugging at my back. But I held there, allowing both of us to settle into the feeling.

"More, please," she begged.

"I'm just getting started," I whispered against her mouth.

As I moved, slowly at first, I wanted to make sure I wasn't

hurting her. Then she bit down on my earlobe, sucking it into her mouth, and the tether on my control snapped in a ragged, messy burst.

There was no thought of finesse or rhythm, no thought of anything other than our mutual pleasure.

Mine started before hers, and I fought to stay with her until the end, even as my chest heaved, my back arched helplessly when heat curled through my veins.

I smothered the sounds coming from my mouth into the curve of her sweat-shiny neck, and when she snapped her thighs against my hips, back curving, my name on her lips, we toppled over the edge together.

I slumped over her. The strength of a hundred men couldn't haven't moved me for how lethargic I felt.

She kissed me softly, running her hands over my back and up into my hair. I rolled to my side, keeping her anchored against me, our legs intertwined as we luxuriated in the taste of each other, the sweet sipping of her mouth against mine.

"I knew you'd wreck me." She sighed happily. I kissed along her jaw, which she tipped so I could reach more of her skin.

"Did you?"

Isabel's fingers traced the features on my face as she nodded. "The day I met you, I think I knew."

The lithe line of her back was damp with sweat, and I touched as much of her as I could manage with long sweeps of my palm. "You've always been smarter than me about this."

She laughed. "Not smarter," she corrected. "More aware, maybe."

I pushed some of her mussed hair out of her face. "If I'd had any idea, I probably never would've walked in the door."

Just like I hoped she would, Isabel smiled at my honesty. "I know."

Even though we were fully enmeshed, as many body parts wound together as humanly possible, I curled myself around her and breathed her in. It was cheesy and poetic, the types of thoughts I was never prone to, but Isabel smelled like the peace that I'd been seeking, that I thought she wasn't capable of bringing. Ironic, given that she blew my life up, resetting it into something that would only work with her presence inside of it.

"I'm glad you did, though," she whispered. "This is where I'm meant to be."

I closed my eyes and held her against me. It was easy to imagine that every step of my life had led to this moment. Not just the moment, but to her.

"Me too," I told her.

Eventually, we pulled the blankets up over us, whispering to each other as the night wore on. I decided, after sweet, gentle touches for the entire time, we were done being in bed.

"You owe me a bath," I told her.

Her smile was wide and happy. "Do I?"

I nuzzled into her neck and decided she smelled best right there. "Yeah. Do you have any idea of how hard it was knowing you were in there?"

Her hand slid down between my legs, and I breathed out a pained laugh. "Tell me."

Pecking a hard kiss against her lips, I extracted her hand and got out of bed. "I'll tell you in there."

Once we were under the water, the deep soaker tub filled with a lather of clean-smelling bubbles, Isabel turned and faced me, folding her long legs around my back so she was situated in my lap. I smoothed her wet hair off her face.

"This is what I pictured," I told her.

She swept some bubbles off my shoulder. "Yeah?"

My hand moved under the water, and she gave me a mock-glare when I merely traced circles just to the side of her chest. "Maybe I pictured something a little more X-rated."

"I think I was too frustrated with you to picture anything dirty," she said.

I swallowed, choosing my words carefully. Before I spoke, I pressed my palm against the skin over her heart, nothing sexual in the touch, despite the warm weight of her that I was now intimately familiar with. "I'm so sorry I kept pulling away. I didn't know how"—I paused with a slight shake of my head—"how to make peace with you. With what you made me feel," I amended.

Isabel wrapped her arms around my neck and hugged me, and we sat like that for a quiet minute, the water lapping gently at our skin.

"Moving on isn't easy," she said, pressing a soft kiss to my shoulder, then setting her chin there.

"It's not."

She pulled back, and her face was so open, so sweet, I had to kiss her again. But when I pulled away, intent on deepening it, she laid a gentle finger on my mouth.

"I think you and I held onto the things that hurt us because it seemed … easier, somehow." She gave me a soft smile. "Yours was your grief, the thing you lost. And mine was"—she screwed up her lips—"sort of the same. I lost something too, but gained something really great in return. But I know I kept a tight rein on the things I could control so that I'd never feel that way again."

I nodded. "No one can hurt you again if you don't let them in." My heart pinched at the understanding I saw in her midnight eyes. For so long and for so many reasons, I'd written her off as wrong, but she was exactly right.

"You have the power to hurt me, Aiden Hennessy," she admitted. Isabel slid a hand over my cheek. "And I'm trusting you not to."

My arms curled around her back, and I sighed contentedly at the strength in our embrace.

When she finally pulled away, her eyes looked a little red, but I knew better than to comment on it.

"You know what you owe me?" she said.

"Hmm?"

She leaned in, whispering some of the X-rated things I'd imagined when she'd been in my own tub, and by the time we left the bathroom, wrapped in plush towels and skin wrinkled, I'd delivered every single one.

CHAPTER 29

Isabel

"**I DON'T BELIEVE YOU.**"

I set my chin on his chest the next morning before the sun had risen in the sky and grinned happily. "It's true."

"You've never tried sushi?"

With a shake of my head, I let my fingers walk up his abdomen. "Nothing could sound worse to me than slimy uncooked fish."

"That is a crime," he muttered, snatching up my fingers to kiss the tips.

"Your turn."

He sighed. "I've never baked a cake."

"I've never baked one *well*," I said. "Add it to the list."

Aiden's hand swept over my lower back. "What else do we have?"

We'd spent the last hour trying to figure out firsts we could experience together, Aiden's attempt at trying to wrap his mind around the fact that I'd never slept with anyone before him. In his mind, he owed me a few of those, and the idea of it made me so warm and melty inside that I was not arguing. I'd just experienced the most perfect night of my entire life, even if I would limp out of this hotel, wearing my bridesmaid dress from the night before.

"Never ran a marathon," I started. "Never successfully baked a cake. We've never worn roller skates. And we've never slept out under the stars."

His face took on a thoughtful expression. "I probably shouldn't admit this one."

"Tell me."

Aiden's fingers slid through my hair, and I closed my eyes at the feel of it, soaking in the affection like a dried-out sponge. It felt so good that I almost missed what he said.

"I've never bought flowers for someone."

My eyes popped open. "Really?"

He shook his head. "Flowers made Beth sneeze like crazy, so I never got her any."

It was the first he'd mentioned her since we left the reception, and I spread my hand out over his chest, laying a soft kiss onto his skin. "What was she like?"

Aiden closed his eyes and took a deep breath. "Funny. She was always smiling. It was the first thing I noticed about her. Smart. Kind. She did everything easily, it seemed like."

It wasn't the time to talk, just to listen.

He wedged a hand under his head and stared down at me. "And she made the best gingersnaps in the world."

I smiled. "Does Anya talk about her a lot?"

"Not as much since we've moved here. I think being in our own house has made a big difference. Being around family. In California, it was just the three of us," he said. "I think … I think she felt the loss of her more there."

Resting my cheek on his chest, I thought about her bright blue eyes, her gap-toothed smile, and found myself smiling too.

He felt it. "What?"

"Just thinking about Anya. She's a great kid, Aiden."

There was a brief pause before he spoke again. "You ready to take that on? When we tell her, I mean."

We'd decided earlier in our conversation to hold off on announcing anything to her just yet. Gain our footing as a couple first. But this was a question I could answer easily.

I rolled up onto my side and scooted higher up on the bed so that I could kiss him. There was no time to deepen it because we both needed to leave soon—him to pick up Anya and me to have a family brunch at Logan and Paige's while Molly and Noah opened some presents before they left on their mini-honeymoon.

"I already love Anya," I told him. "I don't fall out of trees for just anyone, you know."

He laughed. "I hope not."

"That's the thing about my family," I said. Setting my head in my hand, I snuggled up next to him again. "Blood ties don't mean anything in the end, not when it comes down to it. Logan and Paige, my sisters, Emmett ... they are my family because we fight for each other every single day. It was us against the world." I smiled. "We've got a few more bodies now, Noah, Jude, Bauer, and little Gabriel. You and Anya," I said quietly. "She may not know it yet, but she just gained a whole lot of people in her corner."

Aiden tugged me closer for a kiss. "I like the sound of that," he murmured.

I found myself tearing up as he folded me into his arms again. "I do too." I sniffed quietly, but he heard me.

"What is it?"

I shook my head, swiping at my face. "Anytime something big happened to me, I never really understood why. Even if I knew it was coming, even if I hated how I felt, I didn't realize each piece had to happen exactly the way it did"—I pulled my head back so I could see his face—"so I could be here with you. Even the hard things."

Aiden slid his thumb across my cheek.

We didn't have the time for it. I wasn't even sure that physically I could handle more, but he moved over me, gently rocking between my legs, sharing my breath, stealing my heart, and making me fall even more in love with him than I already was.

In my ear, he whispered all sorts of things that pushed me higher and higher, even as he kept his movements slow and steady. It was the relaxed speed and the inexorable strength of his reserve that finally broke me open in a warm wave.

It wasn't fireworks and explosions, but something even better. It was forever.

We dressed quietly. He hooked up the back of my dress, and I buttoned his shirt, stretching on my toes to kiss the edge of his jaw when I was done. And because I could, I slid his jacket over my bridesmaid dress. We entered the elevator hand in hand, trading smiles in the shining reflection on the door as we rode down to the lobby.

At my car, Aiden gave me a deep kiss goodbye, and it took us a few minutes to separate.

"I'll call you later," he told me. "Maybe we can figure out something tomorrow if one of my brothers can help with Anya."

I nodded. "I guess we'll have to be careful at work too, huh?"

He hummed, sliding my hair off my shoulder to drop a kiss onto my neck. "Oh, no. The first day we work together, the second everyone is gone, I have a whole other first to take care of in my office."

My smile was massive. "What's that?"

Aiden lifted his head and pinned me with those green eyes. "You on my desk."

"Okay," I answered breathlessly. "Can we work together tomorrow maybe?"

"Maybe we can both accidentally show up an hour early."

"I *love* showing up to work an hour early."

His laughter was a happy booming sound, and if I was being

honest, I felt a little drugged at the sound of it. We finally said good-bye, and I hurried to my apartment to whip on some clean clothes and slick my hair back into a ponytail. Snatching a Pop-Tarts from my pantry cabinet, I was back in the car and on my way to Logan and Paige's less than fifteen minutes later.

And I knew I was in bad shape when the newlyweds beat me there.

When I walked into the kitchen, the entire family went dead silent.

My face must've been bright red. "Morning."

Molly was grinning like a lunatic. Lia tried to hide her smile behind her coffee. Claire, on the couch with Gabriel, rolled her lips between her teeth.

Paige approached, wearing a deceptively sweet smile on her face, and handed me a massive mug. "Need some coffee, sweetcheeks? You must be tired."

Logan mumbled something from the table, and Emmett held out his hand. My brother dug into his wallet and handed him a dollar.

I took the mug. "I slept *just fine*, thank you."

Lia snorted.

"Are we opening presents or what?" I asked.

Molly set a box aside. "We already started."

"Aiden didn't want to come over with you?" Paige asked, completely undeterred.

I took a slow sip of the coffee and held her eyes.

"He wasn't hungry?"

"Paige," Logan said in a warning tone.

She blinked innocently. "Yes, husband?"

He gave her a look. "If she doesn't want to talk about it, she doesn't have to."

"You can tell me later," she whispered.

Emmett shook his head. "This family is crazy. I'm going outside."

"Coming with you, dude." Bauer stood from the couch with kisses to Gabriel's cheek and Claire's upturned mouth. "Jude, you wanted to show me that thing?"

The big Brit stood with a nod, snagging a soccer ball from the floor. "Be right out." He kissed Lia.

"Geez," I muttered. "I sure know how to clear a room."

"It's probably all the just-had-sex pheromones," Lia added helpfully.

"That's it!" Logan shouted. "I'm outta here."

My brother stalked out of the house, my sisters' laughter following him as he tugged open the slider.

Noah grimaced at the giant pile of unwrapped boxes, then gave Paige and Lia a look. "Can you please stop while I have to be in here?"

Paige patted his cheek. "For my favorite son-in-law? Of course."

"*Now* you stop?" I asked.

Paige sent me a wink, then gestured to Molly and Noah. "Proceed."

Molly started unwrapping a small box but gave me a warm smile. "We're just happy for you."

"I know," I told her. I took a seat on the couch by Claire and held my arms out for the baby. She handed him over with a tiny smile. His warm body cuddled close, I inhaled the top of his head. "Gawd, we should bottle this smell. We'd make a fortune."

I held my nephew away from me, laughing when he gave me a coy little smile.

Claire nudged me with her foot. "How was it?" she whispered.

I blew gently in Gabriel's face, grinning when his eyes widened, his gummy mouth opening in happy surprise. "The wedding was great," I answered. "Which you know, because you were there."

She rolled her eyes at my evasion.

"What is that?" Noah asked.

Molly studied something in her hand, but I couldn't make out what it was. "It's a ring, but I can't tell what the design is."

"Is there a card?" Paige asked.

Noah snatched up a small white envelope and ripped it open, tugging out a card. His gaze darted to Molly. "I think you should read this one."

Molly took the card, and her eyes widened. She handed the ring to Noah, then looked at each one of us.

She let out a deep breath and started reading.

"In Spain, you can find orange blossom trees everywhere you look. It's why they're the flower most traditionally used in weddings here. For Spaniards, or those of us who have made this place home, the orange blossom represents joy and happiness, especially for a newly married couple." She paused, and Noah moved his chair closer so he could wrap an arm around her shoulder. "This ring was given to me by my husband's mother on the day we got married, and I asked her blessing to send it to you. I've found happiness in this path of my life, and I hope you have too, Molly. Thank you for your invitation. I know I didn't deserve it. Beyond my wish that you experience the same joy that this flower represents, I think the best gift I can give you is to let you and your sisters live on the path that you've created since I left."

The room went silent, and I snuggled my face into Gabriel's downy soft hair. I wasn't sure how I felt, but I couldn't help but think about what I'd said to Aiden after hearing Brooke's words. *It's not about deserving, about who's perfect or worthy. It's about finding the right person and choosing them.*

I looked around at my family and smiled.

"How do we feel about this?" Paige asked carefully.

"We?" Claire said with a smile.

"Yeah." Paige gestured vaguely. "You know, the collective we. You. Whatever."

Molly took the ring back from Noah and studied it. "It's pretty. I think I'm just finding it a little funny that we kept holding our breath to see if she'd come, but her answer was sitting right here in a pile of presents for probably the last two weeks."

Lia sighed. "Spain, huh? With a husband?"

"I guess." Molly studied the note again, then handed it across the table to her.

Claire held her hand out, and Gabriel grabbed it. "I think it's a good sign that she's aware enough to know that her presence, even if it was invited, might not be the healthiest thing for all of us. Maybe she's growing up," she said with a rueful smile.

I handed Gabriel back to Claire when he reached for her, and then blinked up when I realized everyone in the room was staring at me.

"What?"

"Feel like punching something?" Paige asked.

I took a deep breath, brows lowered. "No, not really."

Molly smiled.

My fingers picked at the hem of my shirt. "Just seeing the big picture, I guess. We're all on the paths we were supposed to be on." I shrugged. "It's hard to stay angry with her if that's the case."

Molly traded a look with Lia, and Lia traded a look with Claire. Paige's smile curled up slowly.

"Oh my gosh, *what?*" I asked.

"There's only one reason you'd be so chill right now," Lia said. "You totally got laid last night."

Noah threw up his hands and walked outside.

I met her gaze with a lifted eyebrow. "Wouldn't you like to know?"

My sisters dissolved into laughter.

Paige held my eyes. "How many pieces of cake did you have last night, Iz?"

Slowly, I held up three fingers.

Paige grinned, and I hid my smile behind my coffee again. Maybe someday I'd share details, but for now, they were all mine.

CHAPTER 30

Isabel

"**M**INE IS STILL CROOKED."

Aiden tilted his head to the side. "It's not …"

I gave him a look.

"Okay, yes, your cake is crooked." He knocked a kiss on my cheek as he moved his perfectly level cake next to it. "It's a little impressive how bad at this you are."

"Thanks," I answered dryly.

He swatted my butt. "You still successfully baked a cake."

I eyed the baked good in question. "I don't have to decorate it, do I?"

Aiden came up behind me, big hands curling around my hips. "Yes."

He couldn't see my face, but I was glaring.

"We could make it double duty," he suggested.

"In what way?"

His head dropped, and he spoke against the back of my neck. "First time licking frosting off someone's body."

"Sold." I whirled, gripping his T-shirt in my hands so I could tug his head down for a kiss.

And that was the way of it, the way of us, for a couple of weeks after Molly's wedding. Because of Anya, we had short windows of time planned in advance so that we could achieve a few firsts together. Only one of those, she'd joined us, not realizing that he and I were considering it a date because he only touched me when she was in another room.

Logan invited us to a Wolves game, and we watched from the front row, just behind the Wolves' bench. Anya spent most of it, staring wide-eyed at the players and staff. Twice, he'd snuck a kiss, but that was it.

Roller skating had ended in him falling three times because he couldn't keep up with me.

Also, I'd worn short shorts that he said were "categorically unfair" when he was supposed to be keeping his balance.

His family knew we were dating, but I hadn't talked to any of them since we started, mainly because we wanted Anya to be involved whenever I went to his parents' house the first time.

That changed just beyond the two-week mark.

I sat behind the front desk the day after we baked our cakes at my apartment, updating some new member files. Someone opened the door, which was unlocked because I was teaching a class in about an hour's time.

Glancing up with a polite smile, I froze when I recognized her from Aiden's picture.

Her hair was pulled up high on her head, and she had a gym bag slung over her shoulder. "You must be Isabel."

She set her hands on the front desk and studied me unabashedly.

I held out my hand. "You must be Eloise. It's a pleasure to meet you."

"I'm taking your class today," she informed me. "Decided it was worth skipping a day of school and driving back into town."

With a grin, I handed her a form. "You here to form your own opinion?"

"Aiden assures me you are a glorious human being, so I'm inclined to believe him." But she smiled. "But yes, I'm here to make up my own mind about you."

I stood, started wrapping my hands. "Well, Eloise, by the time you finish here, you will either hate me or love me. There's not usually much middle ground with me." I tilted my head toward his office. "He know you're here?"

"Nope. My brothers bet me ten bucks I couldn't get him to take class at the same time as me, especially if you're teaching."

"I'll throw in twenty that I can get him to join."

She laughed. "I don't think I'd take a bet against you, Isabel Ward."

"I'll go talk to him while you fill that out." I walked into Aiden's office and knocked softly before I walked in. He was reading some articles about weight training, and on his face were those sexy as hell glasses. "I think you should take my class today."

He spun in his chair with a thoughtful expression on his face. "Yeah? Why's that."

I approached slowly, finishing up the second wrap with a tight yank to the velcro strap at the end. "Maybe I want to torture you a little."

Aiden widened his legs so I could step between them, sliding his hands up my thighs until he bracketed my hips with his fingers. "You torture me just by walking around here."

Bracing a hand on the top of his chair, I leaned down to give him a kiss. He cupped the back of my neck and slicked his tongue against mine with a contented hum.

"Okay," he said against my lips. "I'll take your class."

I smiled.

"On one condition," he added.

"What's that?"

His eyes held mine steadily. "I want you to come over tonight after Anya goes to bed."

My eyebrows popped up. "Really?"

Aiden stood from the chair and held my face in his hands. "I miss holding you while I sleep. As fun as office sex is, or in your cramped-ass bed in your apartment, I want to know what it feels like to climb into my bed with you right where I've imagined you."

I let out a deep breath. He kissed my forehead, but let me think.

"You're not worried Anya will wake up?"

He shook his head. "She hasn't woken up in the middle of the night in weeks, and the last few times, she always calls for me. As long as we set an alarm, she won't have any idea."

I nodded, excitement building as I imagined it. "Deal."

"You gonna go easy on me in class?"

Up on my tiptoes, I tugged on his earlobe with my teeth, relished in how he tightened his grip when I did. Into his ear, I whispered, "You fucking wish."

His eyes promised retribution a million times over the next hour and a half. When he saw his sister, when I unleashed all my inner dominatrix on him and had his chest heaving and soaked in sweat by the time I brought the class to cool-down. I probably brought it a touch too far when I got down in front of him and told him to lower his ass another inch in the plank he was holding.

And because Anya was dropped off just before we finished, there would be no desk sex for him to give me payback.

But he held onto it. All evening.

With the skies dark, and my backpack hooked onto my shoulders, I knocked gently. He ripped the door open, and without a word in greeting, he dipped, scooping me up over his shoulder.

"Aiden," I laughed breathlessly. "Put me down."

"Trust me, you don't want that." He strode to his bedroom.

"I don't?"

"Nope, because once your feet hit the ground, you are going to pay for that."

I grinned, hair hanging down toward the ground as he shut the door behind us. He tossed me, and I bounced off the mattress with a laugh.

And oh, did he get payback.

My clothes, practically torn from my body, ended in a heap on the floor next to his. And he proceeded to torture me, bringing me to the edge but never quite letting me go all the way, over and over, until I was shaking.

Aiden kept me on my stomach, forced me to hold onto the comforter.

By the time he put us out of our misery, I was mindless, arching my hips to seek the explosive end to an entire day of white-knuck-led anticipation. He covered me with his big body, holding me into place, moving so slowly that I almost wept.

He held still, dragging his lips over my cheek, only stopping when his mouth was over my ear.

"I love you," he whispered.

Slow was over.

Gentle was gone.

In its place was fierce and brutal. It took no more than five seconds, the bruising strength of his hands holding mine down, and I was flung helplessly to a place I didn't actually know existed. He came there with me.

My spine practically cracked from the heat he pulled from inside me, and I managed to hold my sounds into the pillow by my face.

We laid boneless and limp for about ten minutes, just trying to catch our breath.

I wasn't sure how I ever felt complete before this man, before this love.

He watched me pull on my sleep tank and shorts with

heavy-lidded eyes, opening his arms for me to climb into bed next to him.

"This is what I needed," he said into the top of my head. "Thank you."

I sighed. "Thank *you*."

His chest shook with laughter.

We talked for a while, and as I started drifting off, his finger traced the bottom edge of my lip.

I hummed. "That's nice."

"You said that," he added quietly. "The night you were here."

Opening my eyes, I studied him in the dark room. "Did I?"

Aiden nodded.

"I'm glad I got a chance to say it again." I yawned.

"Isabel," he said, nudging me back awake.

"Hmmm?"

"You know you're going to have to marry me, right?"

Eyes still closed, my mouth curled into a smile. "As proposals go, I give that a four."

He laughed quietly. "Just making a general statement. You've ruined me from sleeping alone."

"Good." I turned to my side, and he folded his body around mine, burying his nose in the back of my neck. "Because yeah, I'm going to have to marry you, Aiden Hennessy."

We slept like that, soundly and deeply, until I felt a light stroke on my arm.

When I blinked, I saw a small body standing on my side of the bed. My stomach seized instantly at how she might react.

Anya grinned down at me. "I *knew* it was you," she whispered.

I sat up, glanced over at a still-sleeping Aiden, sprawled on his back with a hand laying on his chest.

My heart raced as I swung my legs over the side of the bed, and she climbed up into my lap.

"You knew it, huh?" I asked her quietly.

Anya nodded, playing with the end of my braid where it hung over my shoulder.

"Want me to bring you back to bed, sweetheart?"

She nodded again, and without waking Aiden, we walked upstairs, and once in her room, I held back the covers on her bed. She pulled the blankets up to her chin and looked over at the picture of Beth. "It's behind there," she said. "You can take it out."

Carefully, I picked up the frame and studied her face. She was pretty. A big smile and laugh lines that told me she'd done both things often.

"Behind the picture?"

Anya nodded.

I pulled the back of the frame off, and a folded-up piece of paper was wedged behind the image of her mom.

When I opened it, it was hard to make sense of what I was seeing. Anya pointed at the side, letters I couldn't really make sense of.

"She told me I'd know," Anya said. "Even if you didn't match the list, I'd know."

My throat thickened, and I smoothed her hair back from her forehead. "Yeah?"

Anya blinked slowly, sleep pulling at her. "I wrote it on the side of the paper, but I don't think Daddy could read that part. Mommy said I'd know because she'd make us all happier. And that's you."

A tear slid down my cheek as I leaned down to place a featherlight kiss on her forehead. Her arms snaked around my neck in a tight squeeze.

"I love you," she whispered.

"I love you, too."

I stood from the bed and turned, stopping short when I saw Aiden watching us from the doorway. He'd tugged on some cotton sleep pants, arms crossed over his chest, and a small smile playing over his mouth. His eyes were red.

"We're busted," I whispered.

He held out a hand, and I took it.

"Ready to go back to bed?" he asked.

I nodded.

I was ready for all of it with him. With her. Most of all, I was just ready for our life together to start, and as I fell asleep in his arms, I had a feeling it just had.

EPILOGUE

Isabel

Six months later

"**I**T'S NOT VERY PRETTY."

Under my breath, I laughed at Anya's dubious expression. We sat on the bed in my bedroom with Aiden, and in front of her was the pink enamel lockbox I'd found online.

"It's pink, though, so that's something."

She gave me a look. "I might have a new favorite color next year. What am I going to do with all my secret stuff then?"

I hummed. "Well, maybe we can spray-paint it if that happens."

She eyed mine. "You never changed yours?"

With a shake of my head, I fished the key out of the small bag and jiggled the lock until I could finagle the box open. "It was a gift from my nan—Logan's mom. She knew I needed a place that was just mine to keep all my special things that should be kept safe."

"What's in it?" Anya leaned forward.

I showed her each item, explaining where they came from, why I felt they were important. When I got to the letter I'd written to her dad, I paused before pulling it out.

"Now this is something I've never shown anyone," I told her.

Her eyes widened. "Really?"

Next to me was another envelope I hadn't shown anyone, but we'd get to that eventually.

Very carefully, I picked up the folded paper and shook my head at the sight of my neat penmanship, the doodles of purple ink along the side.

"I wrote this letter when I was a teenager."

She shifted to her knees, teeth tugging on her bottom lip in her interest. "You never sent it?"

Pulling open the paper, I shook my head. "I decided it should just stay a secret."

It was a risk to show her. But over the last year, this young lady had become my built-in sidekick, my ride or die, outside of her dad.

When I handed her the paper, the diamond on my engagement ring caught the light.

Anya took the letter, her eyes widening on the first line.

"It's for my dad," she whispered.

I nodded.

"And you kept it all this time?" Her finger followed along with the words on the lined paper as she read it.

"Pretty crazy, huh?"

Anya's eyes were bright with excitement. "How'd you know you were going to meet him?"

"I didn't," I answered simply.

When she finished reading, she carefully folded the paper and set it back inside the black metal box.

I knew her well enough now to know she was processing, so I gently twirled my ring while I waited for her to speak.

He'd given it to me a month earlier, tied onto a ribbon, around the stem of a giant bouquet of daisies.

It was the same day I moved in with him and Anya, after five months of trying very hard to pretend we weren't basically living together.

Anya looked at her metal box again and up at me.

"I'm glad you didn't send it to him."

My eyebrows rose. "Yeah?"

"I think maybe he would've remembered when he met you at the gym. And he needed you to be someone new."

A smile spread over my face at how carefully she chose her words.

"I think you might be right," I said quietly.

She scooted forward on the bed and gave me a tight hug. I kissed the side of her head.

"Love you, Iz."

"Love you too," I whispered.

When she hopped off the bed, box clutched to her chest, she looked at mine again. "Are you going to tell Dad about the letter?"

"What letter?" he asked from the doorway.

She looked at me, eyes wide. "Sorry."

I laughed. "It's okay."

Anya scampered off to her room, the pounding of her feet on the stairs had Aiden shaking his head.

As he shut the bedroom door and approached the bed, I studied the way he looked in his button-down shirt and black dress pants.

"I like this look," I told him.

"Yeah?"

He carefully moved aside the metal box and pushed me back onto the bed. My hands tugged his shirt out of his waistband as he gave me a mind-spinning kiss. Aiden always greeted me like this when we were alone—like he hadn't seen me in weeks—and I would never, ever get sick of it.

His kisses moved down my neck as I moved under him, unhooking his belt.

"What letter is she talking about?" he asked, tugging the strap of my bra down and placing a sucking kiss over my heart.

"Umm, nothing?"

He lifted his head, spearing me with a look.

"It's silly," I told him. "But I wanted her to see what kind of stuff I kept in the lockbox from my nan."

Aiden rolled to the side, snatching the box with one big hand and tugging it closer to us. "Show me."

With a burning hot face, I pulled the letter out and handed it to him.

His grin was so pleased, so fricken entertained as he got to the part about the purple dress that he started chuckling.

I covered my face. "Now you know why I literally tripped over nothing when I met you."

He pulled my hands down and took my mouth again. "I love that you kept it," he murmured. "Just goes to show you've always had great taste."

I smacked his chest. "Of course you make this about you."

Aiden settled between my legs as we kissed, his hand smoothing up and down my back, settling on my bottom. Even though we could take it further—Anya knew not to open the door when it was closed—I loved that he seemed just as content to kiss me on our big bed in the middle of the day.

He rolled us, tugging my shirt up so he could reach more of my skin. When I settled onto my back, arching my neck, the crinkle of paper had me freezing.

"What?" he asked.

My hand fumbled on the bed until I found the edge of the envelope. "Something else to show you," I whispered.

His brows lowered as he took it. My hands smoothed up his arms as he pulled it open, and my heart raced as he saw the edge of what was inside.

"Isabel," he breathed. His eyes snapped to mine. "Seriously?"

I nodded, eyes watering at the awe I saw in his face. Aiden brushed a knuckle under his eye as he carefully tugged the sonogram picture out of the envelope.

He stared at it, then at me.

"We're having a baby?" he whispered.

My chin quivered. I couldn't even nod in affirmation because I'd split wide open into happy, messy tears.

"I know …" I paused when my voice cracked, "I know it's sooner than we planned, and I wanted to be sure before I told you."

He wrapped me up in his arms so tight I could hardly breathe. "We're having a baby," he repeated, voice uneven.

I clung to him, tears streaming down the side of my face, disappearing into my hairline. His mouth was on mine in the next moment, and when he broke away, his eyes were red-rimmed and so full of happiness.

"Does this mean I get to marry you sooner?"

I laughed. "I'd marry you tomorrow, Aiden Hennessy."

Resting his forehead against mine, he breathed a shaky exhale. "Of course we'd do this sooner than we planned."

I kissed him again. "It works for us, I think."

Aiden cupped the side of my face, stared down at me with so much adoration, I almost started with the messy weeping again.

"Yeah. It does."

"Should we go tell Anya?"

"In a few minutes," he said, resuming with the lifting of the shirt. He reverently kissed my belly, then moved up until he'd tugged my shirt off.

"Just a few minutes?" I asked skeptically.

Aiden sat up on his knees, between my legs, and yanked his shirt off. "You doubt me?"

With a soft smile on my face, I pulled him back down for a kiss. "Never," I whispered against his mouth.

❧

The End

But first! If you're curious how Logan and Paige got their epic start, here's an excerpt from *The Marriage Effect*.

"So you're like …"

I kept my eyes aimed up when I answered. There was no particular desire to see the look on her face when I told her something I'd managed to keep under the radar for more than two years. "Their legal guardian."

Paige was quiet for a couple of seconds as she processed. "And he wants to be."

"Yeah. He and his wife do."

"And you *don't* want them to be," she clarified.

I dropped my chin so she could see my face again. "Definitely not."

She cupped her cheeks in her hands and stared at me. "And me saying I was your fiancée was …" *Was what?* I wanted to ask. Because I had a few words I could drop into that particular empty space.

Perfectly timed.

Brilliant.

Crazy.

Fate.

Paige didn't say any of those things, though. "It was really stupid, wasn't it?"

I closed my eyes and wiped a hand over my mouth. I didn't know why I thought Paige would make this easy on me. Why I thought her mind would follow the same path that mine was.

Probably because that path was certifiable, padded cell insanity.

Except it wasn't. Not at all.

"I just … didn't think, really. I'm so sorry, Logan. I don't blame you for being furious."

I dropped my hand and stared at her.

"Oh my gosh, would you say something? You're starting to freak me out."

"I'm not furious," I told her.

She blinked a few times. "You're not?"

"Nope."

Paige sat back and exhaled audibly. "Well, that's good. I thought you'd flip the hell out on me, tell me I should think things through better, blah, blah. That's what Allie tells me all the time."

"Oh," I interjected, "you *should* think things through better, but I'm not furious."

"Well, that's good." Her eyes narrowed suspiciously. "Why? You're not exactly Susy Sunshine, if you know what I'm sayin'. I figured you'd be breathing fire right now."

I leaned forward and plucked her hand from her lap, turned it side to side so I could study the ring. When she sucked in an audible breath, I kept my eyes down because I didn't want to know what was on her face. The skin of her long, graceful fingers was smooth and soft. No callouses like the ones covering mine. No scars from broken fingers or skin that had been ripped off by an overzealous lineman.

"Nick is an asshole," I told her as I studied her fingers in mine. "But he's married. He works a job with normal hours. During the season, I probably work a hundred hours a week. My housekeeper just quit, the third in a year. And under my watch, my sixteen-year-old sister just got in a car accident driving around with her drunk friend, so he's going to try to take them from me because of it."

Paige's chest rose and fell with increasing speed. Her pink lips were full and open slightly as she watched me. The bridge of her nose was covered with light freckles, and it worked. All of her separate pieces, they worked really, really well together.

"He's better on paper," she said. "That's what you're trying to say?"

I nodded. "Yeah. He checks a lot of boxes that I don't."

A blanket of quiet fell between us, and I saw the wheels turn behind the bright blue of her eyes.

"What is it that you need, exactly?" she repeated, slowly pulling her hand out of my own.

Her eyes held mine. Turns out, I didn't even need to say the words or try to figure out the best way to say it. She finally tore her gaze away, and it landed on the ring.

"Ohhhh," she drawled. "You need a fiancée."

"Actually," I said slowly, gauging the finely featured face in front of me, "I need a wife."

Paige's face stilled, then the last—absolute fucking last—thing I expected to happen happened.

She smiled.

"Perfect," she breathed.

Keep reading with your KindleUnlimited subscription!

⟲

You can also read the rest of the Ward Sisters series now, free with your Kindle Unlimited subscription.

Focused (Molly and Noah)
Faked (Claire and Bauer)
Floored (Lia and Jude)

AUTHOR'S NOTE

When I wrote *The Bombshell Effect*, and the character of Logan Ward made a comment about how he had four sisters, I never imagined where that one line of dialogue would take me. It wasn't until just before the release of *The Marriage Effect* that I decided to write their stories, and even then, I couldn't have anticipated how my readers would respond to the Wards.

Writing these four books changed my life, and I don't say that lightly. Even when the books were hard (*clears throat* I'm looking at you, Isabel, because she made me WORK FOR IT), I've never felt a connection to my characters like I have to this family.

They feel real, don't they?

Since the release of *Focused*, you've asked me for more. You've begged me to create more siblings out of thin air (I wish I'd given Logan more sisters, trust me!) so that I can stay with this family longer.

So ... I've decided to.

Not create more siblings, but to stay in this world, because I honestly have no desire to leave. Everything I need to be able to do that is already in the books you've read. We have an entire generation of the Washington Wolves that deserve to have their stories told. We have Faith and Lydia Pierson. We have Emmett Ward (you know you need his story too). And maybe after that, we have Anya Hennessy and the little sibling yet to be born.

And for those who subscribe to my newsletter, I have an exclusive bonus epilogue of Isabel and Aiden, to tide you over until I can get the next story out.

My next book, The Lie, will kick off with Luke and Allie's daughter, Faith, who we met in *The Bombshell Effect*. I've got a small snippet for you, because I can't NOT share just a little bit of that opposites attract/bad boy sports romance goodness. It will be available on Amazon and in KU on Sept 15, 2021.

I hope you're as excited about this as I am. It's the greatest gift of a writer, to create a fictional world that doesn't just feel like home to me, but to you, too.

Because without *you*, my dear reader, none of this would be possible.

Thank you for loving them as much as I do.

Karla

Here's your exclusive snippet from *The Lie*!

Allie's door was cracked open, and when I approached, I heard the rumble of a low voice. He came into view before Allie did, and if someone had written a caption for the image of him that I saw, it would've been *pissed-off bad boy bucks authority*. His arms, big and tattooed, were crossed over his chest, and he stared at Allie like she'd done him personal harm.

His jaw was a sharp line coated in dark stubble, and there wasn't a hint of emotion on that chiseled face. For a moment, I stared at him. Something about his demeanor made me feel very much like I was approaching a wild animal, and that danger made the air vibrate at a different frequency.

"There you are, Faith," Allie said as she appeared into view. With a warm smile, she opened the door for me. "Come on in."

"Thank you for waiting," I told her, tucking some of my brown hair behind my ear. "I know I'm a little late."

She rubbed my arm. "Dominic and I were just getting to know each other before you got here."

He snorted, and my brows bent in on my forehead at the derisive sound. Allie's eyes met mine, and I saw a gleam of humor in them, which made me relax a little. Then she gestured toward me. "Dominic, this is my daughter Faith. She runs the foundation I was telling you about."

I gave him a friendly smile and held out my hand. But instead of standing to take it, he gave me a head-to-toe study without rush, then nodded curtly.

Ahh, okay, so he was one of *those* football players. The ego-the-size-of-Everest, I'm-too-talented-for-basic-manners football players who made me want to shove bamboo splints up my fingernails rather than spend time with them.

Those players made it very, very easy not to break my *no*

dating the players rule. Kinda like when you went camping and they told you not to feed the bears because they might eat you alive.

Check out *The Lie* on Amazon and in Kindle Unlimited!

ACKNOWLEDGMENTS

This book. Oh goodness, this book. It should not have surprised me that Isabel would be the most difficult sister to write. She did not, in all her stubborn glory, want me to dig around in her fictional head.

And the only way I was able to survive the writing process was the group of author friends who listened to my endless voice messages as I pieced together this story. They get top billing this round, for plotting, feedback, and encouragement the entire way through— Kathryn Andrews, Fiona Cole, Amy Daws, and Brittainy Cherry.

To Kandi Steiner for slipping in as a last minute beta and all around amazing cheerleader.

To Michelle Clay for providing one last set of eyes to make sure I didn't screw up the story.

To my husband and his endless understanding and support when I ranted and railed about how I'd never get it right, as I locked myself in our bedroom all weekend to write for months.

To Braadyn Penrod for capturing THE MOST PERFECT pictures I could've ever imagined for Aiden and Isabel, and Najla Qamber for the stunning cover and continued rock-star status. (And models Anna and Alex for being stunningly gorgeous and REALLY GOOD at posing together.)

To Jenny and Janice for cleaning up the mess of this manuscript.

To Ginelle and Pauline for doing one last read through.

To my reader group and ARC team, for being as excited about this story as anyone in the universe.

Be strong and courageous. Do not be afraid; do not be discouraged,
for the Lord your God will be with you wherever you go.
Joshua 1:9

OTHER BOOKS BY
KARLA SORENSEN

All books are FREE in Kindle Unlimited

Wilder Family Series
One and Only

The Wolves: a Football Dynasty (second gen)
The Lie (Faith Pierson's story)
The Plan (Lydia Pierson's story)
The Crush (Emmett Ward's story)

The Ward Sisters
Focused
Faked
Floored
Forbidden

The Washington Wolves
The Bombshell Effect
The Ex Effect
The Marriage Effect

The Bachelors of the Ridge
Dylan
Garrett
Cole
Michael
Tristan

Three Little Words
By Your Side
Light Me Up
Tell Them Lies

Love at First Sight
Baking Me Crazy
Batter of Wits
Steal my Magnolia
Worth the Wait

Stay up to date on Karla's upcoming releases!
Subscribe to her newsletter

ABOUT THE AUTHOR

Photo credit: Perrywinkle Photography

Karla Sorensen is an Amazon top 20 bestselling author who refuses to read or write anything without a happily ever after. When she's not devouring historical romance or avoiding the laundry, you can find her watching football (British AND American), HGTV or listening to Enneagram podcasts so she can psychoanalyze everyone in her life, in no particular order of importance. With a degree in Advertising and Public Relations from Grand Valley State University, she made her living in senior healthcare prior to writing full-time. Karla lives in Michigan with her husband, two boys and a big, shaggy rescue dog named Bear.

Find Karla online:

karlasorensen.com

karla@karlasorensen.com

Facebook: www.facebook.com/karlasorensenbooks

Facebook Reader Group: www.facebook.com/groups/
thesorensensorority

Made in United States
Troutdale, OR
10/18/2024